# ALICIA CROFTON

# To My Muse, With Love

First published by Three Dimples Publishing 2019

Copyright © 2019 by Alicia Crofton



This novel is entirely a work of fiction. The names, characters and incidents portrayed in it are the work of the author's imagination. Any resemblance to actual persons, living or dead, events or localities is entirely coincidental.

Alicia Crofton asserts the moral right to be identified as the author of this work.

First edition

ISBN: 978-1-7333994-7-0

Proofreading by Alexandra Ott
Editing by Bethany Robison
Proofreading by Anne Victory

This book was professionally typeset on Reedsy.
Find out more at reedsy.com

*To Erik.*

# Prologue

The buzzing hair clipper trembled in her hand. Nora pulled the strands of her widow's peak over her forehead. One breath in, and she took the vibrating blades to the small triangle of her hairline. A clump of hair fell into the sink in a snakelike coil. The soft brown stubble of her widow's peak remained. She loosely touched the triangle of fuzz with her finger before bringing up her mom's razor blade to shave off the stubble.

She scraped gently, letting the short hairs collect at the base of her blade. The hair was gone, but the triangular shadow of hair follicles was left behind. She looked more ridiculous than she did before, and she would be the laughingstock of sixth grade.

"Mom!" she cried, tears streaming down her cheeks into a sink full of regret. Hearty sobs gurgled deep within her gut until she crumpled to the bathroom floor and cried hot tears onto her wire-rimmed glasses.

Her mother rushed through the bathroom door and surveyed the crime scene—the attempted murder of her daughter's natural hairline. Nora's mother let out a sigh before wrapping her arms around her, squeezing tight. Nora's tears soaked through her mother's pink blouse, but her mother held her tighter.

"What's going on here?" Nora's father's square head appeared from behind the bathroom door. His frown lines deepened as he saw Nora and her mother clutching each other. His thick mustache twitched.

Nora tried to explain through snorts and sobs that she was only trying to buzz off her widow's peak so she could have a perfectly straight hairline like Bridgette from school. When Bridgette pulled her hair up, her face looked flawless, unlike Nora, who was the vampire in gym class. Nora swore she'd heard Jacob from third period call her Dracula.

Nora's father scolded her for being so vain. He gave her yet another lecture on how "beauty is the devil's work in disguise," and then he reclined in his La-Z-Boy to read another passage of the Bible. Nora's mother continued to rock her gently, telling her she was beautiful just the way she was.

"Perhaps bangs will cover up what you have there now."

Nora solemnly agreed to get bangs even though they were definitely not how the cool girls styled their hair at school.

Over time the widow's peak grew into thick, straight hairs, sticking out from her forehead like a unicorn's horn. No amount of bangs or hair gel could conceal the freak of nature that grew on her forehead. At the same time, her dentist slapped on a fresh pair of metal braces to go with her glasses. Had she gone out in a lightning storm, she would have surely been struck by God out of sheer embarrassment to the human race. Nora was too ashamed to be seen. She had no friends and no activities after class aside from hiding in a corner of her parents' bookshop, living vicariously through fictional characters.

There was one particular spot in the bookstore, across from the history section and kitty-corner to the literature section, with a small square piece of orange shag carpet and a red beanbag chair. That was her safe haven. She read mysteries in the fall, historical fiction in the winter, adventure novels in the spring, and she would explore new authors in the summer.

She loved books. She loved the feel of them, the smell of them, and the escape from the traumatic teenage life she led outside the bookshop.

One day, after school, Nora walked into the bookshop—eager to finish the last couple chapters of *Harry Potter and the Sorcerer's Stone* when she heard her father screaming in the back room.

"What kind of animals would do something like this?" he growled.

"What's wrong, Dad?" Nora asked.

"This wretched woman had the nerve to drop off this box of… pornography!"

"What do you mean? For the used book fair?"

"I can't sell this smut in my store!" He threw a pink-covered paperback into the box and shoved it across the floor with his foot.

Nora looked at the box curiously. The book covers were varying shades of pastel, some adorned with floral designs, others with a boy and girl holding hands, or embracing each other in a passionate kiss.

Nora didn't know what porn looked like, but it wasn't how she would have imagined. She'd heard her father say he would never carry romance in his store before; perhaps these were romance novels?

"I can take these for you," Nora said.

"To the trash! Where they belong!" he snarled.

Nora picked up the box with her scrawny arms and hobbled her way to the garbage cans in the back. She plopped the box down to lift the lid, and just as she was about to throw the first book in, she noticed the cover—a hot pink and purple sunset with a faded outline of a man kissing a woman's neck in the clouds. A city skyline nestled between the words "Paradise" and "Judith McNaught."

She chewed on her lip, her father's words echoing in her head. *How could people read such smut.* Nora flipped to the back and read the synopsis. It didn't seem so…naughty. Maybe her father didn't know what he was talking about. The story seemed like it might be kind of sweet.

She took one last glance at the garbage can and then looked behind her shoulder.

She was alone.

Stuffing the book and a few others in her backpack, she threw the rest out as ordered and scurried back to the shop.

"Hey, Dad. I've got a project I have to finish," she lied. "Do you mind if I study at home today?"

Her father was hunched over the computer, pecking at the keyboard. Bright green numbers flashed against the black screen. He nodded without looking in her direction and waved her off. "Your mom should be there. Go ahead."

Nora raced home. Her thin little legs worked so hard she broke a sweat, like guilt pouring down her face. She didn't want to lie to him, but she had to read what the fuss was all about, to see for herself.

At home, she was able to sneak by her mom in a flash. Dinner was going to be ready in one hour. There wasn't that much time. Dumping her bag's contents on her bed, she stared at the books—wide-eyed and breathless.

She tucked the contraband under her bed, grabbed *Paradise*, and ducked into the corner of her closet, where she had strung Christmas lights along the top and set up pillows.

Page after page went by, and she became engrossed with the characters, feeling things she had never felt before. She imagined herself as the beautiful heiress, pretending like she was so effortlessly stunning that she could also make a boy swoon.

At dinner that night, Nora scarfed her food, thanked her parents, and continued with her lie—telling her parents she might need to pull an all-nighter to finish her "project."

Back in her reading nook with the twinkling lights above, Nora devoured her first romance novel. Her heart skipped a beat when the characters kissed for the first time, and when they reached the climax…yes, *that* climax…flutters emerged, deep in her belly. Her face flushed a deep scarlet.

Was this why her father didn't want romance in his store? He didn't want *her* to read it?

Days of sneaking around in her bedroom, reading the books she took from the smut box, came to an end after she'd consumed every last page. Twice.

She wanted more. She *needed* more. She yearned to be like the beautiful, strong women she read about. She hoped that one day she would find her one, true love—just like the stories.

She had to get her hands on more, but how? Asking her parents was out of the question. Perhaps she could check the library, but it was Saturday night, and the library was closed on Sunday.

Nora caught a glimpse of a notebook resting on her desk. Her head tilted to the side and she pursed her lips. A seed of an idea grew in her mind.

What if she *wrote* a romance story?

She picked up the notebook and sharpened a brand-new No. 2 pencil. The tip was so pointy and perfect. So satisfying.

She plopped on her bed, turned to the first blank page, and started writing down all the descriptions of the woman she wished she could be.

*Tall, thin. Long wavy hair—no widow's peak. Straight teeth—no braces. Graceful—not clumsy. Really good at...something. Like throwing parties.*

Scratch that.

*Really good at...playing the piano.*

That was better.

Nora continued until she filled the page. When she flipped to the next blank canvas, she looked down at her pencil. The pointy end had worn into a fat nub. Popping up off the bed, she sprang to her hamburger-shaped pencil sharpener and got back to work.

*My hero.*

*Tall, handsome. Golden-blond hair. Blue eyes. Rippling muscles.*

Nora giggled to herself. None of the boys in school had rippling muscles yet. She scratched that part out.

Tapping the eraser-end against her chin, she pictured Brandon White from school. He was everything she wrote down on paper, and more.

*Freckles across his nose. A dimple just below his right eye. Blue polo shirts his mom made him wear. Really good at sports.*

She scribbled and scrawled the outline of her first story until her hand ached. It was late, and she needed to help her dad at the bookstore in the morning. She read through her outline one more time, grinning from ear to ear. Pleased with herself for coming up with the idea to write her own love story, she tucked her notebook under her mattress and dreamed of what her first kiss would be like.

∗∗∗

By her senior year of high school, Nora had powered through ten notebooks, six short stories, and the beginning of a novel, in secret.

Her widow's peak finally grew naturally into her bangs, which became her trademark look. Apart from normal hair, getting a pair of boobs, and losing the metal contraptions on her face, Nora was still the awkward, sheltered girl at school. She spent all her free time in the bookshop, reading and writing—and writing some more.

Boys called her "cute," but Nora paid no attention, until one day she was approached by Brandon-freaking-White—valedictorian of their class, the head of the Science Club, and the forward for the high school hockey team. He towered over her, asking her if she was ready for the social studies exam.

She was, of course.

Then he did the one thing she had been dreaming about since middle school. He asked her out on a date. *A real date.* Not one of the made-up dates she wrote in her notebook, but an actual night out with the boy of her dreams.

Her stomach flipped. She nodded excitedly, unable to formulate the words that were stuck in her throat. They agreed on Saturday night at eight o'clock, and Nora spent the rest of the day trying to figure out how she was going to convince her dad to let her go out.

Nora's father had made a hard-and-fast rule that she couldn't date until she was eighteen, but her eighteenth birthday happened to be that Friday. It was like the stars had aligned, and the romance gods had given Nora the best birthday present of all time.

It took some begging, but she eventually persuaded her dad to let her go.

On her birthday, Nora's mom made her annual birthday pancakes with whipped cream and sprinkles. She went to school and floated from class to class, thinking of nothing but her date with Brandon, and what her first kiss might actually be like. She had dreamt of it for so long, she worried she might have built it up too much in her head.

Instead of heading to the bookshop after school, she was going to meet her parents at home for her birthday dinner. Her mom was making her favorite—spaghetti and meatballs.

Nora walked into the house and froze. She didn't smell her mom's Italian sauce. She didn't hear the news blasting from the television in the living room. Her dad wasn't on the La-Z-Boy, reading his Bible.

"Mom? Dad?"

She waited for a minute. Her dad's muffled grumbling came from the back of the house, near her bedroom.

Padding lightly down the hall, Nora pushed her door open. Her parents were sitting on her bed—her notebooks spread across the mattress.

*Oh, God. Her stories...*

"You want to explain to me what this is all about?" Nora's dad barked. Thick brows shaded his eyes.

Nora's mom had a hand on her dad's shoulder as if she were trying to keep him calm.

"You read my stories?" Nora's face grew hot, and her mouth went dry.

"I found them while I was flipping your mattress." Her mom's voice was thick with regret.

"What ever happened to privacy?" Nora asked, her voice an

octave higher than normal.

"You of all people should know better than to write this smut!" her father yelled.

"It's not smut, Dad. They are just stories—love stories. You had no right to read my stuff!"

"What has gotten into you, Nora?" her mom asked.

"Nothing! Mom! It's harmless."

"How do you explain these books then?" Her father reached behind him, grabbing the three stacked books she'd taken from the smut box years ago. She'd hidden them deep in her closet. There was no way he could have "accidentally" stumbled upon them.

"You went through my stuff?" A lump formed in her throat. Tears of betrayal flowed from her eyes.

"My daughter will not become a whore, goddammit!" Her father threw the books across the room, slamming them against the wall.

Nora and her mom flinched.

"Rules are rules. No smut in my shop. No smut in this house. You're grounded! You can forget about going on your date."

"No!" Nora looked to her mom for help, begging with her eyes. "Please, no."

"I'm sorry, dear. But your father makes the rules, and we need to stick to them. You know better than to read pornography. And to write it? God have mercy on your soul."

"Mom, please. It's not pornography." Tears streamed down her face. She watched in horror as her parents gathered her notebooks. They were taking her stories away! Her dreams were walking out of the room.

"Please don't throw those away! Please!" Nora cried.

"You're too smart for this garbage," her dad growled. "Stay

in your room and think about what you've done." He slammed the door, leaving Nora crushed in his wake.

Nora launched herself onto the bed, punching the pillows with her fists, soaking her sheets with her tears.

They'd read her books, which meant they'd read her fantasies—all the kissing, the groping, the fondling, and...Nora was too ashamed to think more of it.

She was empty inside. The characters she'd created and fallen in love with were gone. Forever.

Broken-hearted, she buried her face in the floral pillows her grandmother had made. She hadn't done anything wrong, had she? Her parents were completely ridiculous, right?

She had to get out of this small town—away from her parents, where she could figure out who she was and what she wanted on her own terms. Wiping away her tears, she stood up from the bed, composing herself as she marched toward her desk.

Nora picked up the acceptance letter from Northern Michigan University, her parents' favored college, and ripped it to shreds. Pieces fluttered to the floor.

Opening her bottom drawer, she dug through her old homework assignments—essays she kept when she was proud of her work—and pulled out her secret acceptance letter to UC Berkeley. She let out a breath of relief, thankful her parents hadn't found it in their raid.

Holding it tightly, she stared at the bold lettering of her welcome letter and spent the rest of her birthday night researching what it was like to live in the Bay Area, far, far away from home.

I

Part One

# Chapter 1

ora glanced at her watch. Her deadline was in six hours. She should be able to finish evaluating the manuscript on time, but she came in early just in case.

The office was dark and quiet. Too quiet. She flipped the light switch on and walked to her cubicle. Nora tugged at the lamp string until the soft glow illuminated her desk. The thick stack of paper would have to wait for just a second. First, she needed to print out the pickle recipe she found earlier.

Her computer came alive, and the angelic sound came through the speaker: "You have mail."

Clicking on the email she'd sent to herself, she opened the recipe link. While her recipe was printing, she grabbed the manuscript and flipped to where she'd left off yesterday. Red ink and post-it notes were plastered across the first seventy-five pages until she reached a clean page.

Six a.m. Time to get to work.

Her internship at Calico Publishing was a dream come true—but it didn't pay. She was living with her best friend for free and borrowing money from her parents for food—at least, until the internship was over. She only had two more months to impress her boss, beat out the competition, and land a full-time job.

Once she was an assistant editor, she would finally be able to contribute to the rent, no matter how much Jolie refused. Best of all, she'd finally be out of her parents' vise grip on her life—no longer relying on them for money to get by.

She could almost smell the freedom.

An hour later, she heard voices down the hall. Tina and Tracy—her competition. Nora recognized their cackling from a mile away. They were interns too, hired on the same day as Nora. Tina and Tracy became fast friends—bonding over the latest Bachelor episodes and celebrity blogs. Nora didn't make it into their cool-girl club, but she also didn't mind. After twenty-two years of being an outsider, Nora had learned to prefer it. Plus, she was there to work. Not make friends.

Tina and Tracy walked by without saying hi.

Typical.

"Good morning," Nora said to their backs.

Tina looked over her shoulder and gave Nora a smirk, while Tracy continued laughing about something Tina had said moments ago.

Nora rolled her eyes and returned to her work, forgetting about the cackling competition to focus on her dream of becoming a real editor.

*Her dream.* The words bounced around in her head like a pinball machine. It felt like only yesterday she'd dreamed of writing a romance novel, but her parents made good work of squashing that idea. They guilted her so much, Nora was too ashamed to think of it again.

So, Nora compromised. In exchange for her parents' approval to live in San Francisco after college, Nora agreed she would try to write about other things. Other things that just wouldn't cooperate in her imagination—leaving her with blank pages and empty ideas. While she struggled to write, she decided to focus on editing instead. That is, if she could land this job.

Tina and Tracy were gossiping loudly down the hall. Their voices pounded against the back of Nora's skull, reminding her she hadn't had her caffeine for the day. She couldn't focus. Gathering her things to leave, she hoped there might be a perfect spot in the coffee shop on the first floor—her favorite place to work.

***

Nora flipped the page of her manuscript while holding on to her grande macchiato. She inhaled the sweet, nutty aroma before sipping the foamy liquid that flowed down her throat. Like an IV drip keeping her alive, caffeine pulsed through her veins.

Beams of morning light poked through the city landscape behind her, warming her neck. She straightened in response to the sun's kisses and noticed the chatty women sitting at the table nearby, crinkly plastic shopping bags in tow. Their high-pitched dialogue competed with the buzzing sound of the espresso machine from across the coffee shop.

Behind the counter stood four new baristas, listening intently to the store manager as he demonstrated how to steam milk. A tall barista with tattooed arms and a red-and-black-plaid shirt stepped toward the machine and took over.

Nora studied his perfectly manicured eyebrows and thin nose. He looked like any other San Francisco hipster until he caught Nora's inquisitive stare. His honeycomb-brown eyes were surrounded by thick black lashes. The curiosity melted right off Nora's face when she realized he was staring back. The corner of his mouth curled up, and Nora's body reached a low simmer. She frantically looked down toward her manuscript, searching through a swirl of words until she found where she'd left off. She reread the sentence five times before she gave up.

Nora couldn't make sense of her reaction to the coffee shop guy. She preferred guys like Brandon White, the jockey pullover-sweater-and-polo shirt type. Nora's last boyfriend from UC Berkley was on the track team, graduated college with honors, and was currently working for the Peace Corps in Nigeria. Nora had a type, and a coffee shop guy with tattoos was not it.

She fidgeted with her pen, chewing the end. She fought the urge to look back up at the unnervingly hot coffee shop stranger until she realized a lengthy amount of time had gone by and she hadn't gotten through a single paragraph.

*I guess I'll have to sit at my desk today after all.* Stuffing the thick stack of papers under her arm and balancing her coffee on her laptop, she walked a tightrope toward the door.

As she reached for the handle, a harried businessman barreled through the doors, and Nora's coffee cup tipped over onto her cream-colored blouse. Her stack of papers fell in a heap on the floor.

"I'm so sorry," the man said, grabbing napkins and wiping off the coffee spill from her laptop. Nora looked at the scattered papers on the ground, splattered with milky caramel-colored spots. Her blouse had become translucent down the front, and she clutched her computer to cover herself, gathering her papers with one hand.

"Here, let me help." Hot Coffee Shop Guy crouched down beside her. The skin of his knees poked through the holes in his jeans. He picked up the loose papers from the floor and made a stack.

"This is so embarrassing." Nora's voice sounded smaller than she intended.

"Nah, I've seen worse," he said, handing her the final sheet of paper. "I've got the rest."

Nora held his gaze for a moment too long, trying to decode the mixture of mischief and kindness in his eyes. Her insides melted into a pool of hot lava, and she scampered to the elevators.

*** 

When Nora reached the eighth floor, she carefully set her things down at her desk. She looked down at her blouse and thanked her lucky stars she had left a pair of workout clothes in a bag under her desk.

Buzzing stirred from the very bottom of her bag, and she frantically dug through her notebooks until she found her cell phone. Boss Lady flashed on the screen.

"Hi, Evelyn."

"How's the Kline book going?"

"It's good!" Nora looked down at her stained stack of papers. "You'll have my notes by noon today."

"Perfect. And Nora, could you also take another manuscript off my desk? I just got a new deadline, and I'm completely swamped. It's called *Oberdeen*, or *Ovaline*, or something like that. It's on top of my desk—you can't miss it."

"Of course. I'll go in and grab it now."

"One more thing. There's a San Francisco arts event tonight. Sonny Coultren is one of the guests of honor. I'd like for you to join me. There will be lots of people there you should meet."

"Sonny Coultren, as in *the* Sonny Coultren?" Nora's mouth dropped. He was the most celebrated author in San Francisco. Nora had discovered his work in college. He had an amazing ability to write short love stories and poems that made her feel warm all over, and not the least bit guilty. Sonny rarely scheduled book tours or events, and when he did, he typically didn't show up for them. Nora had gone to three different signing events to meet him, but he'd been a no-show all three times. "Of course I'll go with you!"

"Great. Well, actually I'll need you to be my proxy for the first hour. My flight gets in at eight, and the event starts at seven. I'll head straight there."

"Sure, no problem."

"Thank you. You're a lifesaver. See you tonight," Evelyn said before hanging up.

Nora couldn't believe her luck. Maybe tonight would be the night she'd meet her idol. She practically skipped down the hall with her gym bag in tow and changed in the bathroom. She pulled a hooded sweatshirt over her head and teased her bangs back in place, pulling the rest of her hair into a ponytail. On her way toward Evelyn's office, her phone rang again.

"Mom? This isn't a great time to talk."

Over time, her anger toward her parents had healed. Despite their differences, Nora had preserved her relationship with them—not because she needed them, but because she loved them.

"I'll be quick. I have exciting news!"

"And what's that?" Nora hit the speaker button while her

mom talked about a new community group that she and her father had started.

Nora turned on the light in Evelyn's small office. A white leather chair was perched behind a U-shaped white acrylic desk covered by stacks of manuscripts and magazines. A small green plant sat next to the wide-screen computer monitor, browning along the edges. Nora made a mental note to water her boss's plant for her.

"And we've been approved to use the space in the back of the curling club on Wednesday nights and Sunday mornings."

"So, wait a minute. You and Dad started a new church?"

"It's better than that, honey. It's a community center for people like us who are fed up with Pastor Tom's old ways. Plus, it gives your father a sense of purpose now that he's sold the bookshop. Here, talk to your father real quick."

"Wait, what? You sold the shop?" *Without asking me how I felt about it?* That little corner in the shop held most of her childhood memories. It felt like a piece of her was being given away to a stranger she didn't know.

"Nora." Her father's gruff voice came on the other line. There was a lingering silence before Nora could muster the strength to respond with a simple hello.

"Your mom and I decided it was time to retire. We were made a good offer for the shop last week. We would have been fools to turn it down. You know we're not getting any younger."

"Dad, I'm just a little shocked. I guess I thought that bookshop would be in our lives forever."

"Well, pumpkin, it's not going away. The bookshop will always be there, under new ownership. And now your mom and I can focus on the work we've been wanting to do for a long time—God's work."

Nora rolled her eyes. She shouldn't have been surprised it would come to this. Her father always thought he was holier-than-thou.

"What do you even know about starting a church, Dad?"

"It's a community group, and I know enough. We already have thirty people signed up to help build our center."

"That's like half our town."

"Yep. We're giving Pastor Tom a bit of competition. Here, your mother wants to talk to you. I love you, pumpkin."

"Nora?"

"Mom, what the heck is going on there?"

"Isn't it just fantastic? I'm making cookies for our grand opening. The ones with the frosting you like so much. Wish you could be here, honey. I have to go; the oven is calling me!"

"But—"

"Bye!" Her mom clicked off. Nora stared at her phone, feeling like her world had been turned upside down. Her parents had just sold a cornerstone of her childhood. She wasn't sure how she was supposed to feel at twenty-two years old, after moving out of her hometown. She'd only been home a few times since she left for college, but she always kept a piece of that place in her heart.

A small pout formed on her mouth as she got back to her task, flipping through stacks of manuscripts. Nora spotted the manuscript titled *Overlooked.* That must be what Evelyn was talking about. She brought it back to her desk and opened up her original manuscript. She couldn't afford any more distractions.

Just then, a wadded paper ball flew from across the cubicle

wall and hit Nora on the side of the head. A low snicker could be heard behind the gray wall.

"That's not funny, Brent. I have a deadline."

"Oh, come on, Nora. I'm just having a little fun." A freckle-faced grin popped over the cubicle wall and beamed down at Nora, followed by a bow tie.

"Don't you have work to do?"

"Have dinner with me Saturday, and I'll leave you alone now."

"You know I don't date people from work." She chucked the paper ball back across the wall, hitting Brent in the nose.

"I'll quit my job," he quipped.

"No." She could hear him sulk back in his chair. There was a long pause as Nora waited for what she knew was coming next.

"You know you want this," Brent said slyly through the cube wall.

Nora gave an exaggerated sigh. Brent was incorrigible. He had been relentless, flirting with her since the day they started their internship with the cackling twins a year ago.

Brent came from money. He was smart and funny, but Nora wasn't attracted to him. She actually felt sorry for him. His father was some big shot entrepreneur in Silicon Valley who apparently was too busy to spend any time with him. He would make it up to Brent by buying him a Porsche or sending him and his mother on trips to Europe. Despite the fact that Brent had everything he could have ever wanted, he never seemed content. He acted upbeat, but Nora could read between the lines. He had daddy issues.

Nora packed her things again. "Sorry, Brent, but I'm going to work somewhere else today."

"Boo," he said, moping.

Nora made her way out of the building, hiding her face from the mortifying incident at the coffee shop earlier. She walked to the corner and hopped on her second favorite workplace in the city—the San Francisco Muni bus.

***

"These go up in the front. Let me show you."

Kellen dragged the heavy bags of coffee grinds around to the front of the coffee shop, and Richard opened one of the cupboards below the espresso machines.

"Here you go. You put these away, and I'll take care of a few things in the back before the rest of the newbies get here."

Kellen nodded. It wasn't the work he wanted to be doing, but he was grateful for the job while he was figuring out his next steps. Until he could get a job working in a recording studio, he'd be stuck doing the same shit he'd done in high school. Making coffee for yuppie San Francisco businesspeople.

He had graduated from Audio Engineering Tech, and was anxious to do real audio engineering work instead of part-time jobs to pay for the insane rent in the city. Home wasn't an option. His father made sure that was clear after beating the shit out of him last Thanksgiving. He'd been drunk and looking for a fight—choosing Kellen's mom as the victim, until Kellen had had enough. Standing up for his mother cost him a broken collarbone and a black eye that didn't heal for weeks.

It didn't take long for Kellen to get the hint he wasn't welcome anymore. He insisted his mother come with him, but she refused. Kellen was on his own at twenty years old. He took a job as a bartender and moved into a dinky apartment in the Mission. He wasn't sure it was legal to have six people in the apartment, but the rent was barely affordable for his tiny closet space.

He was making it through life as a bartender for a few years, picking up freelance audio gigs on the side, saving a little bit of money, but not enough to buy his own equipment, or to live on his own.

When the restaurant was sold to new management, they laid off the entire staff. Kellen was shit out of luck and desperate for a job, which was how he ended up back in a coffee shop, until he could come up with his next move.

Kellen had been flirting with a waitress named Jenny whose father owned a recording studio. She was smoking hot, but that was about all he could glean from their interactions. She was into him, teasing him during their shifts, touching him every chance she got. He'd been working up to asking her for a favor—to get a foot in the door at her father's studio—but he didn't want to give her the wrong idea. The day they lost their jobs, Jenny took matters into her own hands and asked him out. Their first date was tomorrow.

After the other three new baristas showed up, Richard took them through the rules and regulations of working at Coffee Benz.

They must wear their uniform attire.

They must pay for their own food and drink and were not allowed to eat or drink in front of their "guests."

They must be professional and courteous to all guests no matter what.

The guest was always right.

Richard, the manager, demonstrated how to use the espresso machine to make a twelve-ounce latte.

"Here, Kellen. Why don't you take over, since you already have experience as a barista?"

"Sure." Kellen stepped up to the machine. He packed the portafilter with espresso and locked it into place. As he poured milk into a pitcher, he felt eyes on him from across the room. He looked up, and sure enough, he settled on a curious gaze. Like a deer in headlights, the girl quickly looked down at whatever she was working on. The girl with the bangs had delicate features and perfect porcelain skin. The little ruffle in her cream-colored blouse made her look like she was dressed for church, but there was something sinful about the way she chewed on the tip of her pen. Her succulent lips parted just enough to make the air escape Kellen's lungs.

Kellen focused back on the task at hand and completed the latte in time to take an order from a new customer. Richard hovered over his shoulder as he pointed out each button he needed to press for a tall skinny cappuccino with a shot of vanilla. As Richard demonstrated how to properly give one shot of vanilla flavoring to the steamy beverage, Kellen heard a commotion at the front of the shop. Papers were floating in the air, and the cute girl with bangs stood in shock, her blouse covered in a stain that clung to her petite torso.

He rushed over to help, picking up the coffee-stained papers, inquisitively eyeing the words on the page. She was young, possibly still in college. He couldn't be certain, but he was sure about one thing—she was cute as hell all flustered like that.

"This is so embarrassing," she said.

"Nah, I've seen worse. Here's the last one. I've got the rest."

"Thanks," the girl said. Her face had become the sweetest shade of pink, all the way up to the tips of her ears.

He watched her delicately walk out of the coffee shop and into the elevator. She was so thin, her little frame barely able to hold up her bag while she clutched her laptop to her chest. He suppressed the urge to run out and help her some more. The elevators closed.

As he mopped up the coffee spill, his phone buzzed in his back pocket. It was a text from Jenny.

*Pick u up at six tomorrow?*

*Sure,* he texted back.

*Looking forward to our date.*

Kellen stared at the phone, withdrawing from the text conversation. In truth, he wasn't excited about going on a date with Jenny. *She's beautiful,* he thought, trying to psyche himself up. Surely she had other good qualities.

He looked back toward the elevator and wondered if he would ever see the cute girl at the coffee shop again.

# Chapter 2

Nora walked down the aisle of the Muni bus, passing the honeymooners in the sixth row and a kind-looking old man reading a newspaper. She stepped up onto the stairs leading toward the back seat before plopping her book bag in the corner. The bus pulled forward, and the bumps and creaks set the calming background Nora needed to immerse herself in the Kline story about two teenagers who meet in chemistry class. They fell in love, of course. By the time Nora made it through a full bus route, she'd learned their chemistry teacher was actually the vampire they'd been searching for. Nora pursed her lips at the cute plot twist.

*The young adult audience is going to love this.* She was happy she would be able to write a positive report, knowing that Evelyn could give this author a chance of being published.

The bus hit a pothole, and her pen flew across the seat to land next to an elderly Chinese man. He stood, gripping the bus pole as if his life depended on it. He reached up and handed the pen back to her, smiling sweetly with deep-set crinkles at the edges of his eyes.

"Thank you," Nora said. She studied him for a moment as he shakily sat back down and continued staring out the window. Nora grabbed a spare notebook from her purse and jotted down words that came to mind.

*A wise old soul in khaki pants and mismatched taupe jacket. Long, lonely strands of hair, draped over a spotted scalp. He had the answers to every question in the world, a secret that he planned to take to the grave.*

She closed her notebook and smiled down at the sweet man. He nodded to her as if he knew she had written his description in her notebook, but he looked off into the distance as if he were happy she had. Nora casually flipped through her pages of notes. She had collected hundreds of descriptions since moving to California. Nora hadn't been able to use any of them yet, but she kept adding to the collection in case they might come in handy for a novel one day.

"*Write your first novel, then throw it away*," her college professor had told her. Nora hated that advice. How could she possibly put her heart and soul into a novel that was going to end up in the trash? The pressure of writing her first book to be or not be in the garbage was one of the many reasons she had writer's block. She could write descriptions all day, but when it came to characters and plots, Nora's ideas never strayed from a sweet love story. She was devoid of any good ideas worth pursuing without disappointing her parents.

Nora reached up to grab the bus cord and gathered her things as the bus driver pulled over at the next stop. Rows of pastel-colored apartment buildings lined the steep hill in front of her. Step after step, Nora made the great ascent up to her light blue building with the black door. She stopped to catch her breath while searching through her bag for her keys. Her hand scoured the bottom of her purse, and she realized she'd accidentally left her keys on the kitchen counter.

Time to text Jolie.

*Help! I'm locked out!*

"Did you leave your keys at home again?" a familiar voice boomed from across the street.

Nora twisted around to find Fred, the friendliest homeless man in all of San Francisco, sitting in his usual spot on the park bench with a paper shopping bag by his side. His white beard frayed out like a wide net, catching all the bread crumbs from his meals that week. His cheeks were the shade of a watermelon Jolly Rancher, and the tip of his nose looked like a bumpy wad of Bubblicious gum.

"Hey, Fred." Nora waved.

"That was a mighty fine batch of pickles you made yesterday. I'm almost halfway through them already."

"Aw, thanks. I'm glad you liked them." Nora was pleased she'd found someone who enjoyed her pickles almost as much as she did. She'd tried a new blend of spices over the weekend that gave her pickles a little kick after the initial tangy crunch. Nora made a note to open up a jar once she could get in through the front door.

"How did the people-watching go today?" Nora asked.

"Not like the seventies, my dear, but it was pretty good. Haight-Ashbury will never disappoint. Although I will say I am a little concerned with the sex-trafficking in this city."

"The what?"

"Some young fella came up to me today and asked if I wanted to buy some girl named Molly."

"Oh." Nora giggled. "I think he was trying to sell you drugs."

"Ah, that explains the look on his face when I told him Molly deserved a better home."

Nora and Fred shared a laugh as Jolie opened their front door. Her hair was pulled back into a ponytail with wispy, loose waves framing her sweaty face.

"Hey, Nora," Jolie said breathlessly as she left the door open and got back to her yoga mat. She resumed her upside-down position, and the blood rushed back to her cheeks. Nora waved goodbye to her friend across the street and closed the door behind her.

The kitchen countertop was cluttered with lemon peels, bottles of vinegar, and distilled water. Jolie must have been mixing another one of her healthy concoctions. Nora set her bag down and grabbed a jar of pickles from the fridge.

"What are you doing home early?" Jolie asked, the soles of her feet coming together.

"I couldn't focus at the coffee shop or my desk, so I got on the bus."

Jolie laughed and fell out of her headstand. "You and your bus work. You are so strange."

"*I'm* strange? Now, that's rich coming from you," Nora teased. "What kind of potion are you making this time?"

"It's called a *colon cleanse*. It's only for three days."

Nora rolled her eyes. Jolie was known for ditching her cleansing regimens after only a few hours. She loved food too much, but Nora couldn't blame her. She did too.

"So, how's the blog coming along today?" Nora asked. Jolie had twenty-five thousand followers, mostly men. She lured them in on Instagram with selfie pics in yoga poses on rooftops, beaches, and hiking trails. Her blog was about anything and everything that inspired her, from organic beauty products to her six-week stint as a bisexual.

"Today, I'm writing about my relationship with my anus. I've been on this cleanse since last night, and my stomach feels like it's been washed out with Pine-Sol."

"Good grief." The tips of Nora's ears warmed. "How do you think up this stuff?"

"I don't know, but I do know I'll get a lot of site traffic," Jolie said with a wink.

Nora shook her head and sat down at her desk with her pickles. Through the doorframe, Nora watched Jolie prop herself into King Pigeon pose like a graceful dancer. Her beach-wavy ponytail flowed down her tanned skin. She had long, lean legs, twisting and stretching into positions Nora would never be able to obtain herself. Jolie caught her foot with her hands behind her head, her floral tattoo across her chest pressed up toward the ceiling.

"How are you doing that?" Nora called out from her room.

Jolie smiled, breathing into her pose. She fluttered her almond-shaped eyes. Most people had a hard time pinpointing Jolie's ethnicity. Her father was Israeli and her mother was Chinese. Regardless, she was model-level gorgeous in a way that made "cute" Nora virtually disappear beside her.

Nora would admit she was a little jealous, especially since she lived in Jolie's shadow all the time. There had been a few instances during college when Nora had brought home a boy, and he'd ended up falling in love with Jolie instead. It was their only point of contention…for the most part.

As freshman roommates at Berkeley, they bonded over both being the "only child" and of having tyrant fathers—each toxic in their own ways. Over time, they called themselves "sisters from other misters." Nora learned to accept Jolie's eccentric

San Franciscan lifestyle and her carefree spirit. Likewise, Jolie learned to accept Nora's sheltered Midwestern ways and her slightly hermit-like tendencies.

Opposites attracted in that freshman-year dorm room, and they'd been best friends ever since.

Nora feverishly typed up her notes on the young adult manuscript while Jolie finished her yoga routine. The reverberating sound of meditation bowls competed with the rapid-fire clicking of the keyboard, giving Nora a headache.

*Done.* With five minutes to spare.

Nora hit the send button and popped up off her chair. Her stomach growled, reminding her it was time to eat lunch. She thought of her favorite banh mi place in the Castro, and her mouth watered.

"I'm thinking of going to Dinosaurs. You want to come?" Nora asked.

"Hell yes," Jolie said, leaping out of her tree pose. "I freaking love that place."

"Hey wait, what about your cleanse?"

"Oh yeah. I'll start over tomorrow," Jolie said, putting on her black leather jacket. "My fans will never know." She flipped her long ponytail behind her shoulder and skipped down the steps.

Nora shook her head, smirking to herself as she followed her friend out the door.

✳✳✳

Nora and Jolie hopped off the bus in front of a giant flagpole with a bright rainbow flag that flapped elegantly in the wind. They walked past a cookie shop with penis-shaped cookies featured in the window.

"Yum," Jolie said, licking her lips. "My kind of cookie. Want to tag team one after lunch?"

"You are incorrigible."

"You love it though."

"My parents would die if they visited here," Nora said.

"You mean the gay epicenter of the world wouldn't be the first place you'd take your small-town parents who have never left the state?"

Jolie opened the door to the banh mi place, and they breathed in the smell of pickled vegetables, cilantro, and Vietnamese spices. There were a couple of white folding tables and chairs in the center of the small room. Next to the cash register were unidentified snacks with cartoon shrimp printed on the packaging.

"My parents would definitely be out of their comfort zone." Nora laughed at the thought. "Did I tell you they sold the bookshop?"

"No, you didn't mention it," Jolie said. "Two specials please." She looked back at Nora. "How do you feel about it?"

"I don't know. I feel like they sold a piece of me away without asking for my permission. I realize they didn't have to consult me, but it doesn't make me less sad."

"I'm sorry, Nora," Jolie said as she grabbed napkins from the canister next to the cash register.

"I'm all right. I guess. I don't know, it feels like I lost a friend. I fell in love with books there, and it's where I accidentally came across romance novels. I loved them so much, I started writing my own. Did I ever mention that?" Nora asked.

"You wrote romance? What the hell? How have I known you this long and you never mentioned it before?"

Nora sighed. "I don't know. I guess I don't like to talk about it because my dad made me feel like a whore when he found out."

"You told me your dad was strict, but that's a bit extreme, don't you think? Or were you writing some kinky stuff?" Jolie grinned in jest.

"They were just sweet little love stories. Kind of like what Sonny Coultren writes, but for teenagers, and way more amateur."

"Aren't you naughty." Jolie's words dripped with sarcasm.

"It *was* naughty, for me! I was so sheltered."

"You still are."

"Here's the thing. I want to write a book, but every idea I have leads me to some sort of love story. I'm not sure I want to write anything else."

"Then do it!"

They grabbed their sack of sandwiches and walked up the street toward the busy corner of the Castro that had tables and chairs and the best people-watching in town. Nora felt the heat from the sun seep through her sweatshirt. She slipped it off and put it on her chair.

"I can't write a romance novel. My parents would disown me and stop sending me grocery money before my internship ends."

"Who cares? I can help you out. No questions asked."

"You know I can't ask you to do that. You've already done so much for me." The sick, guilty feeling crept in her stomach, almost making her lose her appetite. "Plus, what if I embarrass them?" Nora stared at her sandwich, ashamed that embarrassing her parents still mattered after all these years. Why couldn't she be more like Jolie and just do what she wanted?

"They don't have to know what you're writing about," Jolie said with a mouth full of banh mi.

"I can't lie. I'm bad at it. And I would get caught somehow. They would find out and then never speak to me again."

"Then I'd say—good riddance. You have to follow your heart. You have to write what you love."

"Coming from the girl who's writing about her anus…"

Jolie scoffed. "Hey! I love my anus!"

The couple sitting at the table next to them turned to look, their eyebrows raised into visor hats.

Jolie ignored them and continued, "I say, tell them you want to write a fucking romance novel, and if they have a problem with it, they can just go to hell."

"I'll get right on that." Nora rolled her eyes and threw a displaced pickled carrot at Jolie, hitting her square between the eyes.

Jolie shot back with a jalapeno. It landed in Nora's lap.

"You brat." Nora laughed.

"Seriously, Nora. The only way you'll become a successful writer is if you write about what you like. You owe it to yourself." Jolie took a big bite, moaning as she chewed her food. "Good grief, this sandwich is as good as sex."

Nora took a bite. The crisp pickled vegetables offered a crunch, paired nicely with the chewy texture of the French baguette, and the salty pork, pâté, and spicy jalapenos were a hearty contrast to the creamy house-made mayonnaise. Nora was in heaven.

"This is good, but I'll have to take your word for it."

Jolie always teased her about her virginity, but Nora had stopped caring long ago. She hadn't found her knight in shining armor yet, and she wouldn't settle for anything less.

A fleck of light sparkled across Jolie's face. When she looked up, her eyes grew round like giant eight balls. "Don't. Look," Jolie muttered under her breath.

Nora froze, waiting until she could see what had sparked her friend's amazement. After a moment Nora could make out in her peripheral vision a naked man strolling down the sidewalk, wearing nothing but a pair of black army boots and a little yellow rubber band around the base of his male parts. Nora nearly choked on a bite of her sandwich as the nudist walked past, his buns in plain sight. He took a seat on the bench underneath the flagpole and casually leaned back to soak in the sun's rays.

"You see, even that park bench has gotten more action than you," Jolie said, and they both giggled quietly in their food while the gentleman pulled out a newspaper from underneath his naked butt.

# Chapter 3

Tonight was the night. The San Francisco event of the year, where local well-known artists, musicians and writers got together to celebrate the art community in the city, by invitation only. Sonny Coultren was expected at the art gallery at any moment. Nora slugged her first glass of wine to ease her jittering nerves.

The art gallery was dimly lit. A small jazz band played in the back corner. All around the room were white columns with sculpted bronze figures. The first sculpture in the main entryway was a man's torso with chiseled muscles and a pair of wings that looked like they had been through war—battered, torn, and broken. Just beyond the entryway, a sculpted eagle perched on a heavy bronze tree branch with a severed hand in its beak.

Nora nervously surveyed the crowd. Everyone there was at least ten years her senior. She bit her lip, wondering how she was going to survive this event until Evelyn showed up.

"Red or white?" a server dressed in black asked, holding a tray of glittering wines.

"White, please." Nora swapped out her empty glass for a new one and pondered the right way to hold her wine. She recalled someone in college saying something about a right way and a wrong way, but she couldn't seem to remember which was which. She glanced at a nearby group of people, but she couldn't see their hands. Nora gripped the stem firmly, pinky up, and decided that would do for now.

She walked to a sculpture of a male figure on his knees, his hands pressed together in prayer, his face contorted in agony. The veins protruded from his skin, and every muscle in his forearms was intricately carved with exquisite detail.

"I wonder what he's praying for," a man with a short white beard and round, wire-rimmed glasses said.

"Begging for forgiveness, probably," a woman with short black hair and a full set of red lips replied.

"Of course, you would assume the man did something wrong, Vicki."

"Don't be so naive. A man on his knees means only one of two things."

"Maybe he's proposing to the woman he loves, but she said 'no' and he's begging for her to reconsider," Nora chimed in. The posh couple looked up at her from their wineglasses and gave polite smiles. Nora immediately felt foolish. She wished she could take it back.

"Quite the imagination you have, darling," Vicki said.

Nora forced a smile at the arrogant pair as they moseyed to the next sculpture without looking back.

Nora looked at her watch. Evelyn wouldn't be there for another hour. How was she supposed to mingle with these people without her? Nora looked around the gallery for a familiar face, but she didn't recognize anyone yet.

Maybe Sonny was there already? She didn't know what he looked like, but she imagined him to look something like Paul Newman, or what he had looked like in his sixties. Scanning the crowd, she didn't see anyone who looked like he could be Sonny.

Across the room, she recognized Barry Johnson, an editor at Calico on the same floor as Evelyn, just a few offices down the hall. She didn't know him, but he always smiled at her in the hallway. This was her chance to introduce herself officially. She mustered the courage to walk to him, reminding herself that possibly one day he might have an open position on his team. It was best for her career to get to know him.

"Mr. Johnson? My name is Nora Miller. I'm an intern working for Evelyn Hampshire."

"It's a pleasure to officially meet you, Nora. This is Joan Spliner. She's an editor on the seventh floor in cozy mysteries. And this is Eric Greenwall, an author I've been working with for the past ten years."

"Oh, wow. Eric Greenwall?" Nora couldn't believe it. "It's a pleasure to meet you! I just finished reading *A Dark Horse Rising*. I really enjoyed it."

"Well, thank you, Nora. That's so kind of you to say." Eric's face crinkled into a smile.

*Okay, so far so good.*

"Do you think Sonny Coultren will actually show up tonight?" Nora asked, finishing the last drop of liquid courage from her wineglass.

"He's such an odd man. I can't say I'd be surprised if he didn't show," Eric said.

"Have you met him before?" Nora asked.

"Yes indeed. And he is not what you'd expect. He's kind of—"

"Eccentric. To say the least," Joan chimed in.

"He's a darn good writer, though. I'll give him that," Barry said.

Nora nodded and grabbed another glass of wine from a passing server. She pretended to listen when the conversation shifted to politics. The gallery felt crowded all of a sudden—there must have been a hundred people crammed into the tiny space, waiting to see the great Sonny Coultren speak. She hoped beyond hope that he wouldn't disappoint them again.

Before she knew it, she'd finished her fourth glass of wine, and she was feeling lighter on her feet. The gallery became less stuffy—and more fun. Her body felt tingly from her head to her toes. With alcohol coursing through her inexperienced veins, she found herself recounting a story about playing flag football in college. And she couldn't stop talking.

"I mean, you should have seen it. Look at me. I was by far the smallest person on the field, and yet I caught that interception like I was some sort of superhero."

*Shut up, Nora. Shut. Up.*

"I started charging down the field as if I were Barry Sanders playing for the Detroit Lions."

Barry and Eric chuckled into their wineglasses.

*Oh, good. They're laughing.* Maybe she wasn't making a fool of herself. She'd come too far. She had to finish the story.

"And that's when I ran smack into this lumberjack-looking dude on the field. His knee made contact with my leg, and snap!"

"Oh my goodness," Joan said. "You broke your leg?"

"I sure did. The only sport I ever played in my life, and I was on crutches for weeks. My poor roommate, Jolie, had to haul me around campus so I could attend my classes."

"That is quite a story," a man said. He had copper skin and

icy blue eyes. His thick, beautiful accent gave away that he was Italian. His arms were crossed as if he had been standing there the whole time. Had he been? Nora hadn't noticed. Her head felt fuzzy. He must have seen the puzzled look on her face because he reached for her hand to introduce himself.

"I'm Antonio Cafarelli. I'm the artist."

Nora blinked a few times, trying to stop the swirling motion in her brain. How did she get this drunk?

"You're the artist that sculpted everything here?" Nora whirled her hand, gesturing around the room. She forced her hands back down, trying to appear normal, but she ended up feeling even more awkward than before.

"I did." He chuckled.

"Wow. You are really, really good. I mean really good. I especially like the woman cradling her baby. Where is that one?" Nora turned and knocked her shoulder into one of the white columns, startling herself. The bronze sculpture perched on the column started to sway. Nora's eyes grew wide as the bronze bust of a man tipped over. Time slowed down as the sculpture soared through the air.

*Boom!*

Nora froze in horror as the bronze sculpture lay on the floor. Her world came crashing down on her, and she stood in complete disbelief.

"Oh no! I am so sorry!" She ran over to inspect the damage. The marble block attached to the bust had broken into several chunks. The tile floor underneath was cracked, with a deep black hole where the sculpture made impact.

Evelyn was going to fire her for this. Nora swallowed, but her throat felt like it was coated with chalk.

"Are you okay, miss?" Antonio asked.

"Am I okay? What about your art? Have I ruined it?"

Antonio and Eric hoisted it up and then placed it back on the column. The nose was dented. The sculpture was *ruined.*

"Oh my God." Nora cupped her mouth.

"What happened here?" Nora heard Evelyn's voice from behind her. Evelyn's mouth was agape. Her face went from confused to worried in a flash of a second.

Nora urged herself not to cry, holding back the waterworks that were about to explode. "I just can't believe I did that." Everyone in the room was staring at her. They didn't even try to hide their gawking and snickering.

Nora felt a rogue tear fall down her cheek.

Evelyn pushed her way to Nora, wrapping her arms around her and giving her a tight squeeze. "Are you okay?"

"I feel terrible. I'm such a klutz."

"Don't you worry about it," Evelyn whispered. "It'll work itself out."

"Am I fired?"

Evelyn pursed her lips. "No, you're not fired. Let me talk with the artist and see if we can figure something out."

Nora pointed toward Antonio, who was hovering around his sculpture with a deep frown. Evelyn walked over to Antonio and led him to the back of the room, where she spoke to him in private, away from the crowd. Eventually, the other guests carried on their conversations, paying little to no attention to Nora standing by herself in the middle of the crowded room.

Nora watched intently as Evelyn spoke with Antonio. He was nodding.

*That's good.*

Then Evelyn put her hand on his forearm.

*That's...interesting.*

Evelyn smiled. Then she giggled.

*What is going on?*

Eventually, Evelyn looked up and smiled at Nora, sending her a long-distance signal that everything would be okay.

"Excuse me, everyone. May I have your attention please?" A woman with frizzy bleached hair and turquoise eye shadow yelled over the hushed conversations in the gallery.

"I'm sorry to inform you all that Sonny Coultren will not be attending tonight's event. He's addressing a personal matter and sends his apologies."

The crowd was silent. No groans, no surprised faces. Sonny never showed up to anything. At least he wasn't there to witness the biggest snafu of Nora's life.

Why would he continue to agree to events and then not come? She contemplated that while she watched Evelyn give Antonio her business card. A slight smile on Antonio's face made Nora question what else those two were talking about.

"Are you okay if I head home, Evelyn? I think I've made a fool of myself enough for one day."

"Yes, of course. Thanks for being my stand-in."

"I'm sorry I'm such a disappointment." Nora looked down at her hands, wishing this horrible day could be over.

"You can make it up to me by finishing the Oberdeen book. Ovaline. Whatever that thing is called." Evelyn smiled. "It was a tight deadline."

Nora nodded, holding onto that string of hope all the way home. She could turn this around. She just needed to do a good job in the office. Who needed to be good at fancy parties anyway?

***

At about five a.m., Nora peeled her face off the manuscript page and rolled herself into the bathroom. Mascara from the night before had drifted under her eyes. A drool mark made a crescent moon shape along the right side of her mouth. Her bangs went several directions at once, and the rest of her brunette hair had formed a little bird's nest at the top of her head. It was definitely going to take longer to get ready this morning.

After showering and drying her hair, Nora stood in the steamy bathroom, rubbing a circle on the sink mirror to see her reflection. Bags under her eyes gave away the fact that she didn't get enough sleep.

She needed to make up for last night's horrible accident. Staying up until two in the morning was the least she could do to get through Evelyn's manuscript. There was still more work to be done, but she'd given herself a head start.

She drew a thin, soft black outline around her blue-green eyes and applied a coat of mascara to her long lashes, all the while rehearsing how she was going to apologize again for ruining that sculpture. The pit of her stomach felt full of needles. Putting on her serious black button-up blouse, she was determined to rewrite her reputation. No more clumsy mistakes.

As she walked down the stairs of her apartment, she waved at Fred, who was sitting on his bench.

"What's on the agenda today, Fred?"

"You're looking at it, kid," he said. "You're looking sharp today. What's the occasion?"

"Trying to impress my boss. I made a real mess of things

last night at this gallery thing. And I really need to make it up to her. Plus she said she would help me with a novel one day. I want to stay on her good side."

"You wrote a novel?"

"Not yet. I'm just waiting on the right idea."

He nodded. "Well, once you've got that book idea, you let me know. I'd be happy to help you too."

Nora smiled and saluted him as she walked onto the Muni bus. On the ride downtown, Nora thought about how lonely it would be to sit on a park bench all day. Her heart hurt for him. She couldn't imagine not having a house to go home to or a bed to sleep in at night. The people-watching in San Francisco might be the best in the country, but there had to have been moments he was bored. Maybe she would ask for his help with her novel if she ever figured out what she wanted to write.

Nora's phone vibrated from somewhere in her tote bag. She clawed her way to the bottom of the bag to find a text message from Evelyn.

*Good morning! Do you mind picking up a latte on your way?*

Nora walked into the coffee shop. It was oddly quiet, with only the soft murmur of Miles Davis playing in the corner speakers of the room. The tables and chairs were empty, and she walked up to the abandoned cash register.

"Hello? Anyone there?"

Nora heard footsteps coming from the back room, and a moment later, the tall barista from yesterday came out, wiping his hands with a washcloth. His tattooed arms stretched behind him as he put his hands in his pockets, his eyes locking on Nora as he smiled.

"Sorry about that. What can I get you?"

Bewitched by his unconventional handsomeness, Nora swallowed the furball in her throat. Her tongue went dry. She had forgotten what she was there for. She looked at the board behind him for inspiration, but the words merged together until they looked like hieroglyphics. She blinked a few times, squinting her eyes, forcing herself to snap out of her incoherent state.

"I'm sorry," Nora said sheepishly. "I'll have a twelve-ounce Americano and a grande skinny latte for my boss."

He rubbed his chin, smiling as he punched the order into the cash register. A white rabbit tattoo on his forearm looked like a page out of *Alice's Adventures in Wonderland*. As she wondered about the significance of it, she glanced up to find that he was looking at her as if he was expecting a response.

"I'm sorry, what was that?" Nora asked.

"That will be six ninety."

He had a dimple in his left cheek, framed by a chiseled jawline that she had only seen in movies. He was beautiful but in a dark kind of way. The top of his chest tattoo peeked along the neckline of his black shirt, and Nora wondered how much of his body was covered in ink. Dark, mysterious, tattooed strangers did not normally appeal to Nora, but she found herself swimming in a confusing, lustful state.

"Did you say sixty-nine?" Nora heard herself ask.

"Six ninety." He chuckled.

"Oh, right." Nora's cheeks flushed, and she felt her neck turn the same shade of red as the rose tattoo on his arm.

He smiled and got to work on her drinks. Nora stepped back, feeling mystified and unsure of whether or not she still had her wits. She had to pull herself together if she was going prove she was ready for the assistant editor position.

*I'm a strong, confident woman*, she repeated to herself. She decided to practice on Hot Coffee Shop Guy while she waited for her drinks.

"So, are you new to the coffee shop?" she asked, talking over the sound of grinding espresso beans.

"Yep."

She looked him over, waiting for more, but he bent over and pulled the skim milk out of the mini fridge.

"You from here?"

"Yep."

Nora narrowed her eyes at him. She swore she saw the corner of his mouth twitch. He was making this difficult on purpose—as if he knew she was trying out her brand-new self on him, and he was going to make it extra challenging for her.

Nora blew her bangs out of her eyes, determined to pull more information out of him.

"Have you been a barista before?"

He placed both drinks on the counter and looked her square in the eyes. "Yep." He smiled, eyes twinkling with mischief.

Nora held his gaze, drowning in his deliberate silence. "Are you usually this laconic?"

"Yep." He winked, then shot up when he noticed another customer had walked through the door.

"See you later, then," Nora drawled. Not her most successful attempt at making small talk, but he was doing that on purpose. She was sure of it.

Nora picked up the two coffees and walked toward the elevators. She looked back through the coffee shop windows, and Hot Coffee Shop Guy was giving her a friendly wave as the elevator doors closed.

He was either toying with her, or he didn't want anything

to do with her. It was probably the latter, but why should she care? It wasn't like he was her type anyway. He looked to be a few years older—working at a coffee shop. No ambition, probably—no goals in life, other than adding another tattoo to his collection. Then why was she so flustered?

She couldn't put her finger on the churning feeling inside, a weird yearning to march back into that coffee shop and demand better answers from a complete stranger who knocked her off her confidence horse. He was only supposed to be practice!

Nora huffed. Yeah, he was cute, but he was not boyfriend material. Her parents would throw a fit if she showed up at home for the holidays in the arms of a guy like that. Hot Coffee Shop Guy would not fit in her world.

As the elevator bell rang on the eighth floor, a light bulb went off above Nora's head.

*She has something to prove.*

*He wants her to fail.*

*She's a...businesswoman...trying to find her confidence.*

*He's a...coffee farmer...and gets in the way of her dreams.*

Like a lightning bolt striking down from above, ideas formed in rapid succession. She rushed to her desk and jotted down her thoughts, one right after the other, until her wrist started to cramp.

"Is this for me?" Evelyn chimed in, interrupting Nora's stream of consciousness spewing from her pen. Nora looked over at the latte on her desk and realized she had forgotten to drop it off.

"I'm so sorry! I got sidetracked with this book idea." Nora's face grew warm. She already messed up by not rushing her boss's coffee to her office. *Get it together, Nora.*

"I can't wait to hear about it," Evelyn said, grabbing her latte and placing a ten-dollar bill in its place.

"Wait. Let me get you some change." Nora reached for her purse.

"Don't bother. Thanks for the coffee. Now, after you finish getting your ideas down on paper, come by my desk and let's talk through your notes on the Kline book."

"That's it? You're not going to reprimand me for getting drunk and knocking over that sculpture last night?"

"I told you already how you could make it up to me. Now, get to work." She turned on her heel. Her short black hair swayed against her shoulders as she walked back to her office, closing the door behind her.

Nora feverishly scribbled down her ideas—before she lost her train of thought. Her words gushed like a waterfall, finally breaking through the icy glacier that had held her back for years.

The beginnings of her book came alive in outline form, and then she paused, remembering the look of disgust on her father's face when he'd discovered her love stories.

Jolie's words sprang into the forefront of her mind. *The only way you'll become a successful writer is if you write about what you like.*

She was right. The only way out of Nora's writer's block was to write what she wanted. To hell with her parents. At least, they didn't need to know about it.

Hot Coffee Shop Guy and Nora might not have a future together, but the sexy plantation owner and the starchy-clean businesswoman did. She almost hugged herself; she finally had her book idea.

# Chapter 4

Nora walked into Evelyn's office and noticed an expression on her face she hadn't seen before. Evelyn's eyes were glossed over, not really looking at anything. The corner of her mouth curled into a wispy smile as she hummed a tune Nora didn't recognize.

"Hey, Evelyn. Is now a good time to talk about the Kline book?"

Shaken from her reverie, Evelyn faced Nora as if she just noticed she wasn't alone.

"Of course, please sit."

"Before we get started, I just have to say that I really appreciate how cool you have been about the whole incident last night."

"Well, let's just say that I see a little of myself in you. I remember what it was like to be young and new to the industry. Not really fitting in, if you don't mind me saying so. I've noticed how Tina and Tracy act around you."

Nora bit her lip, nodding quietly. She hated that her boss noticed.

"Don't worry. You will get to a place where you will feel more comfortable in your skin. I promise. You just need a little boost."

"Well, thanks again for your understanding."

"I wasn't going to tell you this, but after the whole fiasco, Antonio and I got to talking, and he ended up asking me out on a date." Evelyn's face brightened. Nora didn't realize Evelyn was in the market. She had only recently been divorced.

"A date?" Nora asked, bewildered she was having this discussion with her boss.

"Can you believe it? He was just so amazing about the accident last night. Turns out they can just hammer out the nose and create a new base. Plus, he has the dreamiest eyes, don't you think?"

Nora's eyebrows shot up in surprise. Talking about boys with a boss was definitely a first. "I'm so happy for you."

"It's been so long since I've been on a date. I don't know what I'm doing. I'm a little nervous."

"Just be yourself, and everything will work out," Nora said.

"All right, let's get down to business," Evelyn said, putting on her glasses. Her red lips pressed together as she pulled out the manuscript.

***

Back at her desk, Nora's eyes kept trailing to the scribbled notes from her book idea. She felt butterflies in her stomach, as if she were looking at a note from a secret admirer. She yearned to keep working on her outline, but she needed to finish the Overlook manuscript for Evelyn today. She had to prove she was ready for the editor job.

As Nora read, a paper wad hit the top of her head, breaking her concentration.

"Not now, Brent," Nora said, launching it back over the

cubicle wall.

"Come on, Nora. You want to get lunch later?"

Nora pondered the idea. "It's not a date, right?"

"Not a date. I just want to stop at the food trucks down the street."

"Oh, okay then. Let me finish my notes here and I should be ready to go at noon."

"It's a date," Brent said, his grin practically penetrating through the cubicle wall.

"Not a date," Nora clarified.

***

It was twelve o'clock, and Nora had just finished typing up her notes. She relished in the satisfaction that came with pushing send and smiled to herself while she gathered her things. It was turning out to be such a great day. Perhaps Evelyn would let Nora off early to get started on her book.

Nora poked her head out of her cube to find Brent playing videogames on his computer.

"How on earth do you get away with playing videogames at work? Don't you have deadlines?" Nora said, her hand pitched on her hip.

"I'm a speed reader. It takes me half the time to do my job than the average person," Brent said smugly. He turned off his computer and stood up. Nora realized how tall he was compared to her.

"Come on, let's go," Nora said, leading Brent toward the elevators. As they walked past the coffee shop on the main floor, Nora couldn't help but look over to see if Hot Coffee Shop Guy was there. Instead, she saw a girl with short blond hair and a nose ring. She tried not to be disappointed.

Brent burst through the front doors of their building and put sunglasses on to shield himself from the rays that had made their way through the city building jungle.

"Freedom!" Brent yelled. A few tourists carrying shopping bags chuckled as Brent stretched his arms and legs out, making a big scene.

"Can you believe it? Sunny! It's a miracle!" Brent twirled around like a little kid.

"You are embarrassing me; let's go!" Nora laughed. She grabbed his arm and tugged him toward the food trucks. The smell of gyros and tacos grew stronger as they got closer, and Nora took a big whiff.

"Mmm. I'm so hungry," Nora said. "I could eat a horse."

"Not sure they have horse meat here, but they do have an amazing grilled cheese sandwich. And, best of all… fried pickles," Brent said with a grin.

"Did you just say fried pickles?" Nora's jaw dropped. This had become the best day ever. She squealed with joy and ran to the food truck that sold the grilled cheese sandwiches. She jumped up and down like a little schoolgirl until it was her turn to order her grilled cheese with an extra side of fried pickles.

Brent's laughter only fueled Nora's jumps and skips. She danced to the beat of her own excitement. Brent looked down at her with a beaming smile.

"You're adorable," he said.

Nora gave him a little curtsy before looking up to find a stranger in sunglasses standing at a nearby garbage can discarding his trash. The stranger's grin from ear to ear indicated he was a spectator in Nora's little show. Nora squinted to get a clearer picture when she realized it was Hot Coffee Shop Guy. Nora hunched over and stepped behind Brent, hoping his size would block her from any further embarrassment.

"Oh God," Nora said, holding in her breath.

"What?" Brent asked, looking over his shoulder. He scanned the food truck corner as Nora grabbed his shirt at his shoulders and pulled him down to her level.

"Nothing. I just saw someone I know."

"Who?"

"Nobody. Forget it." Nora cautiously peeked over Brent's shoulder to find the coffee shop guy was nowhere in sight. She let out a sigh of relief. Maybe he didn't recognize her from this distance.

The man running the food truck called out their names in his heavy Greek accent. Nora leaped into the air and reached up toward the truck's small window. The man had a bushy mustache and an oversized nose. He handed Nora two baskets of food and asked if she wanted the spicy or regular ketchup to go with her fried pickles.

"Ketchup on pickles? I would never dream of such a thing!" Nora gasped.

Nora and Brent sat at one of the folding tables on the busy street corner. The streets were swarming with people. The food truck lines grew by the second as eager business people flocked from nearby skyscrapers.

Nora took a bite of her fried pickle. The tangy dill flavor and crispy fried coating tasted delicious.

"I'm in heaven," she purred. Nora savored every bite of her lunch while Brent talked about his trip to the Maldives. Nora listened only to the few parts that piqued her interest.

She finished eating before Brent could take his third bite.

"Come on, let's go. I'm hoping to get started on my own novel. I have an idea that is burning a hole in my brain right now and I need to get it all down on paper."

Nora sprang from the table, eager to head back, while Brent packed up his lunch and trudged after her. A familiar buzzing sound from the depths of her tote bag alerted Nora to check her phone. Two missed calls and one text message stopped Nora in her tracks.

*Nora, I noticed you sent your notes on the Overlook manuscript. Thanks. But where is the Oberdeen book?*

Nora's heart fell into her stomach and curdled with her fried pickles. "Oh no," Nora said. "I think I just made another huge mistake."

"What happened?" Brent asked, opening the front door to their building.

"I just worked on the wrong book, and there was a deadline on the other book today." Nora's hands cupped her forehead, and she started to hyperventilate. First the broken sculpture, then Evelyn's coffee, cold and forgotten on her desk, and now this—all in less than twenty-four hours.

This was it. The end of her career as an editor. Tina or Tracy was going to get the job, and she would have to grovel to her parents for more money—or worse, go home and live in her old bedroom until she could figure her life out.

"Nora, I'm sure it's fine," said Brent. "Just talk to Evelyn, and she can give you an extension."

"Don't you get it? I might have just completely ruined my shot at the assistant editor job."

Brent's eyebrows shot up his forehead. "It's just one deadline. I'm sure she'll understand."

Nora growled. "This isn't just one mistake. Oh God. My life is over."

"Stop being so dramatic. There's still a chance everything will be fine."

Nora burst through the elevator doors, picking up her steps as she approached Evelyn's office. She tried catching her breath, bending over and heaving.

Evelyn stood and put her hands on Nora's shoulders.

"Nora, are you okay?"

"Yesterday I searched your desk for the Oberdeen manuscript, but I couldn't find it. When I saw the Overlook one, I figured you might have… well… overlooked the name. I am so sorry."

"It's all right. I figured that's what happened." Evelyn sat back down at her desk and searched the piles of paper for the manuscript. She let out a long, drawn out breath. Nora's heart sank even further. Evelyn had never made that noise before—she was mad.

"Here it is. You're right about one thing. It's not called Oberdeen. It's called *Oberdink*. We were both wrong." She rested her hands on her forehead.

*This is bad. This is very bad.*

"I can fix this. I can plow through it this afternoon and pull an all-nighter if I have to," Nora said, grabbing the thick manuscript.

"Can you work this weekend and finish it by noon tomorrow? I think I could at least get us an extension to Monday morning, but I won't have time on Sunday to review it."

"I'll get started on it right away. Again, I am so sorry. This won't ever happen again. I'll double-check—triple-check the name with you next time."

Evelyn waved her off, letting out another sigh before picking up the phone.

Nora hated to disappoint Evelyn. She had been nothing but kind and understanding. Had Nora pushed her to her limit?

She walked out of Evelyn's office and sank into the realization that the next twenty-four hours were going to be rough. She stood at her desk staring at the scribbled paper that called out to her. She yearned to get back to her book idea, but she would be chained to the *Oberdink* book instead. Maybe this was a sign—God's way of preventing her from writing a romance novel and embarrassing her parents to death.

"You get it all figured out?" Brent asked.

"I have to evaluate this book by noon tomorrow," Nora grumbled.

"Yikes. Can I help?"

"No, but thanks. I'm going to head downstairs for a coffee and will try to knock this out."

# Chapter 5

The coffee shop buzzed with people. The line for coffee was nearly out the door. Nora had to squeeze behind the last person to get into the shop. A small round table in the back corner looked unoccupied, so Nora marched toward it to claim her spot. An outlet for her computer cord was within reach, and the neighboring tables were filled with businessmen and women talking in hushed tones. Nora thanked the coffee-shop gods for giving her the perfect environment to work.

Nora settled into her workspace and plowed through the first half of her manuscript. Hours passed, but she was in the zone. Eventually, her eyes felt droopy. When she looked up, the after-lunch coffee rush was gone. The shop felt quiet. Annoyingly quiet. She couldn't concentrate anymore. Nora set down her pen and grabbed her wallet as she headed toward the register.

Hot Coffee Shop Guy was sitting on top of the back counter, his legs swaying to the tune that must have been playing in his head. He held a textbook across his lap, tapping his right knee with the eraser end of a pencil. He was engrossed in his book. A few strands of hair had fallen out of place and dangled over his eyes.

Nora felt a flutter in her chest but shook it off immediately. She waited a moment for him to look up, but his eyes never left the page.

"Whatcha studying?" Nora interrupted.

Hot Coffee Shop Guy looked up, and the right side of his mouth curled in. Nora's knees felt like putty. She stiffened her back to ensure she didn't turn into a pool of goo on the floor.

"It's a book on audio engineering," he said, hopping down from the countertop and placing the loose strands of hair back in place. Nora's breath hitched at the sight of his eyes, rimmed with the most luscious set of lashes on a man that Nora had ever seen. She somehow managed to order a venti caramel macchiato, or at least she thought that was what she ordered. It all went by so fast, she couldn't remember the last few seconds.

She held up her credit card, waiting for the total to flash on the screen.

"This one is on me," Hot Coffee Shop Guy said.

"Really?" Nora asked, startled at the gesture. He gave her a nod, as the high-pitched whoosh of the steamer turned on.

"Wow, thank you. These coffees do tend to add up. I have a terrible addiction to espresso." Nora stopped herself. She was rambling, and she knew it. "So, what is audio engineering anyway?"

"It's a few different things. I'm learning how to apply it to music."

"You're a musician?"

"I wouldn't call myself that, but I try to mix my own beats on occasion."

Nora pondered what this meant, hoping he would explain

further, but he continued his work on the caramel macchiato. The concept of beats and music was completely foreign to Nora. She had to know more. Her curiosity to learn more about this stranger grew with each breath she took.

"I've never met an audio engineer before. What's it like?"

"I don't actually know. I'm still learning."

"I see."

"And you? What do you do for a living other than put on shows in front of food trucks?"

*Oh crap.* Nora covered her face with her hand, shielding herself from the embarrassment. He *had* seen her at the food trucks, dancing like a fool. Nora's cheeks felt hot as she tried to laugh it off.

"I was excited about fried pickles."

"Pickles?" he said with a laugh. "Yuck."

"You don't like pickles? Well, it's settled then. You're not the one."

"Oh, it's official now? Was there speculation that I might have been the one before this point?"

"Well, no. Er... What I mean is, 'the one' will be someone who will eat pickles with me until I'm old and wrinkly and look like a pickle myself."

Hot Coffee Shop Guy laughed—the kind of laugh that came from deep down. Nora wanted to wrap the sound around her like a warm blanket and never let go.

"It's official then. I'm not 'the one.' But you still haven't answered my question. What do you do for a living other than dance for pickles and search for your pickle soul mate?"

"If you must know, I'm an intern at the publishing company on the eighth floor."

"You're a writer?"

"I wouldn't call myself that, but I dabble in writing on occasion."

"I could have guessed you were a bookworm."

"What is that supposed to mean?"

"I mean, you look like someone who would stay in and read books instead of getting into trouble. It's cute."

Nora crossed her arms and tapped her foot, annoyed that he'd judged her so quickly, even though he was accurate. She never got into trouble. Never.

"I take it you're all kinds of trouble?"

"I am." A smile swept across his face, igniting the sparkle in his eye. "I'm Kellen," he said, wiping his hands on a white towel before reaching out for a handshake. "But you can call me Trouble."

"Nora," she managed to get out as she held his hand for a second longer than what felt appropriate. The cells in her hand simmered, creating waves of tingles up her arm. Nora got lost in the vibrant ink on his arm until her eyes dried out. She snatched her hand back and averted her gaze. "Thanks for the coffee. I have to get back to my bookworm stuff."

Nora heard him chuckling behind her as she walked to her table.

*Ugh.* She hated that he seemed to know he had an effect on her. It wasn't fair.

She made sure Kellen wasn't looking, then smiled at her macchiato. What did a free coffee mean from a guy like Kellen? Was he flirting with her, or was he expecting something in return? Nora chewed on her pencil eraser as she tried to focus on her work. The nagging itch in the back of her mind made her pull out her spare notebook and write down a few ideas for her book.

*She didn't know if she could trust him. Was he only playing with her emotions for his personal gain?*

She finished jotting down her book ideas and got back to work. After a while, Nora looked up to find Kellen wiping down the countertops with a washcloth. The pastry pantry was empty, and the refrigerated section of water bottles was dark. She looked down at her watch. It was almost six o'clock.

Nora was packing up her things when Kellen approached her table. He had pulled a black backpack over his shoulder and looked out the window.

"Do you need me to leave so you can lock up?" Nora asked.

"Nope. The security guys lock this place up later. You can stay."

"Okay, thanks."

"What is it you're working on?"

"I'm reading a manuscript for my boss. I should have been done by now, but I accidentally read the wrong one before," Nora said.

"That sucks."

"It does. Especially today, of all days. On top of everything, I finally have an idea for my first novel. I can't wait to actually get started on it, but I'm stuck making up for my mistakes instead."

"You mind if I sit down while I wait for my ride?"

"Sure," Nora said, feeling her cheeks get warm.

"Thanks," Kellen said, dropping his backpack and taking a seat across the table. "So, is your novel about pickles?" he asked playfully.

"No."

"Is it about your boyfriend?"

Nora scrunched her nose. "Boyfriend? I don't have a boyfriend."

"That guy you were out to lunch with looked like he was."

"Oh, Brent? He is not my boyfriend. He's just another intern."

"I see," Kellen said. His muscles flexed as he leaned more of his weight on the table.

Nora could smell the laundry scent from his shirt. It took every ounce of her willpower not to take a big whiff in front of him. She had to keep her composure—she needed the upper hand.

"So, what's your book about?" he asked.

Nora narrowed her eyes at him. Did he really care, or was he just passing time? He seemed earnest enough. *Oh, what the hell?* She didn't have anything to lose.

"It's about a girl trying to prove herself, and a guy who needs her to fail."

Kellen cocked his head. A whisper of a smile formed at the corner of his mouth. "That sounds intriguing. Is it a love story?"

"More or less," Nora said, ignoring her dad's voice in her head.

"What else can you tell me about it?"

Nora hesitated. "You really want to know?"

He nodded, looking up at her through his thick lashes. He wet his lips, which made Nora tingle all over.

*Keep calm. He's not your type.*

"I…uh…" Nora swallowed. Hard. "I was thinking it would be about a businesswoman and a coffee farmer."

Kellen cocked his eyebrow. "A *coffee* farmer, you say?" He stared at her drink. "And you came up with that idea today?"

Nora's mouth went dry. "Yeah."

"How interesting," he said, gazing deep into Nora's eyes before fixating on her lips.

She licked her lips in response, sparking that devilish grin that made Nora squirm. Her heart thumped so loudly in her chest that she was sure he could hear it. Her eyes darted everywhere and anywhere away from his seductive gaze, and they landed once again on his tattoos—a much-needed distraction.

"What's with the white rabbit tattoo?"

Kellen looked down at his forearm, and the corner of his mouth curled up, revealing the dimple on his left cheek.

"Oh, this? Just something I've been chasing." He looked at it again and traced the outline of it with his pointer finger.

"What are you chasing?" she asked carefully.

He studied her face as if he were calculating something in his head. Nora felt like she was in a chess game, anticipating his next move—and he was about to capture her queen.

"I'm chasing a dream. Hoping that one day I can open up my own studio. Or something like that. I dunno."

*Check. Mate.* He wasn't just a northern California hipster without ambition. He had goals. Dreams.

Nora looked down at her hands, ashamed she had judged him so quickly. There was more to Hot Coffee Shop Guy than she had originally thought. When Nora looked up, a dangerously playful expression spanned across his face.

"You keep looking at me like that," she said breathlessly.

"Like what?" Kellen said with a knowing smile.

She was playing with Trouble with a capital T. She probably should have marched out of the shop, but something was drawing her to him—a gravitational force that teased her curiosity, keeping her there, rooted in her chair. She wanted to know more about Kellen, and more presently, she wanted to know what his mouth tasted like.

She brushed her tongue along her bottom lip in response to the unfamiliar desire to press her lips against a complete stranger's mouth.

Kellen shifted in the chair in front of her.

What was happening? Did he feel the energy between them too? He must have, because he leaned toward her. He was moving toward her mouth.

Nora sucked in a sharp breath.

"Nora," he started to say, inching closer.

"Yes?" Her eyes were partially closed now.

Kellen moved in, brushing his cheek against hers. She felt the tickling whisper in her ear.

"My ride's here. Gotta go." Kellen stood up and walked toward the door. Nora opened her eyes in his wake. Her blood pressure plummeted.

"One more thing," Kellen said, breaking the silent tension that grew with each step he took.

"Yeah?" Nora's voice cracked.

"Good luck with the book," Kellen said as he walked out the door.

Nora sat in her chair in disbelief. While she waited for her heartbeat to regulate itself, she peeked through the windowpanes of the coffee shop and saw Kellen get into a rusty black car. A girl with short pink hair, a full set of lips, and large black studded sunglasses sat in the driver's seat.

As they drove away, Nora let out the breath she had been holding in and nearly passed out.

***

She was there for the taking. Her mouth was ripe with wanting. He could have taken her lips with his, but in the corner of his eye, Jenny had pulled up in front of their building. He couldn't blow his chance with Jenny. She was the key to getting him his first job in a real studio. If she'd seen him kissing a girl in the coffee shop, any potential deal in the making would've been done before it started.

Kellen opened the door to Jenny's beat-up Honda Accord. She flashed him a smile that could have charmed a blind man. Her short pink bob landed just underneath her jawline, exposing her thin long neck.

"How's it going, handsome?"

"It's going."

"Do you like the job?"

"It'll do for now. So, where are we headed?"

"I thought I'd take you to my place and order takeout. Or I can make you a killer bowl of ramen."

"Either sounds good."

Kellen gazed into the passenger side mirror just in time to see Nora step out of the building. She looked so small and frail compared to the concrete buildings surrounding her. Before Kellen could see which direction Nora was headed, they made a turn down Eighth Street, and Nora was out of view.

Kellen's stomach turned into a knot—an anxious ball of twine that he tried to unravel in his thoughts. What was this feeling? Deep in his gut, like a churning black hole with a promise of never being filled. Maybe he was hungry, and he didn't want ramen after all. No, that couldn't be it. He loved ramen. And he wasn't that hungry.

He knew he didn't have feelings for Jenny; was this guilt? He was fine with the idea of going out with her before, so that couldn't be it. He needed that studio job. He needed to move out of the piss-hole apartment and make it on his own. And he was willing to do anything to get it.

Kellen took out a cigarette and pressed it against the car lighter. He offered it to Jenny, and she happily took it from his fingers, pulling in a long drag before blowing the smoke out the crack of her driver's side window. Kellen lit a second cigarette and inhaled the fumes, letting the rush of calm settle his nerves.

Jenny's apartment was on the second floor of a two-story home in Potrero Hill. She was able to live on her own because Daddy helped pay for the rent. A large tapestry of a lotus flower hung above a purple couch with orange and turquoise throw pillows. Beaded curtains reflected flecks of magenta light across the room. It was like walking into a giant-sized jewelry box.

"Can I get you anything to drink? Beer? Wine?"

"I'll take a beer," Kellen said, petting the orange tabby cat that greeted him at the front door.

Jenny pulled out a green bottle from the refrigerator and used a bottle opener to peel the top off. She squeezed her chest together, elongating the cleavage poking out of her white tank top.

"How's your job hunt going?" Kellen asked, diverting his attention back to the cat.

"No luck yet. I've been looking around though. There's this cute little boutique shop down the hill from here. I put in my application today."

"What about your dad's studio? Couldn't you work there?"

"Nah, I'm not really into it," Jenny said as she pulled out another beer for herself. "Are you still interested in working there? I know we briefly talked about it, but—"

"Yeah, absolutely. I would totally love the chance to meet your dad and see the studio."

*Finally.* He had been waiting for this moment. This was his chance. He played off his shaking hand by petting the cat some more—hoping to play it cool.

"I'm sure I can arrange something." She took a sip of her beer and plopped on the couch.

"That would be amazing."

"You want to know what I think would be amazing?" Jenny asked as she dug into her purse and pulled out a cigarette carton.

"What's that?"

"To see how far your tattoos go up your arms." Lighting a new cigarette, she breathed in a puff of smoke and leaned back on the couch, one long, thin leg crossed over the other.

Kellen took off his jacket and rolled up one of his sleeves over his shoulder for her to see.

"More," she said.

Kellen obediently rolled up the other sleeve, but this apparently wasn't enough to please her. She made a flicking motion with her finger, indicating that she wanted Kellen to undress.

Clenching his jaw, he saw where this was headed. A small part of him knew that Jenny would expect something in return for doing him a favor. He'd pushed that possibility deep down in his subconscious, hoping it wouldn't come to this.

"You sure you want me to? I mean, it's only our first date."

"Take it off," she commanded.

Kellen stalled—hoping she would change her mind, but she

only egged him on. He pulled the shirt over his head and stood half-naked before her. A draft from the window sent goose bumps down his chest, as her eyes raked his bare skin.

"Turn around," Jenny said.

He did as he was told, feeling like a prize horse on sale. He felt her eyes on his back, and the hot tar in his stomach turned into heartburn.

"Your back tattoo is hot," she said breathlessly. "Now ask me if I have any tattoos."

Kellen turned to face her. Jenny had kicked off her black Converses and spread her legs open. She pointed to a tiny mark inside her right thigh, less than an inch from her magenta panty line. Kellen swallowed hard as she ushered him closer.

"It's a star, see?"

Kellen took a few steps closer, but the mark was so small, it just looked like a freckle.

"Does the star have any significance to you?" Kellen asked, squinting his eyes.

"It's my lucky star. If you get a real good look at it, you'll find out why it's lucky." Jenny's eyes twinkled as she smiled a slow, seductive smile. She was a girl accustomed to getting what she wanted, and she had a fish hook in Kellen the moment he found out her daddy owned a studio. She had been slowly reeling him in for months, and now it was time to feast on her catch.

"Don't be shy. Come over here and get a closer look."

Kellen approached Jenny, kneeling in front of her. She guided his hand towards her lucky star, locking her eyes on him—daring him to stop. Pulling off her tank top and shimmying out of her jean shorts, she lay on the couch, exposed, reaching out for him and cupping his face, pulling him closer to her mouth. Her plump lips attempted to seduce him until finally, he crashed down into her kiss as she wrapped her legs around his waist.

"Take me," she whispered.

He pushed the little voice out of his mind and succumbed to the fury of hands and limbs.

# Chapter 6

The Oberdink manuscript was garbage. She should have quit halfway. Twenty pages in and Nora concluded it needed a complete rewrite. Her time would have been better spent working on her own book instead.

It was nine in the morning when Nora finished typing up her notes. The characters were unrelatable. The layers of subplots didn't make any sense. The author was trying to be cute and different, but left Nora feeling frustrated and confused.

Nora should've gone to sleep the moment she hit send, but instead she opened up her internet browser. There was something about the Oberdink author's name, Clark Whitcom, that sparked her curiosity. Had this guy written books before, or was this his debut novel?

She opened Google and typed his name. To her horror, she discovered he was the son of Bill Whitcom…the president of Calico Publishing.

*Oh crap.* Not only did she miss a deadline, she missed the deadline for the president's son—and she just sent the toughest critique of her career as an intern.

*Oh, God.* She might as well start looking for waitressing jobs. Nora would need to get right on that…as soon as she got a little sleep.

Nora dreamed of Kellen, working on a coffee plantation in South America. His muscles rippling under a blazing sun. An ache between her legs stirred her awake—leaving her breathless and panting. She wanted to know what it would be like if he touched her. She closed her eyes, imagining Kellen leaning over the table and claiming her mouth. His hands in her hair and around her waist—lifting her out of the chair and…

*Ugh. This is ridiculous. I need my sleep.*

She tossed and turned, trying to release him from the grips of her mind, but something was holding on tight—keeping him close—as if she needed to picture what it was like to be ravished by him in a coffee shop.

Perhaps her imagination running wild was good for her book. Nora jotted down her ideas for a sexy scene in the notepad next to her bed and then fell back asleep.

Thumping made its way into Nora's subconsciousness, waking her from another dream of Kellen. She pulled back her sheets and folded over the cream crocheted blanket that her mother had made for her when she was in school. Her bedroom filled with a softly muted light that shimmered through her sheer window drapery. The floor was dressed in her outfit from the day before.

She rubbed the sleep out of her eyes and reached up toward the ceiling to stretch her tired muscles.

Nora shuffled down the hallway and poked her head around the corner. The bright lights from the kitchen scorched her retinas. As her vision normalized, she saw a colorful array of vegetables scattered across the kitchen island. Heads of purple kale, bunches of carrots, and radishes rested next to a large glass bowl filled with cubed sweet potatoes.

"Whatcha making?"

Jolie looked up from the cutting board and squealed with joy.

"Good morning sunshine! I mean good afternoon!" Jolie said. "I'm making dinner."

"What about your cleanse?"

"Ugh. It's the weekend! I can't cleanse today. I'll pick it up on Monday."

Nora rolled her eyes.

"I have two things I've been dying to tell you. First, I know that this is not normally your thing, but I just got us VIP tickets to one of North Beach's premier nightclubs." Jolie paused to let Nora's elongated sigh come to an end.

"And I got you this," Jolie said, ignoring Nora's blatant dismissal of the nightclub idea. She reached over the counter to grab a black-and-white striped canvas bag. Jolie pulled out a black piece of fabric before tossing it onto Nora's head.

"What is this, a handkerchief?"

"It's a dress, silly. And you're going to look amazing in it. I'll let you borrow my comfy heels too."

"This dress looks like it was made for a slutty doll-sized person. I'm not wearing it," Nora said.

"Yes, you are. And you will look hot. You need to get out of your shell. You're becoming a scary hermit that only has relationships with pickles."

"Hey now," Nora said in protest. "Just because I would rather stay at home and make pickles doesn't make me a scary hermit."

"Well, it won't make you a good writer, either. You need to go out and experience life. No wonder you've had writer's block!"

"Actually, I did come up with a book idea yesterday."

"No way!"

"It's a love story. I decided to take your advice. I need to write what I love. To hell with my parents."

"That-a-girl!"

"I'd really like to get started on it. I don't think I'm up for going out tonight. I'd rather be writing."

"It's only two o'clock. Why don't you write now? You'll need a break eight hours from now. Trust me."

"Yeah, but—"

"No buts! Now tell me about this book idea. I want to hear all about it."

Nora pursed her lips. She was going to lose this battle no matter how hard she tried. When Jolie got something in her head, that was the end of the discussion. She rarely pushed Nora to go out with her, so tonight must have been important to her.

"All right. I'll go if you promise I can get at least seven hours of writing. And as for the book..." Nora sighed, trying not to think of Kellen, but needing him to explain how she came up with the idea.

"I met this guy, and he just sparked something in me, I guess. I dunno."

"What guy?" Jolie's eyes sparkled. She set her knife down, giving Nora her full attention.

"This guy from the coffee shop in my building." Nora blushed.

"Oooh, yes. That is hot. Coffee shop guys are great in bed."

"Again, I wouldn't know anything about that, but yes, Hot Coffee Shop Guy is definitely good looking. He was flirting with me. Or toying with me. I can't tell. Either way, he's got me feeling all…bajigitty inside."

"Bajigitty? God, you really are from a small town."

Nora took a chunk of carrot that rolled off the cutting board and threw it at her.

"Hey! Stop throwing food!"

Nora grabbed a slice of zucchini and pretended like she was going to launch it. Jolie ducked behind the kitchen island. Nora popped it in her mouth instead, smirking at Jolie as she chewed.

"Anyway, Hot Coffee Shop Guy is all kinds of trouble. I should probably stay away from him."

"You see? Sounds like you need a little trouble in your life to inspire a few ideas."

Nora rolled her eyes. She hated when Jolie was right.

"I'm going to check my email to make sure Evelyn has everything she needs from me, and then I'm going to get to work."

"Sounds good. Hey, how about inviting that Brent guy from work? The rich one. He would buy us drinks, right?"

"I'm not going to invite him just to buy us drinks." Nora gave Jolie the judgmental side-eye as she snatched a carrot stick from the cutting board and took a big bite. "But I might invite him because we've become friends. Sort of."

"Perfect! Just you wait—this is going to be so fun!"

***

*Ding dong.*

"That's Brent," Nora said, walking to the front door. Jolie was fixing a vodka soda in the kitchen when she noticed Nora was still in her sweatpants. "Nora! You're not dressed yet? Get a move on!"

"Hi," Nora said, opening up the front door. "Come on in." Brent was wearing a black button-up shirt, gray slacks, and a spicy cologne that caught Nora by surprise. He walked into the apartment confidently, putting his hands on his hips.

"You clean up really nice," Nora said.

"And you look as beautiful as ever," Brent said with a wink.

Nora looked down at her sweatpants and laughed. "Obviously I'm not ready yet. I was working on my book."

Time had gotten away from her. She had pages of notes and the start of a really good outline. She didn't want to stop, but Jolie would have thrown a hissy fit if Nora didn't come through tonight.

"Let me introduce you to my roommate, Jolie. She can make you a drink while I get ready."

Brent looked towards the kitchen to see Jolie squeezing a lime into her drink. Her hair was pulled up in a half updo, her long wavy hair covering her bare back. She was wearing a maroon dress that looked painted on her slim body, with a sweetheart neckline that showcased her perfect C-cup cleavage and the floral tattoo etched across her chest.

Brent's jaw dropped. Open-mouthed, dumbstruck. The same look on every guy's face when they set eyes on Jolie for the first time.

"What's your poison?" Jolie asked from across the counter, holding a vodka bottle in one hand and a rum bottle in the other. Brent stood in a speechless stupor, the drool accumulating at the corners of his mouth. Nora rolled her eyes and left Brent to figure out how to pull himself together on his own.

In her room, Nora slithered her way into the little black dress that Jolie had given her, stretching it over her chest and twisting it around so the plunging neckline fell between her breasts. She tied two thin pieces of fabric around her neck and pulled and tugged at the hem to cover her legs, without success. The farthest her dress would go was halfway down her thighs.

Stepping into Jolie's three-inch black stilettos made her laugh as she struggled to maintain her balance on the fuzzy carpet. *These were the comfy ones?*

She looked in the mirror, not recognizing herself. She never showed this much skin, or this much cleavage. Her parents wouldn't approve…but then again, her parents were thousands of miles away. Resisting the urge to slip into a cardigan, she propped herself up against her bed and jotted down a couple ideas for her book.

*Add Scene: Night at the gala.*

*Lead character hates fancy events, but she has to attend for a business thing.*

*She normally dresses plainly. Forgettable. But tonight she wants to be seen.*

*Slipping on a sexy dress, she musters the courage to make her grand entrance...*

Tapping her pen against her chin, she contemplated what should happen next, but she was stuck. Perhaps going out tonight might give her the inspiration she needed to move her story along. Jolie might've been on to something.

Nora wobbled toward the kitchen. Brent had finally learned how to talk again. He was telling Jolie all about his skydiving adventure in Wyoming while Jolie gave him her I-don't-care-but-I'm-being-nice smile. Nora cleared her throat, and the two of them whipped their heads toward her. Their mouths dropped in unison.

"Holy shit," Brent said.

"Oh my God!" Jolie beamed. "I knew this dress would look amazing on you!"

"Really? You don't think it looks like I'm trying too hard?" Nora asked, looking down and covering her cleavage with her hands.

"I don't think… I mean… you know… Wow," Brent stammered.

"I'm going to need a drink before I head out in public like this," Nora said.

Jolie handed Nora and Brent shot glasses filled with vodka. She held her glass in the air and shouted, "To Nora's first book idea!"

"To Jolie's relationship with her anus!" Nora yelled, clinking her shot glass with Jolie's.

Brent shook off his stunned expression and raised his glass. "To literally the best night of my life!"

***

Nora shivered while they waited for the bouncer to check their IDs. It was a cool summer night, but North Beach was blazing with nightlife energy. People sang in the streets, marijuana smoke billowed from apartment windows, and posh twentysomethings waited in line to get into the grand premiere night at the Fox nightclub.

Nora followed Brent down the dark hallway, lined with

cobalt blue track lights. The beating sound of house music pulsed through her veins. The end of the hallway spilled into a gigantic dance hall with at least three floors that overlooked a high-rise stage for performers. In all four corners of the gigantic dance hall were transgender go-go dancers in oversized bird cages. Masculine features masked by layers of glittering eye shadow and false eyelashes. They swung their hips to the music, their naked, nipple-less breasts flopped from side to side.

Nora blinked a few times, feeling overwhelmed. This was not at all what she was expecting. People dancing to loud music? Yes. A dominatrix in a black leather corset, snapping her whip at the crowd? No.

"Maybe this wasn't a good idea?" Nora screamed over the music.

Jolie turned around. "I can't hear you! Let's head to our table upstairs!"

Nora grabbed Jolie's arm, pleading with her eyes. She wanted to go home. This was too much.

"It's going to be fine," Jolie yelled, reading Nora's expression. "Here, hold my hand."

As they made their way through the crowd of dilated pupils, Nora saw little people carrying trays of Jell-O shots. She followed the yellow brick road towards a bouncer wearing a black pinstripe suit and a top hat.

"We're with Scott!" Jolie yelled. "I'm Jolie, and these are my two friends."

The bouncer looked Nora up and down and nodded. When he glanced at Brent, his brow furrowed, creating deep creases along his forehead. He brought a walkie-talkie to his lips and mumbled something Nora couldn't hear.

They waited for the bouncer to say anything, but he just stared blankly as if he had dismissed them.

"Uh…so can we go or what?" Jolie called out.

"Jolie, you made it!" a guy yelled as he made his way down the steps. His black hair was gelled into pointy spikes, and he had a mole under his eye that looked like a teardrop.

"Nora, this is Scott, the guy who hooked us up. Scott, this is my friend, Nora," Jolie yelled, her arms draped around Scott's neck.

Nora forced a polite smile, but couldn't take her eyes off his mole.

"And this is her date," Jolie said, pointing to Brent. Brent's eyes grew wide as he exchanged an uneasy glance with Nora.

"Friend. Brent's just a friend," Nora chimed in.

"So, can we come up?" Jolie asked.

"Come with me. I've reserved a table for you, beautiful," Scott said.

Nora silenced her inner cynic. If Scott only knew Jolie was just using him for the free drinks and VIP service.

A bottle of champagne and four flutes waited for them at the top of the stairs, tucked away at a table overlooking the dance floor below. Jolie and Brent leapt into their seats, giggling over their special treatment. Nora trailed behind them in a dreamlike state, the buzz from her pre-drinks giving her courage to keep moving forward. She stopped to steady herself on the railing and took in her surroundings. It was as if she were in the middle of a Fellini film. Hundreds of bobbing heads turned purple, then green, then yellow. Bubbles the size of basketballs floated down from the ceiling until the strobe lights came on, and the bubbles inched down with each beat of the music.

Suddenly the heavy bass came to a pause. The dominatrix took the cue to walk off the stage, cracking her whip at a young guy who was wearing a dog collar and crawling on his hands and knees. The room went dark, and clouds of fog flowed from the corners of the stage. Two guys in black shirts and gold chains appeared, and a deep bass beat thumped through the speakers. Another layer of music came on, and Nora found herself entranced by the hypnotic sounds. The music moved through her in a way she had never experienced before, and she found herself pulsing with the beat.

Across the stage was a small, glass room. Three technicians with thick, padded headphones over their ears hovered over a switchboard. *So that's how that works*, Nora thought. Seeing the men behind the curtain made Nora feel more at ease.

There was something familiar about the third guy. She squinted, but the moving glare against the window made it near impossible to see any details. She couldn't get a good look at his face, until he looked up at the crowd. Nora's heart pumped faster in her chest.

*It was him.* Hot Coffee Shop Guy.

He was working at the club? What was she going to do? What *could* she do? It wasn't like she could confront him about being a tease. Or should she?

Her head was swimming in vodka. Perhaps she needed to sit down.

"Drink up!" Jolie yelled across the table, holding out a flute of champagne as Nora sank into the leather seat.

"You look overwhelmed," Brent said, clinking her glass with his.

"I am," Nora said, debating whether she should tell Brent of her discovery.

A waitress in red hot pants, buttcheeks out on display, came to the table with three shot glasses.

"We didn't order these," Nora said.

"These are from Scott," the waitress said, pointing toward the bar.

Nora turned to Jolie and batted her eyes.

"What?" Jolie asked innocently.

"Are you even into him?"

"Oh, I don't know," Jolie said, flipping her wrist. "He's cute, kind of."

"I think you might have your beer goggles on," Nora said, looking into her shot glass.

"Don't you mean champagne goggles?" Jolie giggled.

Nora plugged her nose and let the fiery liquid burn down her throat. Brent chuckled as she took a sip of her champagne to wash away the sting.

"That is so cute," he said.

"I'm tired of being the cute one." Nora's buzz was trumping her inhibitions now. She didn't want to be the timid girl who was left behind in a coffee shop anymore. She wanted to be *wanted*. She leaned over to whisper in Brent's ear. "Just for tonight, can you pretend like *I'm* the sexy one?" The clean scent of his aftershave smelled good. She lingered there for a moment to breathe him in.

"Are you crazy, Nora? Of course you're sexy," Brent whispered back in her ear.

"You want to dance?" Nora asked.

They both stood up and looked across the table to find Jolie's tongue halfway down Scott's throat. His hands roamed up and down her back while she yanked on his hair. Nora couldn't hide her grimace. She knew Jolie would regret making out with him later, but there was no stopping her now.

"We're going to dance," Nora said to the back of Jolie's head. Nora grabbed Brent's shirt and dragged him down the steps toward the dance floor. They were surrounded by a sea of sweaty backs and bouncing boobs. Nora weaved her way through a bachelorette circle of girls in pink and found a spot in the exact center of the hall. A tall man with curly chest hair protruding from his button-up shirt approached Nora and said something incoherent. His pupils were the size of quarters, and his forehead was dripping with sweat. Brent protectively grabbed Nora's waist and pulled her in close. Nora turned to look up at Brent, who was giving the guy a stare down to back away.

"Thanks," Nora mouthed.

Brent's eyes twinkled under the strobe light. He really was a nice guy, underneath his annoying tendencies. He was too confident at times. Persistent to a fault. But he just saved her from a stranger's sweaty chest rubbing against her—a true friend.

They danced for a while until the beat faded away. The lights dimmed, and the two gold-chained singers finished their song. The crowd cheered as they left the stage. Nora clapped for the performers and looked toward the glass window. She locked on Kellen's gaze. He had been staring directly at her, his eyes burning a hole right through her. His face was stone cold.

*Good. She had his attention.* Time to give him a taste of his own medicine. A slow mischievous smile formed on Nora's face and she began to move her body against Brent. She grazed the sides of her breasts with her hands, trailing up her neck and back down again.

"Damn," Brent said under his breath. "You are so hot."

She smiled and looked back toward Kellen, but he was gone. She pocketed her disappointment and continued to flow with the music, letting Brent hold on to her hips as she shifted them from side to side. Alcohol coursed through her veins, giving her the strength to keep moving and grinding against Brent. A bead of sweat accumulated on her forehead, and her bangs clumped together.

Jolie and Scott joined them on the dance floor. Their dance moves, if you could call them that, would make a sex worker blush. Jolie lapped up Scott's mouth with her tongue while Scott pulled Jolie's legs around his hips, revealing her lacey black panties.

Brent and Nora giggled and jumped to the techno music until heat and exhaustion, mixed with large amounts of booze, made Nora feel queasy and the balls of her feet ached. She needed to slow down.

"Do you think we can step outside for a minute? I'm not feeling so great," Nora yelled into Brent's ear. She hiccupped as Brent guided her through the crowd. He led her to an exit at the back of the building that spilled out into an alleyway. The cool air regulated Nora's temperature, but her head felt fuzzy and off-kilter. The alley was poorly lit and smelled of stale garbage. Nora could barely make out the graffiti that spanned across the width of the back wall. The sound of the club pounded through the closed metal door.

Brent tugged on the handle, and they realized they'd locked themselves out of the club. Nora laughed, but her hiccup reminded her she still wasn't feeling great.

"You okay?"

"I'll be fine," Nora said in the middle of another hiccup. She leaned against the brick wall to rest. Brent's hands were still on her shoulders, and she looked down to see if she was just imagining it.

"Nora, you are so sexy. You don't even know," he said.

"I'm not as sexy as *Jolie.*"

"You can't compare yourself to her. You need to embrace your own flavor of sexiness." Brent's hands held her firmly against the wall, intensity building in his face. He looked like a puppy staring at a dog treat. He was too close. His aftershave started to suffocate her. She tried shifting her weight, but he lunged at her mouth. His lips were punishing, forcing her head back against the brick wall. A sharp pain spread across her skull.

"Brent," Nora tried saying with his tongue clanging against her teeth. She tried to push him off of her, but he clamped down harder, pressing his crotch into her hip.

"Brent, stop—" Nora was hushed by his tongue, thrusting its way in before she had a chance to close her mouth. She pushed with all her strength, giving herself an inch to breathe. She heard the crunch of bone hitting bone, and Brent soared into a puddle on the concrete.

"Nora, are you okay?" Kellen came into Nora's vision—hunched over her and panting. He scanned her body for scratches or bruises. "Was I too late? Did he hurt you?"

"Kellen?" Nora could barely get out. The graffiti art on the wall behind him was spinning. She swiveled her head to find Brent clutching his right cheek, running toward the street.

"That's right, get the fuck out of here!" Kellen yelled.

Nora looked up to see Kellen's chest heaving. He was gripping his right hand.

"Brent just got the wrong idea." Nora rubbed the back of her head where she'd hit the brick wall. It stung, but didn't seem to be bleeding.

"Jesus Christ, Nora. He could have…" Kellen slammed his palm on the wall and paced the alley, trying to calm himself down. "Something really bad could have happened."

"Brent wouldn't…" Nora said shakily.

"You don't know that," Kellen snapped. His hands balled into fists. His eyes were wild with fury.

"You didn't have to punch him."

Kellen clenched his jaw, closing his eyes as if he were trying to calm himself down.

"I couldn't just let him… dammit, Nora. I didn't have a choice."

"Yes, you did," Nora said, tears pricking the back of her eyes. She didn't know who she was mad at more: Brent, Kellen, or herself for being such a fool.

"Please don't cry," Kellen said, reaching toward her cheek.

Nora flinched under his touch.

"Come with me. We're going to find your friend," he said, holding out his hand. She stared at it a long while before coming to her senses and placing her palm in his. He led her around the building toward the front entrance, his triceps flexing as he gripped her hand. There was still a line out the door to get in, but they walked toward the front.

"How did you know I was here with someone else?" Nora pressed.

He didn't answer. He looked down at his watch while he said something to the bouncer sitting on a stool. The bouncer patted him on the back before letting them pass.

"Were you watching me?" Nora's voice echoed in the hallway leading toward the dance floor. He continued to ignore her as he scoured the room. He held her hand firmer, marching to the bouncer with the pinstripe suit. Kellen said something to him and got a silent nod before Kellen guided Nora up the stairs.

When they reached the table, it was empty, but Jolie's purse was still there.

"She must be dancing," Nora said. "You can leave now."

"I'm not going anywhere," Kellen said. "Sit."

"What about your job? Aren't you supposed to be working the switchboards up there?" Nora hiccupped.

Kellen looked over his shoulder and shrugged. "Don't worry about it. The dance club can live without strobe lights and bubbles for a minute."

"You came to my rescue," Nora said softly. "I feel like such an idiot."

"You're not an idiot. You're just drunk and you trusted the wrong person." Kellen signaled to the waitress to bring two glasses of water.

"Can I trust you?" Nora asked, more softly than she intended.

Kellen looked away, not answering the question. He grabbed the waters from the tray and handed one to Nora.

"Here, drink this one first."

"Aren't you Mr. Bossypants?" she heard herself slur. Gosh, she really was drunk.

Kellen sighed, but it looked like he was smiling. Was he smiling?

Nora took a swig of cool water, which didn't do much to sober her up. "You see, I am an idiot because I thought you were going to kiss me." Nora laughed at herself. "Back at the coffee shop."

Kellen's smile melted off his face. Why was he so serious all of a sudden? And why did his mouth look so delicious? She stared at it, wondering what it felt like.

"I can't kiss you," Kellen said.

"What?" Nora hiccupped. "Why?"

"Because I'm no good for you."

"Isn't that for me to decide?"

Kellen bit his lip. He put his finger under her chin and looked deep into her eyes.

"You are killing me. And that dress, my God." He rubbed his face with his palms. "You've got me tied up in knots."

Nora's head was spinning around so much, she almost thought she heard a compliment in that statement, but she wasn't sure. She tried to steady her focus on his eyes, but they kept moving. Or she was moving. Either way, she couldn't tell if she was sitting still or rocking like she was on a sailboat.

"I don't understand you," Nora said.

Kellen paused for a moment, pursing his lips, as though conflicted in his own thoughts.

"I wanted to kiss you the moment I first saw you," he said.

Nora couldn't wait anymore. She closed her eyes and leaned in. She waited until she felt the soft pad of his fingertip lightly grazing the center of her lips. She shot her eyes open to find Kellen's tormented expression.

"Not like this," he said.

"But…"

"Nora! I've been looking all over for you. We need to get out of here now. Scott is an asshole. Where's Brent? Who's this?" Jolie's voice came from behind Nora.

"It's a long story. *Hiccup.* This is Kellen."

"Kellen, as in Hot Coffee Shop Guy?"

"That's me." He nodded to Jolie and then turned to give

Nora a knowing smile.

This was normally the moment when the guy Nora was crushing on would break her heart. She held her breath and waited for Kellen to redirect all his attention to Jolie. Instead, Kellen fixated on Nora's eyes. He was unmoving with steadfast loyalty that made Nora want to leap into his arms.

"You should go home now," he said gently.

"But, *hiccup*, you and I have unfinished business," Nora said, as she was being lifted by both Kellen and Jolie.

"Let's go, Nora. I have a ride coming in two minutes." Jolie lifted Nora's arm around her shoulder.

"But—"

"Stay away from assholes," Kellen called out as they made their descent down the stairs.

Nora looked behind her. Kellen stood at the top of the stairs, conflicted, agonized. There was so much more to say, but Jolie tugged her forward, forcing her away from him. Kellen's distraught face was the last thing she remembered before passing out in the Uber.

# Chapter 7

Nora opened her apartment door and found a bouquet of yellow roses in a tall clear vase on her doorstep. A handwritten note was neatly folded and tucked between the stems.

*I'm so sorry. Your friend, Brent.*

Nora shuddered at the thought of confronting Brent. He'd left twelve voice mail messages that morning. The first half dozen were sad and pathetic. He apologized and begged for forgiveness. In the last few voice mail messages, he sounded nervous and defensive. He listed all the reasons he thought he had her consent to touch her. He was preparing for retaliation.

"You were rubbing your body all over me on the dance floor. There would be a video of that at the club. You know that, right? Nora, listen, if you can just promise not to talk to the police about what happened, I will disappear. I promise. I'll quit on Monday."

Nora felt a lump in her throat. The thought of his tongue in her mouth made her sick to her stomach. How could he have taken it so far? Was he really about to…Nora couldn't even finish the thought.

She cursed herself for not following her instincts. She should have stayed home and worked on her book. Nora didn't need a horrible situation to inspire her writing—she just needed her notebook and pen. She could make up the rest.

"He needs to go to jail," Jolie said over her coffee mug.

"But he has a point. I *was* grinding on him on the dance floor."

"Absolutely not an excuse for pinning you to the wall and pressing his crotch against you."

"So, if I just text him to get lost and quit his job, wouldn't that be enough of a punishment for what he did?"

"Think about all the other women out there that you could save from his assaults if you put him behind bars."

"What if I was the only girl he did that to?"

"You don't know that."

"Okay, let's say I'm not. You think six months in jail is going to shape him up?"

"He's a scumbag who deserves to be in jail. That's all I know."

"What if he just got the wrong idea? What if it was a temporary lapse of judgment?"

"Don't be so naive, Nora. He's a rich scumbag who is used to getting everything he wants. He'll do this to someone again. I just know it."

"I need to think. No, actually I need to step away from it for a while. I need to get out of here and write."

"Go then. Hopefully, you'll come back with some common sense."

Nora spent the rest of the evening at the corner coffee shop down the street from their apartment. No Brent, no Kellen, just her and her novel. She poured herself into her writing, escaping the pending decision she would ultimately have to make. Hours passed before her train of thought was interrupted by the buzzing sound of her phone. It was an unknown number. Nora shifted her weight; her heart skipped a beat. She wondered if Kellen might have gotten her phone number somehow. She stalled for a second, then quickly pressed the green call button.

"Hello?"

"Nora, it's Brent."

Blood pounded in her ears. A high-pitched ringing sound prevented her from hearing the words coming through the receiver.

"I'm at the police station. Apparently, they received an anonymous tip that I sexually assaulted you. Can you please come down and explain that I had your consent? Please, Nora."

"Jolie," Nora said, shaking her head, disappointed that Jolie would go behind her back.

"It was Jolie? I knew it. That bitch."

"Jolie was just trying to protect me." Nora scowled. "Which police station?"

"I'm downtown. Oak and Van Ness."

Nora looked at her notebook in front of her. She'd hoped she would find peace in writing about what happened, using it as part of her story, but the truth was…she didn't. She was still mad. Mad at herself, for getting too drunk and putting herself in a precarious situation, and mad at Brent for taking advantage of her.

"I'll be right there."

Nora clicked off and fired a hot text to Jolie.

*I can't believe you called the cops on Brent!*

The ellipses appeared, and Nora rolled her eyes while she

looked up the address to the police station.

*It wasn't me! I swear!* Jolie texted back.

Nora scrunched her eyebrows together. If it wasn't Jolie, who was it?

***

Nora sat behind a female officer's desk. Officer Sheila was from Detroit and specialized in sexual assault cases. She had two framed pictures of her kids, Toni and Bobbi, in matching pigtails. Both were girls, she pointed out. She liked boy names for girls.

"Nora, how do you know Brent Cavanaugh?"

"He works with me."

"And I assume you are aware why he is in jail?"

"He's being accused of sexual assault."

"That's right. And do you think you might be able to help me understand why we would get an anonymous tip that Brent Cavanaugh sexually assaulted someone at 12:03 a.m. at The Fox nightclub?"

"Um…" Nora swallowed hard. Her palms started to sweat.

"Did you know anything about that?"

"The anonymous tipper didn't say who he assaulted, did they?" Nora held her breath, not sure if she was ready to tell the truth just yet. She hated that this situation was completely out of her control.

"They didn't mention it. I think they wanted to protect the girl's privacy."

"I see." Nora was relieved. She still had time.

"So, what brings you to the station, Ms. Nora Miller? Do you have an alibi for Mr. Cavanaugh?"

Maybe she didn't have time. Nora looked down at her hands in tightly balled fists. She remembered the red, puffy knuckles on Kellen's hand after he'd punched Brent in the jaw. He had saved her from Brent, even though she was still not sure Brent meant to go any further than what he did. But she'd told him to stop. He hadn't stopped. A tear escaped her eye and trailed down her cheek.

"Ms. Miller?"

"I, um…" Nora swallowed. "I was the one he assaulted at the Fox last night."

"I am sorry to hear that, Ms. Miller. Are you okay?"

"Yes. I'm fine. He didn't… you know."

"Would you be willing to go to court and testify against Mr. Cavanaugh?"

Nora nodded while Officer Sheila held out a box of tissues. She began to explain to Nora what to expect in the next coming weeks. There would be paperwork, of course, a court hearing, testimonies, and counseling. She handed Nora a business card for a counselor who had done wonders for other sexual assault victims.

*Sexual assault victims.*

The words imprinted on her mind.

Nora blotted her puffy eyes with a tissue and thanked Officer Sheila for her help. She left the station with a heavy heart and a festering uncertainty that she did the right thing.

***

Nora stepped into a cloud. Light rain tickled her nose before she could open up her umbrella. Fred was sitting on the park bench, illuminated by the soft glow of the streetlight immersed in the cotton-candy fog. He waved to her as she took her post at the bus stop.

"Morning, Nora," he said. His cheeks were rosy from the cold. "What seems to be troubling you, dear?"

Nora sighed. "I'm okay. I had kind of a crazy weekend. I didn't get much sleep."

"Oh? Do you want to talk about it?"

Nora stared at the ground, toying with a small rock under her shoe. "I'll spare you the details, but basically my work friend turned out to be a real dirtbag." Nora tried to ignore the sick feeling in her stomach that came up every time she thought of Brent. She shook it off and continued, "But there's this other guy. He's different and unpredictable. I think he's into me, but something is holding him back. I can't seem to figure him out, and I can't stop thinking about him."

"Sounds like you got hit with cupid's arrow."

"Maybe a little bit. It kind of stings, though."

Fred chuckled.

"I mean, I had pegged this guy all wrong when I first met him. I thought he was just your typical tattoo-covered hipster. Moody, and all kinds of trouble. But I'm seeing this whole other side to him."

"Oh, yeah? How so?" Fred asked, stroking his beard.

"Well for one, when I told him about my book idea, he seemed really interested. Like, *really* interested. He actually listened and asked questions—as if he cared."

"Well, that shouldn't be too out of the ordinary, I would hope."

"A guy who listens to me rambling about a silly love story? Ha," Nora deadpanned. "And then, there was the other night. I was drunk and he took care of me. He made sure I was safe.

It was really…sweet."

Fred nodded. "Is he chasing you? Or are you chasing him?"

Nora laughed. "I have no idea. There is this magnetic thing between us, but for some reason, he's resisting it."

"Well, if he's not chasing you, there's something wrong with him."

"Oh, Fred. You are too kind. Perhaps you're right. But I do know one thing. I need answers, and I'm going to get them."

The grinding sound of the bus could be heard from the bottom of the hill as it chugged its way up to the bus stop.

"You finally got that first book idea, eh?" Fred smiled.

"Oh, yeah. I just sent my outline to my boss late last night. Fingers crossed! Hopefully I'm going in the right direction."

"My offer still stands, you know. I'd be happy to read your pages. Anytime."

"You are too sweet, Fred. Thanks for listening." Nora waved and blew him a kiss before taking a seat toward the back of the bus.

***

*Come see me as soon as you're in*, Evelyn texted.

Nora gulped. Evelyn's texts usually weren't so direct. Had she heard about what happened with Brent? Was she in trouble again?

Nora opened the front door to her office building, walked past the coffee shop, and peered in the window. A girl with short blond hair and a lip ring stood behind the cash register. No Kellen. She would have to get her answers later.

She breezed up the elevator and set her bags down at her

desk before softly padding over to Evelyn's office. A desk lamp was on, but the room felt dark. Evelyn had her reading glasses on and was typing. The blue glow from her computer screen outlined her pointy features.

"Good morning, Evelyn. Sorry to interrupt."

"Morning. I read through your outline and your character notes," Evelyn said. "It's a little rough around the edges, but not bad for a first draft. You ready to brainstorm?"

Nora let out the air she had been holding in. "Yes, I'd love to...but, don't you want to talk about Oberdink?"

"Ugh. No. Thank you for putting in the late night to get that done, but you were right. I read the first two chapters and it was garbage. Hot garbage. I already shot him our notes."

"Isn't Mr. Whitcom going to be upset?" Nora flinched, afraid of the response.

"Well, if I can't keep my integrity in this position, then he can kiss my ass."

Nora's eyes grew wide—amazed at Evelyn's sense of gumption. Nora hoped she could be just like her, and she planned to start with Kellen. As soon as she was done, she was going to march to the coffee shop and get her answers, whether he liked it or not.

"Anyway, it's like they say. There are no bad ideas. Just seeds for a new one. Maybe he can take our notes and create something really good, you know?"

Nora smiled at Evelyn's favorite expression. She said it all the time. Evelyn was the most positive person Nora had ever known.

"Now, that's enough of that. Let's get down to what really matters."

Nora nodded and took a seat across from Evelyn's desk.

The chair creaked as she nervously swiveled from side to side, trying to act casual before receiving her first real critique. Her pen and notebook trembled.

"Your male lead character, Luca. Nailed it. I think you can boost his charisma up a notch. Maybe you can show him with another woman before he meets Emery so we can get a feel for a transformation in him. Maybe he's aloof towards women in general, but when he meets Emery, it's sparks and whistles."

"That's a good idea for a scene, in stark contrast to him becoming a hopeless romantic by the end."

"Exactly!" Evelyn pointed.

Nora scribbled in her notebook.

"And for your main character, Emery, she needs some work. She doesn't have anything special or unique. Her character is flat. I think you can add some more pizazz."

"Pizazz, got it," Nora said, jotting down the word. "Like an unhealthy obsession with pickles?"

Evelyn squinted as she thought over the idea. "Mmm, maybe something less juvenile."

*Ouch.* "I'll think of something."

Evelyn continued to rattle off her ideas, and together they refreshed some of the subplots and defining character notes.

Evelyn smiled at Nora. "Whatever happened to you, or whoever happened to you, it is working. Don't lose it and keep writing. I can't wait to read more. Now, if you don't mind, I'm going to need your help with this manuscript that came in over the weekend. I scanned it, and it has potential. Can I get your notes by the end of the week?"

"Of course. And thank you. Was that everything you wanted to talk about?"

"Yeah." Evelyn's head tilted to the side. "Is there something else?"

Nora fidgeted with her fingernails. She shook her head, but her face must have given her away.

"What's wrong? What is it?"

"It's about Brent, the other intern." Nora hesitated; that familiar sick feeling in her stomach was back. "He, um, won't be in today."

"I heard he quit suddenly. Is everything okay?"

Nora couldn't hold back the waterworks any longer. Tears streamed down her face. The vivid memory of him pressing himself against her was still fresh in her mind. She trembled as Evelyn put her arms around her, and Nora told her everything about that night, and about Kellen, and about Officer Sheila. It spilled out of her like an overflowing bathtub. Her feelings could not be contained anymore. Evelyn hugged her tightly.

"You did the right thing," Evelyn said. "What he did was inexcusable."

"Are you sure? I've had so many doubts."

"Yes, and now I understand how you came up with your villain in your book." She winked. "Use it. Work through your feelings and write it down. It's good therapy. But if you ever need to talk to me, you know I'm here for you."

"Thanks, Evelyn." Nora gave her one last squeeze.

"I bet you're dying to talk to your coffee shop hero." Evelyn crossed her arms with a knowing smile.

"I literally cannot wait." Nora's hands were sweating at the thought of confronting Kellen, but it was time. She needed to know how he truly felt about her, and if he was the one who called the police on Brent.

"Go," Evelyn said, motioning towards the door.

*** 

On the way down the elevator, Nora felt the butterflies in her stomach. She needed to know why he kept pushing her away. So many questions ran through her mind, she wasn't confident she would be able to remember them all. She mustered the courage to walk through the coffee shop doors. The smell of roasted coffee gave her soothing comfort that everything was going to be okay. The same blond girl from earlier that morning stood behind the cash register. Nora waited in line, occasionally poking her head around the corner to see if Kellen would appear from the back room.

What would she say to him when she got to the front of the line? *Hey, I'll have a twelve-ounce latte...and why the heck do you keep blowing me off?* That probably wouldn't go over well.

By the time Nora got to the front, she was biting her fingernails.

"What can I get you?" the girl asked.

"I'll have a grande Americano, please. Is Kellen working today?"

"Kellen quit this morning."

"He quit?"

"Yep."

"Wait a minute. Didn't he just start last week?"

"Yeah, well. I guess it didn't work out."

Nora looked at the blond girl as if she had popped her balloon. Mouth agape, she watched as a stranger made her coffee, trying to put together why Kellen would have quit so suddenly. He couldn't disappear on her like that. They only just met.

Nora walked away in a daze, gripping the warm coffee

cup. She lumbered down the street a few blocks toward the Embarcadero waterfront and sat on a park bench overlooking the bay. Seagulls squawked overhead, flocking nearer as Nora pulled a peanut butter sandwich from her purse.

She tried to remember anything about their conversation Saturday night that would have given her a clue that Kellen would be quitting his job, but she struck out. Her memories from that night were hazy. But there was one memory that was as clear and bright as the blue water in front of her. *"I wanted to kiss you the moment I saw you,"* he had said. If that was true, how could he just disappear? Nora didn't even know his last name.

Nora tore off little pieces of her sandwich and threw them to the seagulls. The birds flocked toward the bits of food and fought each other until there was nothing left. She ached inside. He was a virtual stranger, and yet she felt like she'd lost the kindle to her flame. The dark knight had become her muse, and yet he'd vanished without saying goodbye. Without explaining why.

A dull ache settled around her heart, and she spent the rest of the day in a dark fog.

That evening, Nora sat down to work on her book, trying to unravel the unsettled feeling in the pit of her stomach. Creating reasons for why someone would leave so unexpectedly where there were none.

Her writing had become her therapy, and she poured her imagination onto the pages, taking her deep into the night. Grasping onto the few things she knew about Kellen, she built him up as a romantic hero until she finally got her happy ending—even if it was only fiction.

***

"Good luck today!" Jenny called out from the rusty Honda. Her pink hair blew in the breeze of her opened window, and she puckered her thick lips to blow him a kiss.

Kellen sent her off with a polite wave and approached a long line of warehouses. This was it. He finally made it. His first internship at a real studio. All his training and school loans would finally become worth it now that he was on the road to learning how to run his own studio one day.

He nervously swept his hands through his hair and then looked down at his watch. Fifteen minutes early, hoping he might impress his new boss, who also happened to be Jenny's dad.

Not awkward at all.

One of the glass windows stated, "Light House Studios." He took a deep breath and pulled the door handle.

Unlike the dirty white walls of the exterior warehouse, the inside of the building was clean and modern. A small café with barstools stood in the center of the room. The man behind the bar asked if Kellen was meeting someone.

"I'm Kellen, the new intern. I'm here to see Don."

"Welcome, newbie. I'm Matt. Don will probably be here any minute. I can show you around in the meantime."

"That would be great."

Matt took him down the long hallway, opening every door so Kellen could pop his head into each of the studios. Some rooms were empty; others had pianos, drum sets, and microphones in place for the next recording session. The central recording station had state-of-the art systems, with boards that reached the length of the room, covered in dials and knobs. Like a cathedral of buttons, the equipment in the room ready to record the highest quality music. All the things he wished he had at home, but he didn't even have space for his lousy laptop computer.

"Check this out," Matt said as he turned on a switch. He handed Kellen a pair of headphones. Indie rock music filled his ears. The mix was perfectly balanced, and the sound was crystal clear.

Matt smiled proudly. "This is a group based here. We just finished cleaning up their record. Sounds good, right?"

"It's amazing."

"Yeah, this is definitely one of the better recording studios in the city. Come on back and I'll make you a coffee while you wait for Don. Or better yet, I'll teach you how to make the coffee."

Kellen forced a smile.

He sat down at the counter and sipped on his coffee while Matt worked in the kitchen. The mix of caffeine and nerves created a sickening sweet lining along his stomach, but it was nothing he couldn't manage. Jenny had warned him that her dad was an intimidating guy, but that wasn't what was bothering him. He couldn't get Nora off his mind. He knew it was best to keep his distance from her, and he was willing to do anything to break the magnetic pull he felt when he was around her. He couldn't afford the distraction. This was his chance, his big break. Getting a foot in the door at one of the Bay Area's top recording studios was the only thing he needed. Nora's sweet innocence pulled at his heart, but he buried his feelings deep down and tried his best to forget them.

Plus, apparently, he had a girlfriend now. He found this out when Jenny was on the phone with her dad and asked if her *boyfriend* could be their intern for the summer. That was news to Kellen, but he decided to go along with it while he figured out a way to let her down gently.

Pushing his guilt aside, he focused on his half-full coffee cup. He was one step closer to his dream. And another step closer to getting the hell out of his shit-hole apartment. It didn't hurt that Jenny was hot. Maybe he just needed to get to know her better. There could be something there…maybe.

The creaking sound of the front door interrupted his thoughts, and a tall man in a white polo shirt, black denim pants, and a gold link chain around his neck walked through the door. His head was shaved completely bald, and he had deep grooves in his bronzed cheeks.

"You must be Kellen," he said, holding out a firm right hand.

"Don?"

"That'd be me. I hear you're dating my daughter."

"Uh, yeah. I, um, I'm really thankful for the opportunity to be an intern here. I can't thank you enough, sir."

Don crouched down, lowering his voice. His face just inches away from Kellen. "Listen here, boy. You break my baby girl's heart, and this whole summer internship is over. I don't need you here. I'm just doing her a favor, you hear?"

Kellen swallowed hard and nodded.

"All right, good. Glad we got that cleared up. Now let's get you started. I need to get Studio B ready for a recording later this afternoon. Follow me."

Kellen followed behind Don as he strutted down the hall. Had he wanted, Don could have crushed Kellen like a bug. *Better stay on his good side.*

II

Part Two

# Chapter 8



**S**ix years later...

Around the time Nora accepted the assistant editor position at Calico Publishing, she finished her book, titled *Coffee, My Love.* The first draft was sloppy and amateurish, but with Evelyn's help, the book transformed into a beautiful butterfly—a novel that eventually got published with a small publishing house based out of New York.

Eventually, Nora fessed up to her parents that she wrote a romance novel, hoping that maybe somewhere in their hearts they'd find an ounce of pride for their daughter's accomplishment. Of course, they were still stuck in their ways.

Her father, specifically, didn't want to have anything to do with it. "You better not use your real name, missy. It'll tarnish our reputation at the church."

Nora tabled her disappointment and, after pouting for quite some time, she came up with a pen name to preserve her relationship with her parents. Jolie recommended she use her first pet's name and the street she grew up on.

"I can't use Treasure Meadow!" Nora said. "I'd sound like a stripper, which doesn't help my case here. My parents already think I'm writing pornography."

"Your book is not pornography, and you know it. It's as sweet and innocent as you, with the perfect amount of sexy."

"I need to think of something that sounds sweet, but could also be interpreted as not-so-sweet. You know?"

"Oh yeah, like a Georgia O'Keefe painting? Flowers or vaginas? Or both? I love those."

"Yes, just like that." Nora tapped her chin, trying to think of the perfect name. "I've got it!"

"What is it?"

Nora chuckled to herself. "Did I ever tell you about the time some kids tried selling Fred some ecstasy? And he thought they were trying to sell him a girl named Molly?"

Jolie burst out laughing. "Oh. My. God. That's perfect."

"Molly. Molly Ashbury," Nora said.

"Ashbury as in Haight Ashbury?"

"Yeah, the street we lived on together."

"Molly Ashbury it is!"

Nora's novel had mild success in the United States, but it didn't generate a lot of money at first.

Her publicist and agent, Mary Bronson, gave Nora a hard time. "You need to write more books if you want to do this for a living!"

Nora did want to be a full-time writer, but she was back in her slump. Uninspired. She hadn't met anyone who ignited the spark, as Kellen had years ago. (Yes, she did still think about him from time to time, like a faded ghost, lurking in the back of her mind.)

Mary tried everything to increase their revenue on *Coffee, My Love*. She was able to sell the rights in foreign countries and paid to have the book translated into Spanish.

The book eventually became a huge success in Latin America, particularly in Colombia. And to both Mary and Nora's delightful surprise, Quest Productions, a company based out of San Francisco, bought the rights to the book to be filmed and available on a popular streaming network around the world.

Nora couldn't wait to see how the film would come to life. She hoped the movie would stay true to her book, but ultimately it was up to Quest Productions to decide how to adapt the story. Nora was not included in the screenplay or the filming process, so she had no idea what to expect or when it would be ready.

Her life changed one day, standing over her kitchen counter, sorting through a pile of letters. Among the bills and junk mail, she discovered a black matte cardstock invitation with shiny gold trim. She read the metallic calligraphy over and over again until she finally believed it; the day had come.

Her phone rang, and a raspy voice came on the speaker, echoing off the walls of Nora's apartment.

"Pack your bags, honey. We're going to Colombia!" Mary said on the line.

"I still can't believe they're done filming!" Nora said.

"Took them long enough, in my opinion. I'm excited to find hot Colombian men to nibble on while we're there," Mary said, blowing cigarette smoke into the phone receiver.

"Do I go as Molly Ashbury?"

"It's up to you, honey, but you'll be a million miles from Daddy and his small-town mafia. They won't be able to make the connection between their cult leader and his daughter's 'racy' romance novel. If they do, so what? Let them drink the Kool-Aid and shove it."

"You know I can't just—"

"All right, all right. I know you're just trying to keep the peace with your parents. Go as Molly Ashbury. Either way, it'll be great to get you out of your rut. Perhaps being in Colombia will inspire you to write your next book."

"Good grief. You're relentless."

"You know it! But you love me anyway," Mary said playfully.

"And you would love me, too, if I gave you a second book," Nora said.

"Yep. So, I'll see you in Colombia?"

"I guess so," Nora said, overwhelmed at the thought of attending a publicity event.

"Fabulous," Mary said before hanging up the phone.

Much to Mary's chagrin, Nora refused to attend any publicity events or book tours. Part of her tried to maintain her anonymity for the sake of her dad, and the other part made her feel like Sonny Coultren. Only, instead of not showing up to scheduled events, she just didn't let Mary schedule them in the first place.

In a few short weeks, Nora was going to show up to a publicity event as Molly Ashbury, author of *Coffee, My Love*.

***

Before her trip, Nora had plans to meet up with Evelyn for brunch.

"This place is so cute," Nora said, sitting down in her chair. The small cafe in the Castro was bustling with patrons enjoying their Latin-inspired brunches. Salsa music played in the background, and sunshine poured through the windows onto their wooden table for two.

"Can I get you something to drink? Coffee, juice, tea?" the waiter asked. His sideburns were gelled into a swirl, and Nora noted a faint trace of eyeliner under his eyes.

"Coffee for me, please," Nora said.

"Make that two," Evelyn said with a weak smile. Her skin looked pale. She normally wore her dark brown hair down and straight, but today she had it pinned back with loose strands falling around her face.

After Nora's promotion, she and Evelyn became better friends. They occasionally met for brunch on the weekends and tossed around book ideas for fun. None of them seemed to stick for Nora, but she enjoyed it nonetheless.

"They finished the movie," Nora said, unable to contain her news.

"No kidding! That is so exciting!"

"I know! I can't believe it. I'm invited to the premiere. In Colombia! I've always wanted to go there, ever since I wrote that book."

"That is wonderful news. I'm sure the movie won't do your novel justice, but they never do, right?"

The waiter came back with their coffees in large mugs the size of their heads, placing a small metal carafe of milk between them. Nora eagerly grabbed her coffee and took her first sip. It was heaven in a cup. The rich flavor seduced her taste buds, and Nora almost forgot she needed to order her food. She decided to go with the breakfast burrito, and Evelyn asked for scrambled eggs and a side of fruit.

"You're going to make me look like a pig while I eat my big-ass burrito in front of your tiny plate of sides."

"I haven't been feeling well enough to eat much these days. I'm forcing myself to order anything at all."

"What do you mean? What's wrong? Are you not well?"

Evelyn stared into her coffee mug for a long moment. The answer was written on her face. Something *was* wrong. Something was very wrong.

"Is it Antonio? Are you guys having problems?"

"No, no. Antonio is great. Ever since our wedding last year, he has been the perfect husband. It's not that. It's…"

Nora shifted uncomfortably in her seat, waiting for Evelyn to talk.

"I've been diagnosed with leukemia," Evelyn said.

The words lingered in the air while Nora tried to process this new information. She furrowed her brow in confusion.

"I have something called Chronic Lymphocytic Leukemia, Stage III. I went into the doctor because I was feeling so tired, and then the next thing I knew the doctor was explaining chemotherapy options."

"Oh my God, Evelyn. I don't know what to say—" It was a punch to her stomach. To fathom that Evelyn might not survive a silly cell mutation in her body was inconceivable. She had to survive this. She had to. Evelyn was family—family who actually supported Nora's hopes and dreams, instead of squashing them.

"It's going to be okay. I'm scheduled for my first chemotherapy session next week. I'm going to fight this thing, and everything is going to work out."

Nora looked into Evelyn's eyes, and even though they were smiling, she saw fear in their depths. Nora didn't know how to respond. She was stuck. Scared. Frozen in time. She wanted to reach out and comfort her but didn't know how.

"You're doing the thing again," Evelyn said.

"The what?"

"The thing with your nails," Evelyn said kindly.

Nora spat out the sliver from her mouth and looked down to find her right index finger and the middle finger had been ambushed by her nervous habit.

"Listen, I don't want to dwell on it anymore. Okay? I'm fine. I can get through this. And so can you," Evelyn said, putting her hand on Nora's arm and giving her a squeeze. "Now, have you thought of any new book ideas lately you want to run by me?"

Nora shook her head, taking another sip of coffee. Normally, she loved pitching ideas to Evelyn, but she wasn't in the mood.

"What about your trip to Colombia? Can we talk more about that?"

Nora's jittery nerves, mixed with a mild overdose of coffee, made her hands shake. It didn't feel right to talk about her trip while Evelyn was going through such a scary situation in her life. But perhaps she was looking for a distraction. Nora plastered on a smile. If nothing else, she would be strong for Evelyn, just as Evelyn had been for her over the years.

"Well, for one, I'm nervous about going as Molly Ashbury. I haven't been to a single publicity event since the book was published."

"What are you so nervous about?"

"I don't know. Upsetting my parents, for one, even though it sounds completely silly coming from a twenty-eight-year-old."

"What's the worst thing that could happen?"

"Someone from my small town could see my picture and make the connection that I'm Molly Ashbury."

"So? What's wrong with that?" Evelyn tilted her head to the side.

"I told you my dad started a church, right? It just takes one person to learn that Mr. Miller's daughter published a pornographic book, and his church would be ruined."

"But your book isn't pornographic."

"I know that, but they don't. They think that all romance is smut. The entire town is like that. I'd ruin them."

Evelyn reached for Nora's hand, giving it a tight squeeze. Her skin felt clammy, and Nora's heart clenched in her chest.

"Well, I can't say I understand, because I don't, but if it's important for you to protect your family from embarrassment, then maybe stay out of the pictures."

"I guess I can try that," Nora said, swirling her spoon in her coffee.

"And, well, on the off chance your picture happens to make its way onto the internet and into your tiny little hometown, then…so be it. A church not accepting of people because of their personal taste is not a church that is meant to be."

There it was. Evelyn's gumption was back—the very thing that Nora loved so much about her.

Nora smiled. "You always know how to make me feel better."

"Good," Evelyn said. "So, are you bringing anyone with you to Colombia?"

"I asked Jolie to come with me, but her boyfriend didn't want her to go. He's kind of a jerk, but I digress. Mary is going to meet me there."

"I'm glad to hear you'll at least have Mary there with you."

The waiter arrived with a platter over his shoulder. He placed two small plates in front of Evelyn, and then he lowered down a large plate with the biggest burrito Nora had ever seen, smothered in gooey cheese and red pepper sauce.

"See, I told you your tiny plates would make me look like a

pig," Nora said.

Evelyn laughed, a little color coming back into her cheeks.

"Can I get you anything else, ladies?" the waiter asked.

"Yes, a wheelbarrow to roll me out of here when I'm done," Nora said.

***

Nora walked up the bouncy jet bridge, her black Ted Baker roller bag trailing behind her, dressed in a white polka dot blouse and a long, pleated skirt made of chiffon that grazed her knees. Her patent leather red pumps matched her bright red lipstick. "You look like a modern-day Audrey Hepburn," Jolie had said at the curb of the San Francisco airport.

The airport had bright fluorescent lights, palm tree plants, and pastel-colored painted walls, welcoming her to the Miami airport. A crowd of people stood by the gate, waiting to board their flight. Nora found the departure board and searched for her flight to Medellin.

*Delayed.* She had a couple of hours until boarding. Since Jolie wasn't able to come with her to Colombia, Nora decided to give her a phone call.

"Hey, Nora. How was the flight to Miami? Did you make it through takeoff without an anxiety attack?"

"It was only a minor anxiety attack this time. I think the yogi kava tea you gave me helped. Thank you."

"Good, I'm glad to hear. Are you getting on your next flight now?"

"Actually, my flight was delayed, so I'm killing time."

"Well then, listen to this, after I dropped you off at the airport…"

While Jolie was talking, Nora made eye contact with the most beautiful set of baby blues in a gray suit sitting at the bar across the airport hallway. His nose was slightly bent, possibly broken earlier in his life. He had slicked-back blond hair that curled behind his ears and a golden glow to his skin. He looked like a surfer on a business trip. A soft, sexy smile found its way to his perfectly pink lips.

"Hello? Did you hear what I said?" Jolie asked.

"Oh my gosh, I am so sorry, but the most handsome man is smiling at me at the airport bar. I think he's flirting with me," Nora said.

"You're getting eye-fucked by a hot man at the airport?"

"He's definitely undressing me with his eyes."

"Then go talk to him! What do you have to lose?"

"I don't know, he seems so… out of my league," Nora said.

"No one is out of your league."

"Yes, but he looks like a Californian god or a fashion model. There's no way—"

"Get your pretty butt over there, or I'm going to fly to Miami right now and knock some sense into you."

"Ugh. Okay, I will."

"Go get 'em girl."

"Tell Steve I said hi."

"You really weren't listening to me earlier. Steve and I broke up."

"Wait, what?"

"Don't even worry about it. It's fine. I'll tell you all about it later. Now go get your man!"

"Gosh, I'm so sorry, Jolie. I don't feel like I can get off the phone with you now. Will you please tell me what happened… again?"

"Actually, I can't. I'm doing a live video in a few minutes for my fans. Now get over there and put the moves on the hottie at the bar."

"Okay, but we need to talk. I'll call you tomorrow."

Nora hung up and frowned at the screen. Maybe now Jolie could come to Colombia after all? It would be late notice, but that hadn't stopped Jolie from taking trips before. She texted Jolie while she was building up the courage to head over to the sports bar.

*Is it too late to be my plus one?*

She waited a moment, but Jolie didn't respond. Nora lifted her chin and strolled toward the handsome stranger. His head was propped up against his hand as he watched Nora approach him, exuding confidence in all its manly glory. He pulled out a bar stool for her to sit next to him.

"Hi, I'm Jack. Jack Crawford."

"Nora."

"Nora, would you care for a drink?" His smile revealed pristinely white teeth. The skin around his eyes crinkled, just enough to give away his age. Early thirties, Nora thought. As Nora sat next to him at the bar, she noticed blond stubble on his face. He smelled like a sexy forest by the sea.

"I would love one," Nora said.

The bartender set down a pint of beer in front of him and a glass of white wine in front of her.

"Good. I was hoping you would say that. I guessed white wine was your drink of choice," he said.

Nora's mouth dropped open. "How did you know that I would come over here in the first place?" Her sideways smile revealed that she was a little impressed.

He shrugged.

"You must think pretty highly of yourself," she stated, taking the wine glass between her fingertips. "I do like white wine though, thanks."

"You're welcome." Jack's eyes sparkled behind his beer glass as he took a big swig.

There was something about his confidence that Nora couldn't place. He kind of reminded her of a character in a romance novel she once read. She'd imagined falling in love and getting married to a guy like him a hundred times. Her stomach fluttered with excitement, a feeling she almost didn't recognize anymore—it had been too long.

Could this be fate? Nora stifled the idea. Her imagination was starting to run wild. This was good. Maybe she could write about this meet-cute in her next book.

"What do you do for a living, Nora?"

"I'm a writer and editor. You?"

"I'm a producer. Films mostly. I work out of San Francisco."

"Me too. What a small world."

"Born and raised," Jack said.

"Well, I'm not technically from San Francisco. I'm actually from a small town in Michigan. But I left there years ago."

"So… you're just a small-town girl?"

"Living in a lonely world," Nora quipped.

"You took the midnight train to anywhere?"

"Pretty much." Nora giggled. "I studied at Berkeley, got my degree in English and a minor in creative writing. I fell in love with the city, the diversity of people and neighborhoods. You can walk a mile and feel like you're in a completely different country."

"You mean like Chinatown?"

"Well, yeah. Between North Beach's Little Italy and Chinatown, for sure. But even walking between Noe Valley, the Castro, the Mission, Bernal Heights. Each neighborhood has its own special something."

"I grew up in the Sunset," Jack said.

"What was that like?"

"I don't know, it was all right. We had a tiny house, close to the beach. My brother is twelve years older, but he never really amounted to anything. He got me in a ton of trouble growing up. Drinking, smoking, drugs. I didn't have the best influences."

"Seems like you might have turned out all right in the end."

"Yeah, well, luckily, I was able to get my life back on track just in time to apply to college. I went into advertising and lived down in LA for a while. A college buddy of mine was starting a production company in San Francisco and asked me to be his partner, so here I am."

"You like what you do?"

"Are you kidding? I freaking love it. It's stressful at times. But since we cracked that deal with Netflix, our business has been booming."

The twinkle in his eye gave Nora a little flutter deep in her belly.

"I bet you deal with a lot of beautiful actresses all the time." Nora couldn't help herself. She immediately regretted bringing it up. She was talking to the most confident man she'd ever met, and she'd already unleashed her insecurities on him.

*You are a strong, confident woman.*

"None as pretty as you." He winked.

All right, this guy was good at pickup lines. Nora felt a flash of heat on her skin, and she took a sip of her wine to cool down.

"It's cute that you're blushing right now.  I would have thought you get compliments like that all the time."

"I can't say I get out much. Not in my line of work. I spend most of my time with my head down in a book, or talking with middle-aged authors."

"Well then, I'm glad you've come out of your shell today. Where are you traveling to?" he asked, taking another drink of his beer.

"Medellin, Colombia."

"Well, look at that.  You and me both.  What will you be doing in Medellin?"

"I'm attending a premiere."

"For *Coffee, My Love*? That's my movie," Jack said proudly.

"Are you serious?" Nora almost jumped out of her chair. Her heart was beating so loudly she almost couldn't think straight. "How did the movie turn out?"

"It actually turned out pretty good.  It was my first film abroad. But I can honestly say it's one of our better movies. And I'm not just saying that because you're with the press."

"Well, actually I'm not—"

"I think you're going to be really pleased with it.  The director really nailed it. And I don't normally toot a director's horn that much, but Frank really knocked this one out of the park."

Nora nervously swirled her glass until wine dribbled down onto her fingers.

"How's the wine?" he asked with a cocked eyebrow. "May I try it?"

"Sure."

He took the glass from Nora's hand and set it back on the

counter. Nora gave him a puzzled look as he took her hand and examined it against his own. Jack then slowly lifted her finger to his mouth and lightly sucked wine off the tip—just like a character out of a romance novel. Electric bolts shot through her arm, sending tingly sensations everywhere. Nora nearly melted off her chair.

"Yum," he said, releasing her finger.

She stared at him with wide eyes. "Well, that is one way to try the wine," Nora said breathlessly, turning her head so he wouldn't see the blush that accumulated on her face.

"I figured it would be sweeter that way. And it was. You don't have to turn your face away from me. I love it when you blush."

Nora chewed on her lip and slowly swiveled her chair back to face him.

"There, that's better," Jack said.

"I've never met anyone as direct as you."

"And I've never met a beauty as bashful as you are. You're intriguing me, Ms. Nora… what was your last name?"

Nora froze, forgetting which name she was supposed to go by. Crap. She'd intended to go by Molly Ashbury during the press junket. She'd already screwed it up.

Shoot. Well, it was too late now. "Miller," she said. "Nora Miller."

"Well, Ms. Nora Miller, since you lucked out and sat right next to the guy behind it all, did you want to ask me a few questions for your 'exclusive interview'?" Jack signaled to the bartender to get another round of drinks.

"Um, sure." Nora paused, unsure of how to proceed, realizing she was now trapped in this accidental lie and she didn't know how to get out. She needed time to think. Stall.

"That would be great, actually." Nora pulled out one of her notebooks and clicked her pen.

"So…" Nora tapped her pen nervously. "Why this book? Why *Coffee, My Love*?"

"On the record, it got great book reviews and the Latin American market for movies like this has been completely underserved. It was a golden opportunity to make the company a ton of money. Off the record, we got the rights to the story for a freaking steal."

Nora made a mental note to talk to Mary.

"And what is your favorite part of the book? I mean, the movie?" she asked.

"I got to be there for the filming in Colombia during the festival of flowers. We got so many amazing shots. I think the backdrop of the movie is what sets it apart from all the other love stories out there. It'll make the movie really pop."

"Did the movie take any creative licenses and alter any of the original storyline?" Nora asked, afraid of the answer. Please God, no. Please. Say, no.

"The movie is pretty close to the book, actually. Only a couple tweaks here and there."

Nora let out an internal sigh of relief.

"Okay, it's my turn for questions. How did a beautiful girl like you end up being an editor and writer? Have you thought about acting? You would make an adorable lead character in one of our movies."

"No way, I couldn't be an actress. I hate being in the spotlight."

"Good girls always say that," he teased.

The bartender set down three drinks.

Jack elbowed the guy sitting next to him at the bar. "Hey, I got us another round before we head to the gate. Would you like to meet Nora from the press?"

Nora hadn't realized that Jack was sitting next to a colleague. She was mortified that someone he knew was listening to their flirtatious conversation.

She first noticed the tattooed arm leaning against the bar. She stared at the familiar white rabbit, nestled next to a red rose. Nora knew that tattoo so well, it had been imprinted deep in her mind.

"Kellen, let me introduce you to Nora," Jack smiled. "Nora, this is Kellen. He's our audio guy."

Nora followed the trail of tattoos up to Kellen's honeycomb eyes, and the cells in her body froze in time. She was looking at a ghost from six years ago. Memories of Kellen from the coffee shop came flooding back. Her mouth went dry. Kellen reached out his hand to shake hers. She'd felt this same warm strength in his clasp the night he'd brought her back into the club after punching Brent's lights out.

Kellen smiled politely. "It's nice to meet you," he said before turning to yell at the TV screen. "Oh, come on, how can you drop that!" He swiveled toward the football game across from the bar and didn't look back.

He didn't remember her. A brick weighed heavily in her stomach as she watched the side of his face scrunch up at a bad call—not even bothering to give her a second look. Was she that forgettable? Or maybe she didn't mean as much to him as he did to her.

Nora picked up her wine glass and guzzled it down.

"May I suggest a toast?" Jack asked.

Nora nearly choked on the wine gliding down her throat.

Kellen grabbed his beer and lifted it to meet Jack's. Nora

lifted her nearly empty wine glass.

"To the beautiful and talented journalist, Nora. And to *Coffee, My Love* for bringing us all here together," Jack said.

"Cheers," Kellen said flatly.

"Cheers," Nora said under her breath. She touched her wine glass with Jack's beer, but her eyes were on Kellen as he downed his beer in a few strong gulps. Setting the empty bottle down at the bar, he looked up at Nora through his thick black lashes. He held her gaze for a moment before standing up and throwing his bag over his shoulder.

"Thanks for the beers, Jack. I'll see you two at the gate," he said as he walked away.

# Chapter 9

Nora's hands fidgeted as she waited for takeoff. The air felt hot and sticky in her lungs. She reached for the air-conditioning vent above her seat and twisted the dial as far right as it would go. The rumbling of the plane engine indicated it was almost time.

Searching the inside of her purse for a distraction, she gathered a pen and a miniature notepad. She looked at the blank lined paper and started tapping on the notebook. Beads of sweat accumulated on her forehead, and she fanned herself with her notebook to cool her rising body temperature.

Nora felt a tap on her right shoulder. Kellen's concerned face appeared between the seats. He was so tall, his knees pressed into her chair. He wore a raglan henley gray shirt with maroon short sleeves. A leather-made necklace wrapped around his neck and hid underneath the front of his shirt.

"Are you okay?" he asked.

"Is it that obvious that I'm a nervous flyer?"

"The frantic grab for the air conditioner gave it away. Here, try listening to this." He reached over the top of the seat and placed soft, padded headphones over her ears. Roaring airplane engines were replaced by the cooling sounds of a digital ocean. The delicate ambiance and soothing beat washed over her. She wasn't sure if she had ever heard something like this before, but there was something familiar in the sound waves. It reminded her of a foggy day on Ocean Beach, when the ocean and the sand were varying shades of silver and gray and the billowing fog made it feel like she was walking on a different planet.

The flight attendant came over the speaker to announce they had reached ten thousand feet. Nora had survived take-off without a full-blown panic attack. She took off the headphones and handed them back to Kellen.

"Thank you, that actually helped," she said between the seats. "What kind of music was that?"

"I call that downtempo, or ambient music."

"Did you create it yourself?" Nora asked.

"Yep." A small hint of pride made its way to the corner of his mouth.

"It's really good."

Kellen wrapped and unwrapped the cord from his headphones around his fingers. "Are you okay now?"

"I think I am, thank you."

"Excuse me, miss?" The flight attendant tapped Nora on the shoulder. "A man from first class wanted me to give you this, that is if you'll accept it. I trust you're over twenty-one?"

The flight attendant placed a small plastic cup of white wine on Nora's tray.

"Thank you so much." Nora looked under the napkin and found a small handwritten note.

*See you in Medellin. Cheers. X, Jack*

Nora smiled at the note before folding it and putting it in

her purse. She poured herself her drink and sank into her chair. Sipping the fizzy beverage, she thought of his sexy stubble, his buttery pink lips, and his baby blue eyes. He was everything she could have wanted in a man: tall, strong, successful. He was the kind of man that she would gladly introduce to her overly conservative parents, unlike the dark and mysterious tattooed stranger sitting behind her. She peeked over her shoulder through the seats to find that Kellen had his headphones on, his thick-lashed eyes closed tight. He didn't look asleep; he looked as if he were studying something through his headphones.

Nora's thoughts ping-ponged between Jack's intoxicating charisma and Kellen's mysterious demeanor until she settled into a soft slumber. It must have been a few hours later when Nora woke up to the ding of the seatbelt sign, followed by the captain's instructions to keep their seatbelts on when seated in the cabin. She drowsily made her way toward the restroom in the back of the plane.

The fluorescent light made her look pale and sickly. Nora pinched her cheeks and fluffed up her bangs before pulling on the sliding door. She stared at the towering wall of Kellen, who stood impatiently outside the bathroom door.

"Can I have a second?" he asked.

Nora was too confused to respond, and he guided her into the galley. The rattling of metal against metal in the shelving units above Nora's head made it hard to hear what Kellen was trying to say.

"What did you say? I can't hear you."

He was still holding her elbow. There was less than an inch between them. He peeked down the aisle to see if they were in the clear, then bent down to whisper in her ear.

"Listen to me. You should stay away from Jack."

"What?" Nora stared back at him in astonishment. Who did he think he was? "Why? Jack seems nice."

"He's an asshole."

Nora blinked in surprise. "What's it to you? You don't even know me."

"I told you to stay away from assholes, didn't I?"

Nora gasped. "Oh, so you *do* remember me? Why didn't you say anything before?"

She shoved his shoulder, but he didn't budge.

"I didn't want to make a scene in front of Jack. He was obviously staking his claim on you."

"Stake his claim? I'm not property."

"Exactly."

"Forget about Jack." Nora had to take a few seconds to conjure up some of the things she had wanted to say to him so many years ago.

"You vanished into thin air."

"I know."

"You didn't even say goodbye."

"I know, but—

"Were you the one who called the police on Brent?"

Kellen's hand balled up into a fist. Nora saw the click in his jaw and the flare of his nostrils.

"Yes."

"Why?"

"Because he needed to go behind bars. I will never forgive him for what he did to you."

"I am so confused. You saved me from what could have been the worst night of my life. You told me things... things that made me think there was this connection between us. But then you just left. Without saying goodbye."

"I know, about that—"

"Why?"

Kellen let out a sigh and shook his head.

"It's complicated."

"Then uncomplicate it." Nora crossed her arms and looked up at him as he shoved his hands in his pockets.

"That night I saw you, I was offered a job."

"You got a new gig? So what? I would have understood that."

"The guy that offered me the job was this girl's dad."

"What girl?"

"Her name was Jenny. She had a thing for me. She offered to talk to her dad, who owned a studio. And, well, things between me and Jenny kind of turned into a relationship."

"She was your girlfriend?"

"No. I mean, yes. Kind of. I don't know. If Jenny thought for a second that I wasn't into her, I would have blown the whole deal. I couldn't afford the temptation."

"I was the temptation?"

"Well, yeah. Look at you. You're beautiful."

"Don't flatter me," Nora said. "You used that girl to get a job?"

Kellen shook his head no at first, but then a shadow swept over his features.

"This is ridiculous," Nora said. "I need to go."

Nora tried to pass him, but he clasped on to her arm.

"Nora—"

"Let me pass."

"Just stay away from Jack, okay? He's an asshole."

"Takes one to know one."

Nora broke free from his grasp and walked into the aisle. She collided with the beverage cart, her hip ramming the metal corner, and she keeled over in pain.

"Are you okay?" the flight attendant asked.

"I'm fine," Nora said slowly, straightening her posture. A throbbing pain shot from her hip down her leg. She hobbled down the aisle and slumped into her seat. Nora couldn't shake off the disappointment that lingered in the air. She'd imagined a million reasons why Kellen had left without saying goodbye. Not one of them had anything to do with "not being able to afford the temptation." She sat for a moment in the stale airplane air, grateful she'd dodged the gigantic tattooed bullet so many years ago.

Nora felt a prickling sensation on her neck as Kellen sat back in his seat behind her. She ignored the heavy tension between them, took out her pen, and started scribbling angrily on her notepad.

***

Jack escorted Nora through customs, holding her hand or playing with the loose strands of hair that framed her face. He teased her for putting on glasses, and she made fun of his sandpaper face.

"You're the cutest thing I've ever seen," Jack said.

Nora blushed.

"Especially when your cheeks get all pink like that," he said, poking her cheek with his finger.

"Hey. I'm not blushing," Nora lied. "You're blushing."

Jack tilted his head back and laughed heartily. Nora felt warm inside and out.

They waited by the carousel for their bags while Kellen leaned against a cement column and listened to his music in silence. A dark cloud seemed to hover over Kellen as he avoided eye contact with Jack and Nora.

"Wonder what's up his ass," Jack said.

Nora shrugged. She would never understand that man.

"He's usually pretty mellow, but he seems downright moody today."

"At least he got his luggage," Nora said.

"Here's mine," Jack said, grabbing his black suitcase off the moving conveyor belt.

Nora pouted. "Not fair." Her eyes darted around the carousel.

"I'm sure yours will turn up," Jack said.

Passengers claimed their bags until only one remained, and it was not Nora's. Then, a new wave of luggage came bumping down the conveyor belt.

*Crap.* Nora's dress for the premiere was in her luggage.

"Would you like me to walk with you to the baggage claim office?" Jack asked.

"Yeah, I guess. Shoot. I was really hoping it was going to turn up."

He placed his hand on her back, and goose bumps branched from his fingertips, as he guided her toward the back of the baggage claim area.

"Excuse me," Nora said. "Can you please help me track down my bag?"

The short man was wearing a blue airport uniform and had a mustache that looked like a fuzzy caterpillar resting on his upper lip. He grabbed the baggage receipt and typed a few numbers into the keyboard, pecking at each number, one by one. He frowned as he scrolled down his computer screen.

"One hour," he said in a heavy Colombian accent.

"Oh no," Nora said. She looked up at Jack, who was scrolling on his phone. "You guys go on ahead without me. I'll wait here for my luggage," Nora said.

"I can't leave you here alone," Jack said, as he stroked her back. Nora felt protected, like she was wrapped in a warm blanket, despite the setback. She looked up into his glittering eyes, and she almost kissed him right then and there.

"You can go ahead, really. I will be fine," she said. Hundreds of people scurried across the baggage claim floor. Crying babies, families with oversized luggage, and security guards swarmed the room.

"Here's the thing," Jack said hesitantly. "I was supposed to meet up with my partner tonight. We were going to talk about our plans for our next film. I don't think I'll have time to meet with him tomorrow or the next day."

"Then go. I'll be fine. Okay?" she said, pushing down the pang of disappointment. She had hoped they could take the long ride to the plantation together.

"It's just one hour, right?" Jack asked. "How about this, I'll head to the site now. And then I'll meet you for a drink when you get there? I'll be done with my meeting by the time you arrive."

Nora smiled; a nervous swirl of emotions formed in the pit of her stomach. Did she just get asked out on a date? She couldn't remember the last time she went out with a man. "That sounds good to me."

"Perfect! I'll have Kellen stay back with you so he can escort you to the plantation."

Nora's eyes shot up toward Kellen. He was drumming on

the tops of his thighs. His headphones were on, completely unaware of Nora's situation.

"No, really that's not necessary." She didn't want to be left alone with Trouble with a capital T. She'd fallen into that trap before, and she did not intend to do it again.

Jack took Nora's hand. "Don't worry. Mr. Grumps won't bother you. He's in his own little musical world right now. Look at him."

Kellen's eyes were closed. He had a soft sway to his head, moving to the music ever so slightly. Nora wondered what he was listening to that enraptured him so much.

"Come on." Jack led her to Kellen, despite her resistance. "Nora, he won't bite."

Nora cocked her eyebrow at him. "I don't need a babysitter."

"I just want you protected." Jack gave Kellen a pat on the back, knocking him out of his trance. "Our lady of the press needs to wait an hour for her bag."

"I'll stay with her," Kellen said. "You go ahead."

Nora blinked at Kellen, surprised he was so quick to offer to stay after she yelled at him in the galley. She shook her head, unable to predict what Kellen would do next. "Seriously, I don't need an escort. I'm fine," Nora said.

"Text me the driver's information," Kellen said.

"Why aren't you guys listening to me? I'm not a child!"

"This is not the place for you to be alone," Kellen warned. "I'm staying. End of discussion."

"Here's my card," Jack said, placing it in her hand. "Call me when you arrive, and I'll see you at the bar."

"But—" Nora started.

"Take care of her for me, Kellen," Jack said, backing out of the airport and blowing her a kiss on the way out.

Kellen scoffed. Placing his headphones back on, he unceremoniously plopped down on the floor and leaned against the column. He looked straight ahead, avoiding Nora's eyes.

"What is your problem with Jack?" she asked, tapping on his headphones.

"What?" Kellen turned off his music.

"What is your problem with Jack?"

Kellen's jaw twitched and his eyes narrowed. "He's not good enough for you. And he has a reputation."

Nora crossed her arms, waiting for him to go on.

"He has a bad reputation with women, all right? He plays the field. A lot. You deserve someone better."

Nora softened her stance—unsure of Kellen's intentions. Was he trying to protect her, or did he just not want her with anyone else?

She leaned in closer, studying his face. He was every bit as beautiful now as he was six years ago, and every bit as protective.

"I don't get you," Nora said. "How can you be so protective and distant at the same time?"

"How can I be distant when you are only a few inches away from me?" A mischievous smile swept across his face.

She might not understand him, but she couldn't seem to stay mad at him anymore. Letting out a large sigh, she released the anger that had been tugging at her heart. Perhaps they could be...friends.

"I'm sorry for what I said earlier. I might have overreacted," Nora said.

"It's all right. I deserved it."

"No, you didn't. We hardly knew each other then, and I certainly don't know you now. So, I'm really sorry."

"It's okay. I get it."

There was a long silence. Nora watched people grab their bags and greet their family members who came to pick them up.

"Are you still with that girlfriend? Jenny?"

"No, we broke up. And of course, after we split, her father gave me the boot."

"So, what did you do next?"

"A little this and that. I was bartending most days and DJ'ing on the side. I finally got a job with Quest Productions as an assistant audio engineer. When we took on the *Coffee, My Love* project, they promoted me to Lead Audio Engineer."

"Sounds like your dream job."

"It's close. I want to own my own studio one day, but I'm still figuring all that out. What about you? You're a big-time journalist now?"

"I'm an editor." Nora smiled. "And I dabble in writing."

"Oh yeah." He smiled, revealing the dimple in his cheek. "What ever happened to that book you started? Did you ever end up finishing it?"

"I did," Nora said, fidgeting with her baggage claim ticket. "But I haven't written anything since."

"What's stopping you?" he asked.

"I guess I'm just waiting for the next inspiration bolt to strike."

"What inspired you last time?"

Nora swallowed hard. She remembered the moment she came up with the idea after she met Kellen in the coffee shop. She had spent hours fantasizing about him. Nora bit her lip and shook her head. "I don't remember," she lied.

"Well, I'm sure it'll happen again," he said, looking into her eyes.

"Possibly."

When the conveyor belt started moving in front of baggage claim nine, Nora's heart raced. She stood anxiously by the opening where bags popped out. And there it was. Her black luggage with the red bow she'd tied on it, specifically for this trip.

Thank God. She snagged her bag.

"You ready to check out the coffee plantation?" Kellen asked.

"I can't wait." Nora yawned. "That is, if I can keep myself awake. But I'm supposed to meet up with Jack for drinks."

Kellen shook his head. "You know how I feel about that. Just don't come crying to me when you find out I'm right."

"Yeah, yeah. I get it. Jack's a player. I'll be careful. I can handle it."

# Chapter 10

The sea of headlights and honking horns welcomed Kellen and Nora as they stepped out of the baggage claim area. A blast of warm smoke coated Nora's throat, and she coughed into her sleeve. A man leaning against the airport wall, wearing all black with a silver belt buckle, was taking a long draw from his cigarette and said something in Spanish directly to Nora.

"Lo siento. No hablo español," Nora said, using the only Spanish words she learned before her trip.

The man leered, revealing one solid gold tooth among a crowded set of brown chicklets. He started to approach her until Kellen's arm protectively wrapped around Nora's shoulders. He bent down to whisper in her ear. "This is why I didn't want you to wait alone." He held her tight, rubbing her arm up and down, softly pressing a kiss on the top of her head, claiming his territory in front of the lurking stranger. It was just an act, of course, but Nora couldn't prevent the shivers down her spine as he held her close.

The man with the gold tooth finally walked away and approached another woman standing on the curb.

Kellen released Nora, and the absence of him disheartened her more than she cared to admit.

"Thanks," Nora said softly, as Kellen pulled a cigarette from his bag.

"It's nothing." He placed the cigarette between his lips and flicked the lighter.

Next to them was a couple, seemingly on their honeymoon, passionately kissing each other under the Delta Airlines sign. The young man's hands were roaming his new wife's back and down to her rear end. The woman squealed as he squeezed her butt.

Nora observed the way they looked at each other. Their soft caresses. Fingers tangled in her hair. The visual image of two lovebirds in an airport brought an idea to her mind. She reached for her notebook and started scribbling her descriptions.

"Whatcha writing?" Kellen asked.

"Just some ideas for a book." Nora smiled.

Kellen looked at her with what appeared to be a proud smile.

"What?" Nora asked.

"Are you going to tell me about it?"

"It's not a fully formed idea yet."

"You promise to tell me when it is?"

Nora narrowed her eyes on him, bewildered by his curiosity in her writing. It was so unexpectedly sweet.

Kellen took a drag of his cigarette and looked out toward the rows of cars waiting to pick up their passengers. The square lines of his jaw seemed more pronounced in the shadows of the airport lights. His eyelashes were so thick, they cast small shadows underneath his eyes. With his black leather jacket and his hair falling out of place, he looked like a modern-day James Dean.

A black car pulled up; the driver quickly got out of the car and looked at Kellen.

"Kevin?" he asked.

"It's Kellen," he said, putting out his cigarette.

"Oh, okay." The driver took their luggage and secured it in his trunk while Nora and Kellen got in the backseat of the man's car. The driver sat down in his seat and spoke to Kellen in Spanish.

"I'm sorry, man. I don't speak Spanish," Kellen said. "Do you know where you're going?"

The driver smiled and nodded. He said a few more Spanish words and drove them out of the city and into the beautiful green country. A full moon cast a spellbinding glow on the peaks of the mountains in the far distance.

"Check out the moon over here. It looks like we're on a different planet," Nora said.

"Oh yeah?" Kellen leaned over her to see out her window. Nora could smell the clean scent from his aftershave mixed with the earthy tobacco from his cigarette, and she breathed him in. He lingered in front of her, resting his weight on her lap as he peered out into the moonlit landscape.

"Do you have any other music you've made that I could listen to?" Nora asked.

Kellen pulled out his headphones and placed them on Nora's ears. He scrolled through his phone and selected one. A proud smile appeared at the corner of his mouth as he watched Nora listen to the electronic sound waves.

She closed her eyes, letting the rhythm penetrate her subconsciousness, and she dozed off into a deep, relaxing sleep.

***

Nora woke up to the sound of a car door closing. Her head was resting on something warm, and she was wrapped in a strong embrace. It took her a moment to realize where she was, tucked into Kellen's arm. She looked up and saw that he was still sleeping.

"Kellen," she said, trying to gently remove his arm from around her waist. "I think we're here."

He fluttered his eyes open and started to stretch.

"That was weird," he said. "I almost never sleep in cars."

"Me neither. We must be tired."

They thanked the driver and rolled their luggage to the front of the coffee plantation. It was very dark, with only a few lights leading them to the front door. Gentle rain pattered in the distance. A breeze cooled them off from their warm slumber as they walked up the steps to the plantation house.

The plantation was quiet. She hadn't been to a film press junket before, but she was expecting more people to be out and about at midnight. Kellen had an equally confused look on his face as they opened the front door.

An elderly man with a sweet face greeted them with a smile.

"Hola. You must be Kevin and Amy," he said. "I'm Jose."

Kellen and Nora looked at each other.

"I'm sorry, did you say Kevin and Amy?" Nora asked. "This is Kellen, and I'm Nora. We're here for the press junket."

Jose looked down at his planning book and then back at Kellen and Nora. "What press junket?"

"Is this the Hacienda Coffee Farm?" Kellen asked.

"Lo siento. You are at the Buenavista Coffee plantation." Jose's phone rang. "Pardon me for one moment." He stepped in the back room to take his call while Kellen got out his phone to dial the car driver.

"Are we seriously at the wrong place?" Nora asked. "I wonder how far we are from the Hacienda." She got out her phone and pulled up her maps app. "Oh my God, we are almost two hours away." Nora looked at Kellen in disbelief.

"Yes, I believe there has been a mistake," Kellen said into his phone receiver. "Your driver took us to Buenavista. We were supposed to go to Manizales. Is there anyone that can take us to Manizales right now?"

Kellen waited for the person on the other line to respond.

"First thing tomorrow?" Kellen waited again.

"All right, I'm not sure we have any other options here. That will have to do."

"What will have to do?" Nora asked.

"They couldn't get someone to help us tonight. We'll just have to wait here until nine a.m. tomorrow."

"Mary is going to kill me." Nora was supposed to be in interviews the next morning. Her first ever appearance as Molly Ashbury, and she was going to be a no-show. She was going to get the same reputation as Sonny Coultren at this rate—a complete flake.

"Who's Mary?" Kellen asked.

"Excuse me," Jose interrupted. "That was Kevin and Amy on the phone. It sounds like you two got picked up by each other's drivers. They are at the Hacienda now."

"Oh my God," Nora said. "What are the odds?"

"They said they can't get a car to bring them out here until tomorrow, so they are offering to give you their room reservation if they can have yours. Just for one night."

"So, we're staying here then?" Nora gasped.

"We're staying here," Kellen said, coolly.

"In one room?" Nora asked.

"The honeymoon suite," Jose said.

Jose led them outside into a garden, dimly lit by globe lights. Chirping crickets surrounded them as they walked toward a secluded bungalow. A trail of stepping stones guided their path. Jose unlocked the door, and it creaked open.

Along the back wall was a queen-sized bed with a white lace coverlet. Two small night stands, one on either side of the bed, had potted plants with wide green leaves. It was a simple and modest room—one Nora imagined would be a perfect place to write with the buzzing sounds of nature seeping through the paper-thin walls.

Across the room was a large window without curtains that took up most of the front wall. The moonlight illuminated the vast jungle in the distance. She felt secluded and hidden.

Maybe this situation wasn't so bad after all. She could relax here, at least for a little bit, before the frenzy began.

"I need to take a shower," Kellen said. "Do you need the bathroom first?"

"You go ahead. I need to make a call, anyway."

"Suit yourself." He shrugged and headed into the bathroom.

Nora pulled out her phone. No Wi-Fi. Crap. Service looked spotty, but she dialed Mary's number anyway. The phone rang and rang until finally Mary's sleepy voice came on the line.

"Nora? Is everything all right?"

"Mary, hey. There was a mix-up with my ride to the plantation. I'm at this other place right now, and I won't be able to get a cab ride until tomorrow morning. I'm so sorry, but I think I'm going to be missing some of the interviews."

"Are you serious? Is this just your cold feet about being in public?"

"I swear it's not. It was a complete accident. We think we

can be there by about eleven in the morning."

"We?"

Nora sighed. "It's a long story."

The flick of a lighter came through over the speaker, and Mary took a deep inhale and blew her cigarette smoke into the receiver. "I'm not sure I'm going to be able to reschedule the early morning interviews."

"Crap. I am so sorry, Mary. I'll make it up to you. Listen, I've got some ideas for a new book that I can share with you tomorrow."

"Good. Write me another damn book."

"Please don't be mad, Mary. Please."

There was a long pause with smoky breathing on Mary's end. "I can't stay mad at you, dear. You know I love you too much."

Nora felt a wave of relief. "Thanks, Mary."

"Now get some sleep. You're going to have a big day tomorrow, and I need you fresh-faced and fabulous. I'll do my best to recover some of the interviews."

"Thanks, again. Good night."

Nora looked down at her phone. It was past midnight. She pulled out Jack's business card from her bag and stared at it for a while. Kellen's warning about Jack nagged at her, but maybe Kellen had the wrong idea. Or maybe he was jealous. Jack seemed so romantic. Straight out of a book.

The least she could do was let him know she wasn't going to meet up for a drink. She could figure out what was going on between them tomorrow. Nora typed his number in her phone and opened a new text message.

*Hey, Jack. This is Nora. There was a mix up with our cab ride, and I'm at the wrong plantation. I'll be there tomorrow morning.*

The ellipses appeared right away. Nora's heart pounded.

*Oh no! I was hoping to see your beautiful face one more time before I go to bed. Text me tomorrow when you get in?*

Nora blushed.

*I will.*

*Goodnight, gorgeous. X*

Nora frowned. Was he really the player that Kellen made him out to be? Or was Kellen just hanging on to some residual feelings from the past? Nora didn't know what to think or how to feel.

After his shower, Kellen walked out with a towel wrapped around his waist. Tattoos covered his arms and spanned across his broad shoulders and chest. The crevices of his abs and the tiny trail of hair around his belly button stirred Nora's nerves. *He left without a trace, remember? He would do it again. He's just a friend.*

"You can use the bathroom now." He smiled.

Nora fortified the protective wall around her heart and broke free from her frozen stare at his half-naked body. Tiptoeing across the room, the wooden floorboards creaked underneath her light steps. She glanced over her shoulder, watching him sort through his duffel bag. Muscles rippled along his ribcage while he reached into the depths of his luggage. Nora bit her lip.

*Just a friend.*

Taking a deep inhale, Nora clicked the bathroom door shut. The air smelled like the aftermath of Kellen's shower. Wafts of pine and cedarwood filled the steamy bathroom. She stepped into the shower and let the water wash away her unclean thoughts of Kellen.

After she dried herself off, she wrapped herself in her towel and stepped out of the bathroom. Steam billowed out from behind her into the cool room.

Kellen was propped up on the bed with his headphones on. His eyes flicked over her for a brief moment before he closed them, focusing on his music.

She shuffled through her outfits, her underwear, and her dresses. She took out her makeup bag, her curling iron, and shoes.

"Crap," she said under her breath.

Kellen set his headphones down. "What's wrong?"

"I am pretty sure I forgot to pack pj's."

"I can lend you a shirt." He reached in his bag and threw a black T-shirt across the room.

Nora grabbed the shirt with one hand, but lost her grip with the other. Her towel crumpled to the floor. The air grazed her bare skin. "Oh God!" Nora frantically covered herself with the shirt, bending over to make sure her lady bits were not on full display.

Kellen's sparkling smile stifled a laugh.

"Turn around, please!" Nora's face was flaming hot as she put on her underwear and threw on Kellen's band T-shirt over her head. She tugged on the shirt to see if it would go any lower, but it barely covered her butt. She blew her bangs out of her eyes and quickly ran to the bed and burrowed under the covers. Kellen's shoulders were shaking from quiet chuckles.

"Please tell me you didn't see anything."

"I didn't see anything."

"Liar."

"Can I turn around now?"

"Yes."

Kellen pulled his feet back up on the bed and looked over at Nora, covered up to her chin with the white coverlet.

"Damn, I was hoping I would see you in my favorite shirt," he said.

"Absolutely not. It's barely covering my butt."

"Exactly." He smiled.

"Who's Incubus?" she asked, peeking at the bold lettering on the front of the shirt.

Kellen lay on top of the covers, resting his head in his hand.

"You haven't heard of Incubus? Did you live under a rock growing up?"

"Basically, yes."

"They used to be my favorite band. Listening to them is what got me into music." He paused. "Where is this rock that you grew up under?"

"Ishpeming, Michigan. My parents were very strict and didn't let me out much."

"How did you end up in San Francisco?"

"I went to school at Berkeley, and before I knew it, my best friend Jolie and I were getting an apartment together. You've met Jolie actually, at the club. I'm sure you remember her."

"I can't say I do."

Nora looked at him quizzically. "Well, that's strange. Everybody remembers Jolie. Even in the slightest passing glance. She always makes an impression."

Kellen narrowed his eyes on Nora. "You made more of an impression on me with spilled coffee all over yourself than your friend."

Nora rolled her eyes. "Right, because I'm a complete mess. It's hard to forget."

"I remember you in your church clothes, with your papers flying everywhere. Dancing over pickles and talking about a love story you made up in your head. *You* made an impression on me. Not your friend."

Nora's mouth dropped open. Words were caught in the back of her throat.

He was staring at the wall above them, his hands behind his head now. He appeared to be deep in thought.

"So, what got you into writing in the first place?"

"It's a silly story."

"I want to hear it." His eyes sparkled.

"My parents owned a bookshop—"

"Well, there's a surprise," he quipped.

"Ha. Ha. Anyway, my parents didn't carry the romance genre. They consider it pornography, and against God's will for people to read good, clean literature."

"Whoa, that's strict."

"You're telling me. One day, some lady dropped off a whole box of used romance novels and my dad ordered me to throw them away. I was so curious. I had to read at least a few of them. So, I snuck around reading romance novels like I was doing something terribly wrong."

Kellen chuckled.

"When I ran out of romance books to read and I didn't have any way of getting more, I started writing them myself."

"Look at you. The rebel romance writer. Who would have

thought?"

"Ha. Ha. I eventually got caught, and my dad made me feel horrible for years. I stopped writing and became an editor instead."

"How raunchy was your stuff?"

"Not even the slightest! Kissing! At most!"

"Damn…"

"I know. It was all very traumatic."

"So, what about that book you wrote? Wasn't that a love story?"

Nora smiled, shyly. "It was a love story. And it took a little bit of inspiration and a lot of gumption to get over my hang-ups."

"Did you ever get it published?"

Nora felt her cheeks burn. Was this when she was supposed to tell him who she was? She mulled it over, chewing on her bottom lip in the process. Perhaps she could just have one more night without someone knowing she was Molly Ashbury.

"I did, but it wasn't a big success in the United States." She could tell him the rest later. "What about you? What got you into tattoos?"

Kellen smirked. "It's a long story. Can I tell you tomorrow?"

He reached over and pulled a strand of Nora's hair behind her ear. His touch sent electric currents through Nora's body. She didn't want him to stop. They looked into each other's eyes for a lingering moment just as Kellen pulled his hand back to his side.

"Probably should get to sleep," he said through a yawn.

Nora ignored her disappointment while he turned his back. She would have talked to him all night if he had wanted to.

"Okay," Nora said.

He reached over to switch off the light. "One more thing."

"What's that?"

"You've got a rocking body."

"I'm going to go ahead and keep thinking you didn't see anything."

"I saw everything, and you are stunning."

# Chapter 11

Nora woke up to a warm sun bath pouring through the window. She fluttered her eyes open and saw Kellen's silhouette standing by the window with his headphones on. She admired the outline of his muscular shoulders down to his trim waist. A pair of black sweatpants rested just below his narrow hips, revealing the top band from his gray boxer shorts underneath.

As if Kellen could feel Nora's eyes on him, he looked over his shoulder. His face was still shadowed from the light coming directly behind him, but Nora could tell he was smiling.

"You've got to see this. Come over here," he said.

Nora rolled the blankets off her legs and stepped onto the cold wooden floor. As she wiped the sleep from her eyes, she approached the window that overlooked a vast coffee plantation that dipped into the valley of a lush mountainside. A thick blanket of clouds hovered just below the top of the mountain and moved delicately across the fields, where the workers were picking from the trees.

"Wow," Nora breathed. It was just how she imagined.

Kellen pulled off his headphones and placed them on her ears. Classical piano became the backdrop to the majestic view in front of her. The piano notes glided from one octave to the next and swept her away like the birds that soared across the sky. The sun poked holes through the clouds, creating a glittering effect on the fields that had been covered in the morning misty rain. The beauty of the moment struck her so unexpectedly.

Nora looked up at Kellen to find he had been watching her. Studying her face, searching for something, but giving nothing. He carefully brought his thumb to catch the solo tear that had escaped Nora's eye.

"It's just so beautiful." Nora smiled, wiping the rest of her tear away with the back of her hand. "And I wasn't expecting you to be listening to classical piano. I guess I got overwhelmed and—"

"Shh," he whispered. "You don't need to explain." He wrapped his arms around her in a strong hug, bringing her cheek to rest on his chest. She could feel the warmth of his skin, and the steady beating of his heart. He held her tight, then let her go, holding her an arm's distance away. He looked down at Nora's shirt and pulled back a sly grin.

"You look good in my shirt," he said, staring at her bare legs.

Nora snapped back into reality. She reached for the hem and pulled it to her knees. She was so carried away by the beauty of the moment, she forgot she needed to get dressed.

"You weren't supposed to look!" she said, grabbing her black slacks and slipping them on.

"Can you blame me?" he said, taking his headphones back. "We better hurry. I think the cab is coming soon."

"Oh, right." A cloud formed over Nora's mood. Their little excursion was coming to an end, and Mary would ensure Nora would be too busy at the premiere to spend time with him.

Walking toward the bathroom, his tattoo was visible in the morning glow. It had vibrant colors and abstract lines that created a pattern across his back. Before Nora could make out the figures, he closed the bathroom door.

She took the opportunity to change into her blue maxi dress and long dangling earrings that flirted with the tops of her shoulders. After pulling her hair into a top bun and teasing her bangs, Nora was applying a thin coat of ChapStick to her lips when Kellen reappeared from the bathroom.

"Can you tell me the story of your back tattoo now?" Nora asked, pressing her lips together.

Kellen took a seat on the edge of the bed and rubbed his chin as if he were thinking over her request. He looked out the large window and fixated on a spot in the distance. "I found this tattoo artist in San Jose and let him go to town."

There was sadness behind his eyes. Something was left unsaid. It hung in the air like a storm cloud only he could see.

"What's the real story?" Nora blurted—immediately regretting her direct question.

Kellen gave her a knowing smile. "Am I that transparent?"

"It's written all over your face."

Kellen leaned back on the bed. "I don't normally tell the real story, and we don't have a lot of time."

"Tell me everything." Nora didn't care if she was late anymore. She needed to know more about him—and what was troubling him.

Kellen let out a sigh. "My dad used to knock my mom around." He swallowed, hard. Like the words nipped at his throat. "Sometimes he would lock me in my room, while he would go to town on her."

"Oh my God." Nora's hands shot over her mouth.

"I couldn't stand the screaming. And the crying. And there was nothing I could do. If I got in the way, I'd end up with a black eye or a kick to the stomach. While my mom was crying, I would put on my headphones to block out the noise, ya know?"

"I'm so sorry."

"Anyway, there were a few toys I kept around as a kid. I used to pretend they would swoop in and save me and my mom. There were three toys in particular that stuck with me: a plastic fish that was gold with blue fins, a plush monkey that jingled when I shook him, and a Spiderman action figure. Even when I got a little bit older, like in my teens, those toys always came to mind whenever my dad would go on one of his rampages. The toys became my protectors. I know that sounds silly."

"That's not silly at all." Nora hugged herself, desperately trying not to wrap him up in her arms.

"So, the point of that story is that these toys, in my mind, became my shield, my armor. Even after I moved out of the house, they stuck in the back of my mind when times got tough. I think I might have been nineteen or twenty—living in a closet with six other guys—when I came up with the idea for the tattoo. It was around that time when I met this tattoo artist. He happened to be thinking about submitting a large-scale piece of work for a competition, and he liked my idea. He did the tattoo for super cheap so he could experiment a little bit with the design. It actually turned out better than I had imagined."

Kellen twisted around on the bed, exposing his broad back.

"If you look closer, it's basically a fish, a monkey, and a spider conquering a city. It sounds stupid saying it out loud, but the design is what makes it so unique. This is the fish," he pointed with his arm stretched around his neck. "And just below it is the spider, which was supposed to represent the source of Spiderman's powers."

"Wow. I see it now. It's so simple, and yet not simple at all." Nora scanned the artwork for the monkey and found it climbing an abstract skyscraper.

"Found your monkey," she said, grazing it with her finger. The softness of his skin made her weak. With his broad back on display before her, she couldn't resist the urge to touch him anymore. She stopped thinking and followed her heart. Her fingertip connected with his skin again.

He didn't flinch, giving Nora the courage to keep tracing the lines of his tattoo down his back. His muscles flexed under her touch, and little trails of goose bumps spread along his skin—driving her wild.

She bit her lip in self-restraint, only allowing her fingertip to slowly glide its way down and around the entire shape of the tattoo. But she wanted more. She needed more.

Kellen closed his eyes, and his breathing deepened.

"It really is a work of art," Nora said breathlessly.

"Thanks." His voice was raspy, and hot. She was pushing it too far. She had to stop. But she couldn't. She rested her hand on the center of his back and felt the rise and fall of his ribcage as he breathed.

"I'm sorry about your dad," Nora whispered.

"It could have been worse." Suddenly, he got up and pulled on his T-shirt, creating a barrier over his bare skin. "Hey, we should probably get our stuff together before the driver gets here."

"Do you always do that?"

"Do what?"

"Let people in for a second and then shut them out?"

Kellen sighed. "I don't usually let people in at all. You probably know more about me than anyone else at this point."

"Why me?"

"What?"

"Why did you open up to me?"

Kellen shoved clothes into his bag. His eyebrows pinched together. He looked up to meet Nora's gaze. "I don't like a lot of people. But I like you."

Nora swallowed. Her world was shimmering in a sea of confusion. She knew better than to fall for him again. She had been heartbroken when he left the first time, and she hadn't even known him.

Her heart ached. She wanted to wrap her arms around him and kiss away the pain that was buried deep inside.

A buzz startled her. Her phone vibrated on the nightstand next to Kellen.

"I got it." Kellen grabbed her phone. They both glanced at the screen as he handed it to her.

"Jack The Hottie" was emblazoned across her phone.

Her face turned scarlet. Why did she have to put that name in her phone?

Kellen's features darkened. "I'll let you get that. See you in the lobby."

"Kellen—"

The door shut behind him, and Nora felt the room's emptiness like a slap in the face. It was only a matter of time before he would leave again, this time for good. She stared at her phone, not able to decide if she should pick up the call. She let it go to voicemail and texted him instead.

*On our way to the plantation. Will text you later.*

It was going to be a long car ride alone with Kellen. Better to distract herself than put herself out there again. She pulled out her notebook and pen, determined to get some decent writing in on the way to the plantation so at least something good might come of this.

*** 

The first hour of the car ride to the Hacienda had been long and quiet. Nora spent her time jotting down novel ideas in her notebook. She thought back to the feeling of her fingertip on Kellen's bare skin, and her imagination swept her away.

*Her fingers left a trail of goose bumps as she spanned across his broad back. His hand clasped on hers, and he pulled her into his lap. His arms wrapped around her as she melted into him. Their eyes locked, and she knew. She was in trouble.*

*His hand caressed her knee and played with the hem of her T-shirt. His finger slipped under the fabric, tickling the inside of her leg until he found the lace of her panties. She opened up for him and—*

"Hey, check out this song. It reminds me of you," Kellen said, jarring Nora out of her story.

Nora slapped her notebook shut—her face was burning hot. She tried normalizing her breath while Kellen placed his headphones on her ears.

A breathy trumpet twinkled against the playful notes of a piano. When Louis Armstrong's raspy voice came over the speakers, she recalled the tune, "La Vie En Rose."It was the last thing she would've expected to be on Kellen's mp3 player, but she couldn't be any more surprised by this man.

"That song reminds you of me?"

"Yeah." He smiled. "It's classic and sweet. Just like you."

Nora blushed, unable to keep up with his mood swings. He had become the most confusing, unpredictable man she had ever met.

"What are you writing about over there?"

Nora hugged her notebook closer to her chest. "Nothing. Just some ideas."

"Let me read."

"Absolutely not." She playfully nudged him away.

"All right, all right." He placed the headphones back on his head. For the rest of the car ride, he tried to get a glimpse of her notebook until he got a friendly elbow to the ribs instead.

They didn't talk much on their trip, but Nora enjoyed the nearness of him. She couldn't help feeling a little sad when the driver pulled up to the resort hotel.

Kellen grabbed her luggage out of the back and handed it to her.

"Thank you," Nora said, taking her bag. "We finally made it."

"Yep," he said flatly. "Back to reality."

Nora pondered his words as they approached the grand entrance—a far comparison to the humble plantation they had stayed at the night before. The main lobby had white painted stucco walls and a terracotta tiled roof. Large palm trees stood on either side of the open doorway. Beyond the main lobby building, an outdoor event space held hundreds of people drinking champagne and snapping photos.

The frenzy was in full flight, and Nora was about to get sucked into the storm of interviews in a matter of seconds. Her heart raced; she still wasn't sure she was ready to face the press.

Inside the main lobby was a woman sitting at a white folding table. She had a deep wrinkle across her forehead, thin wrinkly lips painted in hot pink lipstick, and a nametag attached to a strap looped around her neck that read NANCY in bold capital letters.

"Welcome to the Hacienda Velencia. Can I get your name?" Nancy asked.

Nora's mouth went dry. She couldn't remember if Mary reserved her hotel room under her real name or under Molly Ashbury.

"Nora Miller?" she guessed, posing it more as a question than she intended.

"One second, please." Nancy searched the roster, flipping the pages one by one. Her brow furrowed as she struggled to read the list through her bifocals.

*This is it.* Nora would have to come clean about her author name in front of Kellen.

Just then, a high-pitched squeal darted across the lobby as Mary rushed down the hall with her hands waving wildly in the air. Her hair was frizzy, and her skin was dewy from the heat. Her lips were a bright shade of red, and she had a cigarette locked between her fingers.

*Oh no.* Nora exchanged a glance with Kellen, not able to get the words out. She needed to explain.

"Nora! Darling!" Mary trotted over, grabbing one of the photographers standing idly in the corner.

*No. No photographers.* They had agreed no photography.

Mary gave Nora a kiss on each cheek. "I know you just got here, but I'll need Pablo to take your picture." Mary caught a glimpse of Kellen, who was watching the whole scene unfold. "My goodness, aren't you a tall drink of water."

"Mary, I thought we agreed we wouldn't do pictures," Nora said.

"Yes, yes. Of course. Minimal photography. Got it. Sorry, Pablo. Run along."

Kellen tilted his head to the side, as if trying to piece together the puzzle. It was time Nora told him.

"Mary, this is Kellen," Nora said. "He stayed back with me while my luggage was being delivered, and then got stuck with me when the driver took us to the wrong plantation."

Mary looked Kellen up and down and blew out a puff of smoke. "Nora was lucky to have a strong, handsome man like you by her side during that whole fiasco."

Kellen gave her a polite smile, then turned back to Nora. "Kellen, I—"

"Excuse me, miss. I'm sorry, but I don't have a Nora Miller listed on our roster," Nancy interrupted.

"Oh!" Mary cut in. "Her room is under Molly Ashbury."

Nora whipped around to face Mary, sending darts through her eyes. Mary and her big mouth! She was just about to tell Kellen.

The hairs on Nora's neck stood on end. She could feel Kellen's glare on the back of her head.

"¿Puedes sonreír por la foto, por favor?" Pablo, the photographer, said.

"What?"

*Flash!*

The bright light blinded Nora. She blinked away the spots

until her vision came back to normal.

"Oh shit, sorry, Nora. I forgot Pablo doesn't know a lick of English," Mary said. "Gracias, Pablo. You can go now." Mary shoed him away.

"Wait a minute, Nora," Kellen interrupted. "You're Molly Ashbury? The author of *Coffee, My Love*?"

It was all happening so fast. Nora couldn't keep up anymore. She nodded apologetically as Mary put her arms around her.

"The very one," Mary said proudly.

"I was going to tell you—" Nora started to say.

"Sorry, dear, but I have to take Nora, I mean Ms. *Ashbury*. She has people to meet and interviews set up all day."

Mary swept Nora away, practically dragging her down the hall. Nora looked over her shoulder to find Kellen standing in a cloud of Mary's cigarette smoke.

# Chapter 12

Nora barely survived the interviews. There were so many questions in rapid-fire succession, her head was still reeling despite her long hot shower in the hotel room. Slipping on her red dress, she looked at her reflection, hardly recognizing herself.

*Molly Ashbury was hot.*

She wondered if she would see Kellen at the cocktail hour. Maybe he had already slipped out of her life again. She ignored the uneasiness in her stomach and wished away the affect he had on her—like a vise grip on her soul. She tried to overcome it.

Then there was Jack—charming and confident. He had texted her all day long—eager to get together for a drink before the premiere. At the very least, she would need to find him and tell him about her pen name. Nora pulled up her text messages.

*Heading down for cocktail hour. Meet me there?*

*Can't wait. X.*

***

Nora grabbed a champagne flute from the server's tray while she pitched her new book idea to Mary. She had to shout over the crowd of people adorned in gowns, tuxedos, or an armory of photography equipment. Large round lanterns were strung above the grassy courtyard where the cocktail hour took place before the grand premiere of the film.

"What brought back the creative juices?" Mary asked as she pulled out another cigarette from her purse. "And by the way, I can't stop staring at you in that sexy little red dress. I mean, va va voom!"

Nora looked down to check her cleavage. Thin straps held up the slinky red dress that flowed down to her gold stiletto heels.

"Do you think it's too sexy?"

"There's no such thing, honey. I just didn't know you had it in you. You normally dress like you're in the church choir."

Nora chuckled. She smoothed out her bangs and took a sip of her champagne, hoping to ease her nerves. She looked around the sea of people as they mingled. Still no sign of Kellen. Or Jack.

Mary led Nora to a tall, handsome man in a purple button-up shirt that sparkled against the constant flickering of camera flashes. His skin was a leathery umber, his eyes an electric blue. He smiled at Nora as they approached, accentuating perfectly placed dimples on either side of his neon white teeth.

"Alejandro, this is Molly Ashbury, the author of *Coffee, My Love*. Molly, this is the fabulous Alejandro. He played Luca in the film."

Alejandro's arms flew up in the air in a delighted squeal and then wrapped around Nora in a light hug. He kissed both of Nora's cheeks.

"It is so amazing to meet you," he said in a soft voice with a thick Argentinian accent. "I just loved the book!"

"Wow. It's like my book came to real life. This is so weird," Nora said, scanning his tall, muscular body.

"I can't tell you how much I loved playing Luca. I'm anxious to hear what you think of the movie." Alejandro took a sip of the orange and yellow drink, moving the tiny pink cocktail umbrella out of the way.

"Alejandro is a big-time movie star in Argentina. Quest Productions was lucky to snag him," Mary said.

"You are too kind!" Alejandro said before posing for another picture.

A shorter man with fair skin and soft blond hair came up behind Alejandro and placed a hand on his back. He had to perch up on his toes to be able to whisper in Alejandro's ear. Alejandro's face lit up. He turned to face the man and planted a big kiss on his lips.

"You made it!" Alejandro said to the short man. "Pardon me, Molly, I must catch up with my partner before the movie begins. I'll see you after the show!"

Alejandro and his boyfriend glided up the grassy hill toward the brightly lit hotel building.

"Well, he definitely looks the part." Nora smiled.

"I was told the chemistry between him and the girl who played Emery was electrifying," Mary said. "Speaking of the devil, there she is right now. Let's go meet her." Mary took Nora by the hand and grabbed a champagne flute from one of the passing servers. They struggled through the crowd, making their way across the party.

From a distance, the actress who played Emery looked like a Cosmopolitan model. She was a tall blonde wearing a form-fitting white dress with thin straps and thick false lashes. Her red full lips contrasted with the shimmering glow of her pale skin. As Nora got closer, she noted a small brown freckle above the right corner of her lip. Her hair was parted heavily across one side and softly cascaded down her shoulder. She grabbed the man next to her and posed for a few pictures, placing her hand on her hip and pouting her lips toward the flashing lights.

Nora stretched her neck to see who the blond bombshell was holding.

Her eyes landed on Kellen.

He looked up, locking eyes on Nora, and the room came to a halt. The swarming crowd froze in time. A high-pitched ringing filled Nora's ears.

Kellen's face paled, his beer glass glued to his bottom lip. His other arm wrapped around the blond beauty under the constant flashing from the cameras.

Nora felt daggers in her stomach. As the buzzing of the crowd returned to her consciousness and the swarm of people reappeared in her periphery, she spent the last few steps toward him gathering her strength.

"You must be Cindi. I've heard so much about you," Mary said, shaking the actress's hand. "I would like to introduce you to Molly Ashbury, the author of *Coffee, My Love*. Molly, this is Cindi. She played the role of Emery. She's been in several films for Quest Productions including *Mi Amore,* my personal favorite."

"It's a pleasure to meet you," Nora said, collecting Cindi's limp hand in hers.

"Oh my God. You are, like, totally a legend down here. For reals," Cindi slurred.

"A legend? I wouldn't say that."

"No, really. The people here are *obsessed.* They are dying for the next book."

"That's what I've been telling her." Mary arched her brow.

Nora gave Mary a playful nudge.

"I just *loved* playing Emery as a badass business woman."

Nora smiled politely, not quite picturing how this drunk girl could play a good Emery.

"Honey," Cindi said to Kellen's back. "Honey, turn around. You have to meet the author of the book!"

Kellen reluctantly faced Nora. "We've met," he said. "Although she neglected to tell me she was the author."

"And you neglected to tell me you had such an enchanting girlfriend," Nora said flatly. "Cindi, you are far more beautiful than how I imagined Emery."

"Aww. That's so sweet," Cindi cooed. "And you are way younger than I thought the writer would be. For some reason, I picture all novelists as frumpy old hermits like my tenth grade English teacher, Mrs. Ramsey."

"Thanks, I think." Nora smirked.

"What inspired you to write the book?" Cindi asked, wrapping her arms around Kellen's waist. Nora felt a wave of nausea. She looked into Kellen's eyes for a moment and decided she had nothing to lose anymore.

"It started with a guy I met in a coffee shop." Nora grabbed another glass of champagne. Kellen's head cocked to the side. She gathered the strength to continue. "He was so different than anyone else I had known. In the very short time I knew him, he triggered something for me. It felt like I had been walking in black and white my whole life, and when I met him, I discovered color for the first time. But as quickly as he came into my life, he was gone without a trace. I was left with nothing but a faint memory of what color looked like. So, I wrote down as much as I could before I forgot the feeling I had when I was with him. And that's what got me through the book."

"Wow," Cindi said. "That is quite the story."

Nora looked up at Kellen. He was tracing his lower lip with his thumb. His tattoos poked out of the sleeves of his black suit jacket.

"And Molly hasn't written anything ever since, much to my chagrin," Mary chimed in, a cigarette hanging out the side of her mouth.

Nora gave her an exaggerated eye roll.

"Although, she came to me with a few ideas today. Something's got her creative juices flowing again."

Nora furrowed her brow. Mary was right. She was writing again. Was Kellen showing up in her life the common thread? But why?

Kellen chugged the rest of his beer and set it down on the table. He offered Cindi another drink before he brushed past Nora and headed to the bar.

"Cindi, how did you and Kellen meet?" Mary asked.

"I met him at the studio. He had just walked out of his interview and was trying to find the exit. He looked like a lost puppy, so I helped him out. He asked me if I wanted to grab a coffee. The next thing I knew, I was pulling a few strings to help him land the job, and we've been dating ever since."

Nora frowned. Kellen had a pattern, and it did not sit well in Nora's stomach.

Cindi continued to rattle on about how hard it was to be away from him while she was filming in Colombia. "We were both so busy, we hardly talked on the phone."

Nora downed her glass of champagne just as Jack approached her with open arms. He was dressed in a perfectly tailored black suit, his hair pulled back in a short ponytail. His strong jaw was still dusted with light blond stubble.

"Nora from the press!" Jack bellowed. "I've been looking all over for you. I see you've met Cindi. Hello, Cindi. I assume you're behaving yourself?"

"This isn't Nora, silly. This is Molly, the author of the book." Cindi stumbled over her drunken words.

"What book?" Jack asked.

"*The* book! *Coffee, My Love!*"

Jack's jaw dropped as Nora gave him a sheepish grin.

"I'm sorry I didn't mention it earlier," Nora said, leaning up to his ear to whisper. "I'm not using my real name here, if you don't mind calling me Molly."

Jack's eyes sparkled. "Well, I'll be damned. You are just full of interesting surprises. This must be fate then. You're the beautiful brains behind the story, and I just brought it to the big screen. We were great partners throughout this whole thing, and we didn't even know it."

"Great partners, huh? I hear you got the rights to the book for a *steal*," Nora said, her hand perched on her hip.

"Oh yeah, about that…" He cringed, his hands up in surrender. "I'll make it up to you. I promise."

"What do you mean you got the book rights for a steal?" Mary perked up. "I need to talk to you, mister."

"Hey! Ouch!" Jack bent over as Mary grabbed his ear between her manicured fingers and dragged him across the room, making the nearby press laugh out loud. "Go get 'em, Mary!" Nora chuckled.

Kellen returned from the bar with two drinks in hand. "I've seen women drag Jack out of parties before, but never like that," he sneered.

Before Nora could give him a piece of her mind, Cindi cut in and grabbed a drink out of Kellen's hand.

"Thanks, sweetie," she said, sipping through the red straw. "I'm going to the little girl's room. I'll be right back." Cindi tripped over her own feet and almost collided with a server holding a tray full of champagne. She pulled herself together before cautiously wobbling up the grassy hill toward the main building.

"She seems fun." Nora crossed her arms.

"She's a mess," Kellen said with a frown.

"Why didn't you tell me about her?"

"Why didn't you tell me you were the author of *Coffee, My Love*?"

"I didn't tell you because I've been trying to be anonymous. The only reason I agreed to come here was because I thought I could compartmentalize. Nora at home. Molly down here. I wasn't expecting to run into someone I knew at a movie premiere in Colombia."

"Why do you want to be anonymous?"

"It's a long story."

"Tell me." His hand rested on Nora's arm, sending tingles up her spine.

Nora fidgeted with the champagne flute in her hands, trying to ignore the effect he still had on her. She wasn't sure how much she wanted to share with Kellen. She wasn't sure if she could even trust him. The amber hues of his eyes softened as he leaned into her.

"I need to be anonymous to protect my relationship with

my parents. I don't want to hurt their reputations back home."

"What? I don't get it."

"I already told you what they think about romance novels. They consider it smut and a disgrace to literature."

"That's ridiculous."

*What's ridiculous is this conversation.* "Why didn't you mention you have a girlfriend?"

"Jesus, Nora. It's not like anything happened between you and me."

It felt like the air was taken from her lungs. She stood still, but her chest heaved.

"Physically, I mean," Kellen corrected himself, toying with the label of his beer bottle. "I didn't mention Cindi because it's a dead relationship."

"Then why are you with her?"

He let out a hard sigh.

"Because she helped me get to where I am. She's Jack's niece. Did you know that? I could lose my job if I break up with her." Kellen looked down at his feet.

"That sounds familiar."

Kellen's head snapped up. "What's that supposed to mean?"

"Why are you relying on these women to get you jobs when you're good enough without them?"

"How do you know? I ain't shit. Nobody cares about my music. Don't you get it? I've got to make a living somehow, and it's about who you know."

"That's bullshit," Nora snapped.

"Oh look, the small-town girl does swear after all. Well, listen up. I'd love to have my own studio, but that's just not possible right now."

"How would you know? You haven't even tried."

Kellen's jaw clenched. "Because I know."

Nora shook her head. "I've heard your music. It's like nothing I've ever heard before. You have a gift. You don't need anyone but yourself."

Kellen shifted his weight, his eyes dropping to her mouth. He stared at her lips as if he couldn't comprehend the words that came out of them.

"You believe me, right?" Nora asked.

Kellen shook his head, avoiding her glare.

"Then you're a coward."

"I'm the coward?" Kellen snapped. "Said the girl who used a pseudonym because she doesn't want to embarrass her parents. How old are you, twelve? Who gives a shit what they think?"

"I..."

"What is it?"

"Maybe I'm a little embarrassed, too. I don't know. The snooty literary world looks down on romance all the time."

"And *I'm* the coward?" Kellen took a swig of his beer. The fire in his eyes was smoldering. "Maybe you should give yourself a hard look in the mirror."

Nora simmered with rage—hating herself for opening up to him. She scolded herself for her feelings—for caring about what he thought of her—for building up this imagined person in her mind that he could never live up to.

"Well, good luck with Cindi. Hope it's all worth it." Nora took a step away before Kellen grabbed her arm.

"Nora, wait. Was your story true?"

"What story?"

"About what inspired you. Your book."

*Damn him.* She wouldn't cry over him. She couldn't. She was too smart to fall into his trap again. "It doesn't matter anymore."

"But it is true."

Nora said nothing.

"Please, just, whatever you do. Stay away from Jack."

"You have no right to tell me who I should or shouldn't be with."

Nora stormed away toward Mary and Jack's yelling match in the courtyard. She couldn't tell if they were having fun, or if they were seriously rebargaining the terms of their agreement. Nora got between them and reached out to stop the shouting.

"Mary, do you mind postponing this argument? I have a few things I need to work out with Jack," Nora said.

"He's all yours, honey."

"Thank you for saving me from that *devil woman!*" he shouted at Mary as she playfully gave him the middle finger while walking away.

"What was that all about?" Nora asked.

"She's trying to get another percent of the profits. But it's a done deal. Enough business now. May I just say, you look absolutely gorgeous in that red dress. You have taken my breath away tonight."

"Thank you," Nora said, feeling warmth in her cheeks.

"So, you're the infamous Molly Ashbury?"

"I am." She still wasn't used to being recognized for her book. It was an odd feeling, like her two worlds were crashing together.

"Would you care to be my date to the movie premiere...*Molly?*"

"I would love to." Nora smiled. "Under one condition."

"What's that?"

"No pictures."

Jack looked at her curiously, rubbing the stubble on his face. "Whatever you say, beautiful."

# Chapter 13

Kellen's fingernails dug into his palm as he watched Nora walk up to Jack. He gritted his teeth, trying not to punch something or someone.

Seeing Nora under Jack's arm made his blood pressure rise. She was taunting him. Especially in that dress. God, *that dress*. She couldn't have looked more perfect, and it was driving him wild. It took every ounce of his self-restraint to keep from marching up to her, throwing her over his shoulder, and taking her to bed.

He watched Jack lead Nora back through the crowd until Cindi approached him holding a tumbler glass.

*Great, the lush is back.*

"You wouldn't believe the heifer inside the bathroom. She was busting out of her dress like an overstuffed sausage link," Cindi said into her drink.

Kellen grimaced. "Why do you have to be like that?"

"Like what?"

"Mean."

"Oh, come on, Kellen. I haven't eaten in like five days. I'm allowed to be a little moody."

Cindi's arm crept around his waist, but he brushed it off. He'd had enough of her bullshit.

"What's wrong?"

"You're drunk." *And you're a horrible person.*

"So? It's a cocktail party."

"You're always drunk."

"I like to have a little fun. What's your problem?"

"Nothing," he snapped.

Kellen watched Nora walking up the hill with Jack. He wanted to run to her, stop her from spending another second with that weasel. He was going to break her heart. But that wasn't why he wanted to take her away.

She was his. And he was hers. They were both too stubborn to admit it.

"You've been a bear ever since you got here," Cindi grumbled into her glass.

"Yeah, well. Maybe things aren't working out between us."

Cindi cackled and dug into her clutch purse, pulling out a tube of blood red lipstick. She carefully glided the waxy coating on her lips before pursing them together.

"You don't mean that," she taunted.

"I do."

"You are nothing without me."

Cindi grabbed ahold of Kellen's chin and pulled it down toward her mouth. Her sultry lips no longer tempted him, and he pulled away.

"Watch it, Kellen. You could lose everything."

Kellen glared into Cindi's threatening eyes. His nostrils flared as he suppressed the urge to scream at her in front of all the cast and crew. He knew he could lose his job if he broke it off with her. He'd have to find an apartment, give back the equipment she'd bought him, and completely start over. But Nora was right. He didn't need Cindi. Their relationship was over, and it wasn't worth staying in it anymore.

"Kellen. Come to your senses. We'll talk in the morning. For now, can we just get through this premiere together? You and me?" Cindi's glare melted into a sweet, pathetic beg. Her hands clutched his lapel as she swayed, almost pulling him off balance.

"Please, Kellen."

Kellen propped her up and let out a sigh. "Fine, but we need to talk. Tomorrow."

"Tomorrow." Cindi saluted him in that mocking way she always did when she wasn't taking him seriously.

# Chapter 14

Nora wiped the tear from her eye as the closing credits scrolled up the big screen. The movie was everything she'd hoped for and more. A Colombian melody filled the ballroom, but it was quickly overshadowed by the rolling shower of applause. Across the row of seats in front of her, the director stood up to take a bow. The crowd rose to their feet, continuing to clap. Nora joined in.

"What did you think?" Jack asked, handing her a white handkerchief as they followed the crowd out of the ballroom.

"I'm very happy with it," Nora said, blotting her eyes. "Honestly."

"Whew! I'm not going to lie, I was a little worried you wouldn't like it. In my experience, most writers aren't satisfied with how their movie adaptations turn out."

Across the hallway, Nora noticed a girl who looked like Jolie arguing with the lady in bifocals behind the receptionist desk.

"Oh my God, is that…"

"Who?" Jack asked.

"My best friend, Jolie!" Nora rushed down the hallway, her arms flying in the air.

*She made it.* Her best friend actually flew thousands of miles to surprise her. Nora's heart filled with joy.

"Jolie, what are you doing here?" Nora wrapping her arms around Jolie's neck.

"You asked me to come, didn't you? I'm sorry I missed the premiere. This lady wouldn't let me in because I wasn't on the list."

Nora looked up at Jack, who was smiling down at both of them. "My God, how can it be possible to see such beauty from two women at the same time? I'm afraid I might go blind."

He was good. A pro, even. He wasn't ogling over Jolie like other men. He made Nora feel like Jolie's equal, which made Nora feel fuzzy and warm from the inside.

"Jack, this is Jolie. Jolie, this is Jack," Nora said.

"Here. Let me take care of the list," Jack said, sliding past them to talk to Nancy.

"Who is Jack?" Jolie whispered, her eyes as big as saucers.

"He's the movie producer. The guy from the airport bar."

"No way! He is hot."

"I know." Nora smiled to herself.

"All right, you're all set," Jack said. "Why don't you two get caught up, and I'll see you at the after party?"

***

Jolie applied mascara while Nora filled her in on all the details from the last couple of days. "Wait, a minute. You slept in the same bed as Kellen, and he didn't put the moves on you? I'm confused why you're mad at him. Because he didn't tell you he had a girlfriend or because he didn't fondle your tatas?"

Nora laughed, then bit her lip at the thought of Kellen's hands on her. She'd wanted him to touch her that night, but that was before she knew he had a girlfriend. Before she knew *why* he had a girlfriend.

"Don't you see that he uses women to get what he wants? He's not in love with Cindi. He's only with her because of his job. And when I met him years ago, he was in the same situation. I'm mad because he's not the guy I thought he was! He's not the guy I built up in my head all those years ago."

"So what if he uses a couple of bimbos to boost his career? I use men all the time to make a living, and you're still friends with me. You are being unreasonable." Jolie blotted her lips.

"What's unreasonable is that he thinks he can tell me what to do and who to be with. He's demanding that I stay away from Jack. Which is precisely the opposite of what I intend to do."

"Are you going after Jack because you like him or because you want to make Kellen jealous?"

"Does it matter? I have no future with Kellen, so why not give Jack a shot? He's ridiculously handsome, successful and... and..."

"Sexy," Jolie added.

"Totally sexy."

"What about the movie? How did it turn out?"

"I was actually really happy with it. The chemistry between Luca and Emery was hot. It was missing something, though. I can't quite put my finger on it."

"Like what?"

"I don't know. I guess when I was writing the story, I was fantasizing about myself in Emery's shoes. Maybe it was the fact that Emery was played by Kellen's girlfriend, who is an obnoxious drunk, by the way. I couldn't bring myself to identify with Cindi because I had just met her."

"That is seriously so weird. I mean, you made up Luca's character loosely based off of Kellen, and Emery's character loosely off of you, and now Kellen is actually dating your Emery."

"She's not my Emery."

"Yeah, but you know what I mean. It's weird. Like, Twilight Zone kind of weird."

"I guess so," Nora said, pondering if Kellen had made that connection. It was probably weird to have worked on a movie all this time and then be slapped in the face with the news that the main character was based off their brief encounter all those years ago.

"Was the guy who played Luca good looking?"

"Alejandro? He's super hot. But don't get too excited about meeting him. He and his partner couldn't keep their hands off each other during the entire movie." Nora giggled.

"Got it. Well, I can't wait to meet everyone. Let's go to this after party!"

"Wait a minute. Do you want to talk about your breakup first?" Nora asked.

Jolie shook her head. "Ugh. No. I'm so ready to just move on. Let's find me a hottie to help me forget about him."

Nora and Jolie walked into the main ballroom of the hotel. A DJ played Latin club music through oversized speakers. The dance floor glowed in bright red and purple moving lights. Nora recognized a few of the dancers on the dance floor, including Cindi, who was sandwiched between Alejandro and the young guy who played Luca's nephew. Cindi's hair whipped from one side to the other, her body gyrating between the two men. Nora scanned the party and found Kellen drinking a beer in the corner of the room, staring blankly toward the dance floor.

Mary came running toward Nora, screeching about how happy she was with the movie. Her hair stuck to the sides of her face where she had been sweating. She smelled of smoke and pineapple-flavored rum. She continued to remind Nora of how important it was to get started on her next book so she could convince Quest Productions to do this again. Nora introduced Mary to Jolie and excused herself to find Jack.

She thought she spotted Jack by the bar, but on her way, she was stopped by a young journalist with a recorder in his hand. His hair was greased back, and his creamy caramel-color skin shone in the bright moving lights.

"Molly, can I ask you a couple of questions? Were there any creative differences while writing the screenplay or making the movie? When will there be a sequel?"

"Um, I sold the rights, so the screenplay and filmmaking was completely done by Quest Productions. Even though I didn't have any part in it, I was very happy with how it turned out. There is no plan for a sequel yet, but I am working on ideas for my next book."

"Can you tell me what your next book might be about? Any chance it will be based in Colombia again?"

"I can't say yet," Nora said, locking eyes on Jack from across the ballroom, who had started to head her way.

"All right, that's enough questions for now." Jack approached with a glass of something fizzy with lime and handed it to Nora.

The journalist nodded and politely thanked Nora for her time before disappearing into the crowd of people.

"You're my hero." Nora clinked her glass with his beer bottle. "Congratulations, Jack. Your movie seems to be a big hit."

"Congratulations to you. It's your story." They both took a sip of their drinks and watched people dancing to the salsa beat.

"Did your friend get settled in okay?" Jack asked.

"You mean Jolie? Yeah, she's over there talking to Mary. Or at least, she was." Nora scanned the red and purple bobbing heads until she found the wavy-haired vixen on the dance floor. Jolie and Mary were trying their hand at salsa dancing with one of the Colombian photographers. "She's over there."

"Do you want to dance?" He motioned toward the fun.

"Do you know how to salsa?"

"Once I finish this drink, I will know how to salsa."

Nora giggled while he downed the rest of his beer. They joined in on the mini salsa lesson with Jolie and Mary. Nora tried moving her hips like the Colombian photographer, swaying from one side to the next with coordinated footsteps. The Colombian didn't speak any English, so he put his hands on Nora's hips to help guide her. Jolie and Mary shouted with delight when Nora seemed to catch on to the rhythm. The four of them danced and laughed and danced some more. Nora couldn't remember the last time she had so much fun.

After a few songs, Nora felt a sharp ache at the bottom of her feet and gave Jolie the signal that she needed to sit down. While Nora rested her feet, she watched as the crowded dance floor circled around Cindi, who was shimmying and shaking her way to the center of attention. Her white dress had slipped up her legs, giving a peep show of her white silk panties every time she squatted toward the floor.

When Jack noticed the show Cindi was putting on for everyone, he stormed toward her, snatched her by the arm, and pulled her across the party to Kellen, who was still by the bar. Jack yelled at Kellen while Cindi swayed in Jack's grasp. Her eyes closed and her knees gave way. She started to crumple to the floor, but Jack grabbed under her arms in time to hold her up.

Nora took off her gold heels and put them under her chair. She ran over to help, shoving the cameraman out of the way before he could snap a picture.

"Get her out of here," Jack said as he handed Cindi over to Kellen.

"Can I help?" Nora asked.

"Go sit down, Nora," Jack commanded. "Kellen's taking care of this."

Nora ignored the direct order and slipped her shoulder under Cindi's limp arm. She didn't like Cindi, but she couldn't bear seeing Kellen deal with her on his own.

Cindi grunted something incoherent under her breath and pointed to the dance floor.

"Let's go." Kellen hoisted her up on the other side. Cindi slumped onto Kellen's and Nora's shoulders, and together they walked her out of the party while Jack stayed back to handle the photographers.

Cindi's dress inched above her underwear, and people in the hallways were staring. Nora paused, trying to pull down the skin-tight fabric. She tugged at the hem, but she couldn't get a firm grip, leaving Cindi's panties exposed to the passersby in the lobby.

"Just let it be. We're almost there," Kellen said, breathing heavily. He'd been holding most of her weight.

When Kellen and Nora reached Cindi's hotel room, Kellen pulled out the key from his pocket and unlocked the door to their hotel suite. A living room with white padded furniture and large potted plants overlooked the vast plantation through wide french doors. They rested Cindi on the bed, taking off her shoes and tucking her in.

Nora was catching her breath while Kellen brought the garbage can in from the bathroom and placed it next to the bed. Cindi was snoring by the time they walked out of the bedroom.

"Thanks for the help," Kellen said.

"You're welcome," Nora said, making her way to the door. She felt a hand on hers before she could reach the doorknob.

"Please stay and talk with me," Kellen said.

Nora couldn't fall in his trap again. She was too tired, too emotionally drained from the past forty-eight hours, and yet she couldn't resist the small window of opportunity to spend time with him.

"What is there to talk about?"

Kellen motioned for her to follow him as he pulled out a cigarette from his coat pocket and opened the French doors to the patio. The chirping sounds of plantation wildlife filled the room, and the soft moonlight shown down on Kellen's dark features. Nora softly padded to the porch and folded her arms around her waist as the cool night air breezed over her bare shoulders.

"Here." Kellen took off his suit jacket and gingerly placed it on Nora's shoulders. Then he lit his cigarette.

"Nora, I'm a fucking mess."

"You're damn right about that."

Kellen blew out a puff of smoke, subtly smiling at her jab. The deep crescent moon on his cheek appeared, reawakening the butterflies in her stomach.

"I knew there was something between us when I met you in

the coffee shop."

Nora's heart clenched. The words she had dreamed of hearing for so long, laid out in front of her on a silver platter. She thought back to the hours she'd spent agonizing over whether she had made up their feelings in her head.

"Then why did you leave?"

"I was an idiot. But now, fuck. You can't deny there's something here. I've been a wreck since you showed up at that airport bar and let that scumbag put the moves on you. I don't know how to act. I don't how to breathe."

Nora looked at the deep creases in his frown. He flicked the ashes of his cigarette into the nearby ashtray.

"I want you," he said.

Nora sucked in her breath, wishing he had said those words to her long ago. Tears welled in her eyes, and her heart pounded in her chest. She knew deep down she wanted him too, but she didn't want to get hurt. She couldn't go through that again.

Kellen placed his hand on her cheek in time to catch the escaped tear. She rested her face in his palm, feeling the magnetic pull between them. A force bigger than her—and one that would consume her entirely if she wasn't careful. She looked up at his troubled face and held his gaze.

She wanted him too. To feel him under her hands. To kiss him softly. To bite his lower lip. A growing sense of need churned deep in her core. As she leaned toward him, she heard the sound of Cindi puking into the garbage bucket.

Kellen stood like a statue, unwilling to pay any attention to the distraction. Nora peeled his hand off her cheek.

"You need to take care of your girlfriend now." Nora took off his suit jacket and reached for the door.

"Wait."

"I can't." Nora opened the French door and walked out of the hotel room. She stood in the hall, not sure what she was waiting for. Her head was buzzing. Her skin felt cold and damp, yearning for Kellen's touch again. She was mad at herself for feeling this way. She needed to get back to Jack, to forget how she felt about Kellen.

The soft carpet under her feet reminded her that she'd left her shoes in the ballroom. She lightly tiptoed back down the hall. The music had slowed down to a sultry pace. Nora picked up her shoes off the table and looked up toward the dance floor. Only a few couples were left. Nora had to squint through the darting lights to make out the details of figures. She found Mary in the far corner by the bar, gesticulating wildly as she tried communicating with the Colombian photographer. She playfully patted his shoulder and took another drink of her cocktail.

Nora scoured the room for Jack or Jolie, but neither could be found. She marched toward the lobby, where a few patrons sat leisurely on couches and photographers and journalists were packing up their equipment.

"Nora."

She turned around to find Kellen towering over her. Out of breath.

"Kellen, what are you doing here? You're supposed to be taking care of your girl—"

"I just...," Kellen started. His eyes darted from side to side. "I just wanted to make sure you were okay. Can I walk you back to your room?"

Nora needed her distance from him. She had to get away and claw herself back to reality.

"No. I need to find Jolie."

Nora started walking toward the outdoor courtyard when Kellen grabbed her arm.

"Stop."

"Let go of me, Kellen." Nora struggled out of his grasp.

"Don't go that way," he urged.

"Why?"

"Just, don't. Please."

Nora saw it written all over his face. He had seen something he shouldn't have.  Her heart pounding in her ears, she stormed out through the doors. In the shadowed corner of the courtyard, two figures groped each other. Jack's hands cupped Jolie's upper thigh, his mouth on hers in a feral kiss.

Nora stood there, stuck in what felt like quicksand, as the handsome devil pawed her best friend.

"How could you?"

Jack released Jolie, and they both looked back at Nora in horror. Jolie's lips were swollen as if they had been making out for hours.

Jack rushed toward Nora. "Nora, it's not what you think."

"It's exactly what I think," Nora said as she whirled around and hurried back inside, where she wouldn't have to look at either of them.  Kellen was there, waiting for her at the door—pity written all over his face. She couldn't face him, either.

"Nora, I'm so sorry," Kellen said.

"I don't want to hear it." Nora stormed past him in a fury that almost blazed the hotel carpet.

Nora slammed the hotel room door, then saw Jolie's suitcase lying near the nightstand. That was the last time. She was tired of men fawning all over Jolie, choosing her over Nora.

Every. Single. Time. Enough was enough.

She shoved makeup and hair products into Jolie's case and threw it out in the hallway. Jolie would have no problem finding a room tonight. Hell, she could sleep with Kellen, too, for all Nora cared.

No. No, she couldn't. Kellen was the only guy who didn't get wrapped up in Jolie's spell. If Jolie ever laid a hand on Kellen she'd…

It didn't matter. Nora sobbed into her hands. Kellen wasn't Nora's to begin with. And neither was Jack.

# Chapter 15

A girl had to be pretty low to flee a resort hotel in the tropical fields of Colombia and fly spur-of-the-moment to Michigan to visit her parents. Especially when those parents didn't support her career choices.

And yet, there Nora was in her parents' driveway with no one else to talk to and nowhere else to go. She had been home a few times since she'd moved to California, but it still felt weird being back, given all the tension that had built up between them over the years.

Nevertheless, her mom rushed out to greet her, jumping up and down and screaming, "My baby is home! My baby is home!" It was like therapy for Nora's heart. Even though her parents drove her nuts, sometimes she still needed them for comfort. This was why she'd agreed to use a pen name. This was why she was willing to compromise with her parents, ridiculous as it seemed to everyone else. She still needed them in her life.

***

Nora blew her nose while her mom rubbed her shoulders. Her childhood room was more or less unchanged, but now her bed was covered in crumpled tissues. A carton of uneaten chunky monkey ice cream with two spoons sat melting on the nightstand.

"What did you do when Kellen confessed he had feelings for you?" Nora's mom asked.

"Nothing. His girlfriend started puking, and that brought me back to reality. I thought that maybe Jack would help pull me out of the Kellen spiral, but that clearly didn't work out either."

"Are you more upset about Kellen having a girlfriend or about Jack kissing your friend?"

"I don't know. Both."

"Can I tell you what I think?"

Nora blew into another tissue, wiping the remaining tears that had streamed down her face.

"I think you're more upset that Kellen didn't dump his girlfriend the second you showed back up in his life."

"I wouldn't have expected him to dump his girlfriend. I just don't understand how he could be with someone so awful for so long. Just to protect his job. His priorities are all messed up."

"Yeah, well. That doesn't mean he can't get them straight. You didn't even give him the chance to straighten out. Instead, you were eager to jump into McDreamy Producer's arms to spite him."

Nora grabbed the ice cream carton and dug out a scoop with her spoon. She offered it to her mom first, who respectfully declined, and then let the sweet gooey goodness cover her tongue.

"Maybe you're right. But I'm still mad at him. No matter how rational it is. He left me once. His second chance was in

Colombia, and he still messed up."

"Okay, honey."

"Plus, he doesn't even like pickles. I mean, who doesn't like pickles? Maybe that was my sign."

Nora took another scoop of ice cream and stuffed it in her mouth.

"You can't honestly think that, Nora."

"I have to.  Otherwise, I'm going to start doubting my decision to cut my Colombia trip short."

"You did the right thing, I think. Anyway, I'm so glad to have you home. We hadn't seen you in a long time. You should come with us to the center tonight. I'd love to show you what we've been up to."

Nora cringed at the thought.  Seeing her father and his followers was the last thing she wanted to do, but her mom would have been disappointed if she didn't go. If Nora ever wanted her parents to respect her choice to write romance novels, she would have to respect what they chose for a living, too.

***

The sounds of meditative music echoed off the gymnasium walls. Her father sat on a pillow, perched in front of a semicircle of his followers dressed in golden robes. Their eyes were closed, listening to the soft hum of their own breathing.

Sunbeams cascaded from the tall windows of the gymnasium, giving light to all the dust particles that danced above Daddy's little seance. Nora felt a nudge on her left side. Her mother handed her a pillow so they could both join the group. Nora reluctantly took the pillow and followed her mother.

Her weight sank into the cushion beneath her. She looked around at the contented faces and wondered in awe how and why they were following her father in this madness.

The sound of a gong broke the spell, and they all pressed their hands together in front of their hearts.

"Let the light in you flow unto others. May the grace of God be with you." Nora's father bowed his head. Quietly to himself, he whispered, "Amen."

"Amen," the group saluted back.

"For those of you sticking around for tonight's peace and light ceremony, we will be meeting back here at six o'clock sharp."

One by one, the group lifted themselves from their pillows and walked across the gymnasium, leaving her father behind. He sat up in amazement as he laid his eyes on his daughter.

"Nora, you're home." His arms opened wide, inviting her in for a hug. Nora walked over to him and knelt down. She wrapped her arms around his neck and wondered if he was the same man that she grew up with. He seemed so peaceful and calm.

"What are you doing here?" he asked.

"I needed a break from real life."

Her father stood and offered Nora his hand to help her up. "Is everything okay?"

*No. Everything is not okay.* "I'm fine, Dad."

"Will you be staying for the peace and light ceremony?"

Nora looked up at her mom for guidance.

"You should stay," her mom said. "I'll head home and make your favorite spaghetti and meatballs."

Nora nodded. It just so happened that Nora needed peace and light. Anything to help heal her broken heart.

***

Nora took a candle from her father and passed it to the man next to her. She grabbed another candle and passed it again. And again. Finally, the circle of patrons stood around the center court. Her father said a prayer while lighting his candle. He reached his flame to light hers, and together the group sent the glow around the circle, warming their faces.

Her father spoke of light and love—being kind to one another—at peace with the things that had gripped their hearts and minds so hard that they couldn't see straight.

She thought of Kellen, and how she had been holding on to her anger for so long, she couldn't see what had been in front of her. He wanted her. He even told her so. But she had been so scared of getting hurt again that she wasn't giving him a chance.

The flickering candles danced and swayed. The warm glow seemed to melt the icicles around Nora's heart, and she started to forgive. Almost.

A woman on the other side of the circle started to cry. Nora's father walked over to her and handed her a tissue before putting his hand on her shoulder.

"It's okay, dear. Let it out. This is the place you can be free."

Her father was so tender-hearted and sweet. A proud smile swept across Nora's face. Maybe he had changed? Maybe he could finally accept Nora and what she loved to write about. She could only hope.

They finished their service by blowing out their candles and walking out of the gymnasium in comforting silence.

Afterward, Nora got into her father's car and closed the door, shutting out the cold night air.

"Well, Dad. You seem to be helping those people in there. It was really impressive."

"Thanks, pumpkin."

"What's with the robes, though? They feel a little unnecessary." She was treading in dangerous territory, and she knew it.

"Don't you dare say it," her father said sternly.

"Say what?"

"That cult nonsense you keep telling your mom." His mood flipped the switch from peaceful to agitated. He was back to the father she recognized, the vein in his neck bulging through his reddening skin.

"I'm sorry." Nora looked down at her hands. She'd poked the bear. The tension was rising.

"I take it you're still writing that smutty garbage." Just like that, their same pattern was back, the argument they'd had over and over again since the day he'd found her love stories.

"Dad, it is not smut! I'm tired of telling you," Nora snapped back.

"Well, whatever you want to call it, I don't want it getting around town that my daughter is into porn."

"Oh my God, I can't handle this anymore. It is not porn!"

"And my community group is not a cult!"

Nora crossed her arms, glaring out the window as her father turned into their neighborhood. It was painfully clear that no matter how hard she tried to see her father's side, he would never see hers. He pulled into the driveway and took the keys out of the ignition.

"I'm sorry I yelled," her father said more calmly. "But I really think you should consider a different genre. Thriller, mystery, adventure… you like those types of books, right?"

"It doesn't work like that, Dad. You can't tell me what to do, or what to write. You can't keep me from being successful, either. Not anymore. If I write a second book, I'm not going to say no to the publicity this time."

"Don't you dare, Nora," her father growled. "You'll ruin me."

"The only person who can ruin you is *you*, and your naive conception that a romance novel, written by your very own *daughter*, can create some sort of scandal, tainting this 'oh-so-perfect world' you've created for yourself. You are completely and utterly delusional to think my book would have any kind of impact on the cult-like empire you are building here. I don't know who you think you are, but you are not *God*. And you do not determine what is good and what is evil. I will not let you determine what I do or how I should do it any longer!" Nora slammed the car door, raced up the front steps, passed through the kitchen, and locked herself in her bedroom. Not even the smell of her mom's home-cooked meatballs could keep her in this town anymore. She packed her bags to go home. Her real home.

# Chapter 16

I t was a quiet morning in the coffee shop on the ground floor of Nora's office building.  She finished reading a manuscript and set her pen down when her phone buzzed. Jolie. Again. Nora clicked the ignore button and decided to get another coffee.

It had been two weeks since she'd left Colombia. There had been many missed calls from Jolie and Jack. She wasn't ready to face either one of them.

Nora played with the lid of her coffee cup and tried shoving all of the drama from the movie premiere night to the back of her mind. She'd become numb to any emotion that tried to make its way to the surface, and she'd coasted through the last few days by getting into a routine. Work. Write. Sleep. Repeat.

Her phone buzzed again.

"Hey, Mary," Nora said, holding her coffee cup under her lips, letting the steam warm her cold nose.

"You've been a tough cookie to get ahold of. How are you holding up?" Mary asked.

"I'm all right. I've gotten through the first three chapters. I can send you the pages."

"That's not what I'm talking about. You want to talk about

what happened with Jack?"

"I really don't."

"Well, I'm afraid I'm not giving you a choice. Jack is an ass. Apparently, he has a reputation for being a scumbag."

Nora grimaced, remembering Kellen's warning. Nora had been too stubborn to listen.

"I don't know if he felt bad about what happened or what, but he's willing to renegotiate our deal, giving us an extra percent in royalty fees."

"I don't want his filthy money."

"Tough shit," Mary said, blowing out her cigarette smoke into the phone receiver. "This is a deal we can't pass up. Now here's the catch. He refuses to negotiate with me, and he wants to book a meeting with you today."

"Absolutely not," Nora said.

"I'm sorry; this isn't up to me. He told me he was going to show up at your office this morning. I'm giving you a heads-up. Don't blow this. I want that extra percent."

"Please don't do this to me," Nora begged.

"I'm sorry, honey. It's just business. Call me after you've met with him. He'll probably be there any minute."

Nora's heart pounded. She looked around the coffee shop in time to see a dark figure walk in through the doors. She had to blink a few times before she realized it was Kellen, not Jack.

Kellen wore a black T-shirt and dark jeans. He looked so much bigger than she remembered him in this place. His shoulders were wider, his biceps more pronounced. He approached her cautiously. "Can we talk?"

Nora felt her heartbeat in her ears.

"I'm expecting someone. I actually need to get back up to

my office."

"Just a minute. Nora, please."

"How did you know I was here?"

"I've been here every morning since last Friday. Thought I might run into you at some point."

"What do you want, Kellen?"

He swallowed hard, then sat down. His leg jittered while he looked down at his hands.

"I just wanted to say I'm sorry."

"For what?"

"For being an idiot, mostly."

Nora nodded, although he wasn't the only idiot. She'd never given him a chance.

"I broke up with Cindi."

Nora gulped. "I see."

"I should've done it a long time ago. I didn't love her. But of course, after she kicked me out of the apartment, Quest Productions gave me the boot."

"I'm so sorry."

"It's all right. You've made me realize that I would rather be doing something I've earned, not something I've slept my way to get."

Nora flinched at the thought of him sleeping with someone else. "I'm glad you've come to that epiphany."

"Took me long enough, but I finally got there."

Nora toyed with the rim of her coffee cup. He looked so beautiful. His sad eyes drew her in. She wanted to comfort him, wrap him in her arms and tell him everything was going to be okay.

"That was very brave of you, but I know you're going to be fine. You have so much talent."

Kellen ran his fingers through his hair. "I don't know."

"You do. You really do." She looked up in time to see the glimmer of a dimple. He was holding back his smile, maybe because he was waiting for her to make her move?

"What are you going to do now?"

"I don't know. Maybe finally try to open up my own studio."

"I'm happy to hear that."

"What about you? Are you doing okay after Jack and your friend—"

"I'm fine."

"I warned you about him."

"You did."

Kellen leaned forward on the small table, closing the space between them.

"Nora, I don't know why, but I have this urge..."

"Urge?"

"Yeah, this feeling that I need to protect you. Maybe because I wasn't successful in protecting my mom, and I need to make it up somehow, as messed up as that sounds."

"It doesn't sound messed up, but you can't protect me from everything," Nora said with a cocked brow.

"I can try." There was so much meaning in those three little words. He was willing to try...to be with her? To stay with her? Nora's heart almost leapt out of her chest.

"Nora, you are one of the most precious little creatures I've ever met. You are beautiful and smart and funny. Do you know how hard it was to quit my coffee shop job without saying goodbye to you? How often I've looked at pickles and remembered your cute little dance in front of the food truck? Do you know how badly I wanted to put my hands all over you that night in the honeymoon suite? I don't think I slept more than a minute that night because I was trying to justify wrapping you in my arms. I couldn't stand the fact that I couldn't have you. I wasn't good for you before, and I'm not good for you now. I have nothing to offer. Not even a place to stay. You deserve better than me."

Nora swallowed as her walls crumbled. It was her move. She needed to make the choice to take a chance on him or walk away.

"Did you say you came here every day since last Friday?" Nora asked.

Kellen smiled. Just as he was about to open his mouth again, Jack showed up behind him, clamping his hands on Kellen's shoulders.

"I thought that was you in the window. Mr. Atwood, I'm sorry to kick you out, but I have a meeting with Nora right now."

Kellen's hand clenched into a fist.

"I see how it is," Kellen said, focusing on Nora as he rose from the table.

"Kellen, it's not like that. Please wait."

But Kellen stormed out of the coffee shop.

"Jack, you have a lot of nerve," Nora said.

"Do you have an office somewhere we can talk in private?"

"I'm not going anywhere with you."

Jack let out a sigh before sitting down at the table across from her. "First of all, I am really sorry about what happened that night with Jolie."

"Sorry that it happened, or sorry that I saw it?" The vision of him pawing at Jolie made her sick to her stomach.

"Both. Honestly. I was crazy drunk. I wasn't thinking straight. I made a mistake. Can you please forgive me?"

"What am I supposed to say to that? Yes? It doesn't work like that. You made out with my best friend."

"Listen, I'd like to make it up to you. I want to prove to you that it was a one-time mistake. Can I take you out to dinner tonight?"

"No."

"Tomorrow?"

"No."

"Okay, you need your space. I get it. Then let me make it up in another way until you change your mind. I'd like to renegotiate our terms for the rights of your book. The film got incredible reviews, but it was because of the story. I'm willing to bump your royalty fee another percentage point if you give us exclusive rights to your next book."

Nora put her computer in her bag and stood up. She looked down into his blue eyes and traced her finger along the edges of his face. On one hand, he was beautiful and successful. On the surface, he was everything she'd dreamed her one true love would be. On the other hand, he'd had his tongue down Jolie's throat less than five hours after meeting her.

"Jack, go to hell." Nora stormed out of the shop and into the street, looking left and right for any sign of where Kellen might have gone until she spotted his back. He turned the corner into the alleyway behind her building, and she shuffled down the sidewalk with her computer bag in tow, her black heels clicking on the cement.

"Kellen!" She turned the corner and saw him walking down the alleyway, his hands in his pockets. Nora called his name again, but he didn't respond. She trotted up to him and touched his shoulder. But when he turned to face her, the man she'd been following wasn't Kellen. This man had deep sunken eyes and large dark patches on his paper-thin skin. He snarled at her, revealing two gaping holes where his teeth used to be. Nora yelped and took a step back. "I'm sorry. I thought you were Kellen."

"You can call me whatever you want, sweetheart." He lunged at her. Nora barely got out a scream before his dirty palm covered her mouth. A knife blade, cold and hard, pressed against her neck as she was pinned to the back wall.

"Hand over your bag," the man growled.

With Nora's shaky hand, she dropped the bag on the ground. The man kept the blade at Nora's throat as he reached down, then pulled the strap over his shoulder. Nora whimpered under her hand as the knife nicked her skin.

"Don't you say a word now, you hear? Or I'll come back and finish the job my knife started." The man backed away, still holding the knife towards her.

***

"What the fuck?" Kellen ran down the alleyway. His pounding footsteps echoed off the walls as he darted at the man with a knife at Nora's throat. Kellen pulled back his fist and rammed it into the man's jaw. He crumpled in a heap, and the knife skipped off the cement.

Nora was shaking, holding her throat and staring blankly at Kellen. Kellen cupped her fragile face in his hands and scanned her neck.

"Shit, you're bleeding," Kellen said. "Do you have a tissue in your purse?"

Nora eventually mustered a nod. Kellen looked at the unconscious man and found her black bag beside him on the ground. He searched through it, pushing aside multiple notebooks until he finally pulled out a package of tissues. He placed a fresh one on her cut.

"Here, hold this." Kellen placed her hand on the tissue to apply pressure. "Let's get you out of this alley." He wrapped his arm around her thin shoulders and guided her shaky body to the street.

"What the hell is going on?" Jack demanded, approaching them.

*Oh great. Just fucking great.* "Nora was just attacked. I'm calling 911."

"Nora, are you okay?" Jack placed his hands on her shoulders, snatching her from Kellen's arms.

*Piece of shit.*

While Kellen spoke with the police dispatcher, he watched Jack embrace her, and she wept on his shoulder. Like a dagger to his heart—it pained him to see Jack touching her.

"The police are coming now," Kellen said, clicking off the phone. "You can take your hands off her now."

"You go on. I got this," Jack said, holding Nora tighter.

Kellen's blood pressure spiked. "I'm not going anywhere." He pulled out a cigarette and looked behind him. The perpetrator was gone. He must have slipped out of the alleyway while Kellen was on the phone. "Shit, he got away."

Blood from Nora's neck seeped through her tissue, dripping onto Jack's pants.

"You should really get this stitched up," Jack said.

*Damn your fancy pants, Jack, and get the hell out of here.*

"Really dude, I can handle it from here," Kellen said.

Two police officers soon arrived and proceeded to ask them a series of questions, filing their police report. A moment later, the ambulance arrived. Flashing lights and sirens were everywhere, and Nora remained in a semishocked state as they placed her on a stretcher.

"Where are you taking her?" Kellen asked one of the paramedics.

"Saint Francis," the medic said as she placed a heavy bandage on Nora's neck.

The doors to the ambulance closed, and both the ambulance and police officers took off, leaving Jack and Kellen on the street in their wake.

"I'm heading to the hospital," Jack said.

"I'm coming too," Kellen said.

"No, you're not. You need to back off. Nora and I are working things out."

"What?" Everything went quiet. The sirens had left, and the flashing lights had stopped. The world was put on pause. "You guys are together?"

"Yes. And I'm in the process of arranging a deal for exclusive rights to her next book. I can't have you interfering."

"Fuck you, Jack. You don't give a shit about Nora. You just care about your business."

"Listen here, asshole. I told you to back off, and I mean it."

"Nora doesn't want you."

"She does. She said so herself. In fact, she came out here to tell you in person, but the mugger got to her first."

"You're not serious."

"Sorry, bro, but she made her choice. Now get lost."

Every muscle in Kellen's body clenched. He reached back to give a solid crack at Jack's nose when a cab pulled up to the curb. Jack got in and slammed the door shut.

The cab zoomed away, leaving Kellen in a swirling rage. He

couldn't believe that Nora would go back to that asshole, but then again, she had been clutching Jack after the accident. And Nora mentioned she was expecting Jack in the coffee shop.

Fuck. His world came closing in on him. He was too late. Pouring his heart out like a complete moron, and all the while, she'd been waiting for Jack to come to her rescue. From *him*.

After a while, Nora's choice finally sank in. After everything Jack did to her? If she was that naive, then she wasn't the person Kellen thought she was after all.

***

"You're all set," Doctor Stephens said after placing the bandage over the stitches in Nora's neck.

"Thank you so much, Doctor," Nora said.

"I suggest you go home and get some rest. That was quite the traumatic experience, I'm sure."

A nurse in purple scrubs peeled back the curtain. "Doctor, someone is here to see Nora."

Nora's heart leapt in her throat, expecting to see Kellen. She walked out of the exam room toward the main lobby.

Jack stood with his hands in his pants pockets. The weight of disappointment settled in her stomach.

"Jack. What are you doing here?"

"I came to see if you were okay."

"I'm fine," she lied, wondering why Kellen hadn't come instead.

"Let me take you home then," Jack said.

"There's no need."

"How bad was the cut?"

"I just needed a couple of stitches, and a tetanus shot as a precaution. You didn't need to come."

Jack placed his large hands on Nora's shoulders and looked squarely into her eyes.

"I was worried sick about you. Please, let me take you home at least. Make sure you get into bed safe and sound."

"Where did Kellen go?" Nora asked quietly.

"He took off soon after you got in the ambulance."

Nora almost dropped to her knees. The wounds in her heart that had started to heal had been ripped open. He was gone. Again. Nora didn't get to tell Kellen how she really felt about him, and how proud she was that he was giving up everything to start with a clean slate.

Nora reluctantly agreed and let Jack order a ride. They stood in silence, waiting for a guy named Damion in a red Prius to show up at the front doors. The hospital lobby's light jazz music filled the awkward void between them. When the Prius pulled up, Nora and Jack sat in the back seat. The air in the car smelled of licorice and berry-scented car freshener. Nora's stomach churned. She rolled down the window for fresh air.

Thick clouds of fog spilled over Twin Peaks as they made their way up Corbett Avenue. The temperature dropped ten degrees, and Nora shivered against the cool wet air that blew against her cheek.

"Here," Jack said, putting his arm around her shoulders. Nora flinched at his touch.

"Whoa there, it's just me."

It wasn't just him. She couldn't stand to be around him, or anyone. She was suffocating, and she needed to be alone. She needed to walk off her frustration instead of sitting in the putrid sweet scent of the Uber with Jack's sleazy arms around her.

"I need to get out of the car," Nora said, reaching for the door handle. "Stop the car, please."

"Whoa, whoa, Nora. Wait. Don't go."

The car pulled over to the side of the street, and Nora stepped out.

"Jack, I know what you're doing. You're being sweet and trying to help, but I know what you're trying to do, and it's not happening. I won't sleep with you." The rolling fog blew strands of hair into her mouth. She slammed the door shut while trying to tame her hair down.

"Come on, Nora. I thought we had something special," Jack said, sticking his head out of the car window.

"Something special? Jack, I liked you. Yes. But then you had your tongue down my friend's throat! That's not really something I can get over."

"Fine," Jack huffed, sitting back in his seat. "Our deal is off then."

"What deal?"

"The extra percent in royalty fees, and an exclusive deal on your next book. That deal. It's over."

"I didn't want that deal anyway!"

"Fine!"

"Fine!"

The car window rolled up, and the red Prius drove up the rest of the hill. Nora would now have to climb that hill on foot to get to her apartment. Perhaps if she told Mary the whole story about getting mugged in the alleyway, she wouldn't be so hard on her for losing the deal with Jack.

***

Nora logged onto her computer. She was the first one in the office that morning. The air was still. The lights were off except for the single lamp she had at her desk. It had been several days since the mugging, and she was barely starting to feel normal again. Despite the stack of manuscripts on her desk and the ninety-nine unread emails in her inbox, she typed Kellen Atwood's name into the Google search bar. She'd done this a hundred times before to no avail, but she hoped that one day she would find some trace of him. Where he went. What he was doing. Anything to connect her back to him.

Something new came up in her search. It was an Instagram page. He hadn't had this before. Could this be him? She clicked on his name to find one post; a photo taken from inside a car, through the back window, with a view of the bay city in the distant background, warmed by a pink and orange glittering sunset. The caption read, "Left my heart in San Francisco. Goodbye for now. #freshstart."

Nora stared at the image for a long time, letting the realization settle in. He'd left again. Without saying goodbye. Again. Her heart felt heavy, and she sank into the familiar sadness she'd felt so many years ago.

It was over. For good, this time.

# III

# Part Three

# Chapter 17

*wo years later...*

The room quieted to a low murmur. People shifted in their seats, waiting for Nora to begin her reading. Nora picked up her book and smiled at the audience. Fifty, maybe sixty people filled the space. Their bright eyes and eager faces looked up at her with so much anticipation. Nora's nerves got the best of her and her hands began to shake.

It was her thirtieth and last appearance of her book tour, but that didn't make her feel less nervous. She was home in San Francisco, at the historic City Lights bookstore. Not only was she doing a reading at one of the most famous bookstores in America, but she was grouped with other romance novelists and poets, including the infamous Sonny Coultren.

If he showed up.

Nora wasn't sure if he was in the audience or finding another excuse to flake out of the event. Either way, Nora had to focus on calming her anxiety. She steadied her hands as she flipped to her chapter.

She read out loud, finding her stride in the lyrical tone of her book. She used inflections to convey the feelings behind the written words. Nora couldn't help but think of Kellen.

Her new novel invoked feelings she'd tried to bury deep down, but every time she read it, she dredged them back up again. Anguish, when she learned he had left San Francisco for good. Despair, knowing she would never see him again.

Her heartbreak made for a romantic drama that made it to the New York Times Bestsellers list. One would think making it on the bestsellers list would make her happy, but she still felt this gaping hole in her heart that couldn't be filled. At thirty years old, she read and wrote about love, but the only real romance she'd ever experienced firsthand had been gone from her life for years.

As she read her passage, she noticed a familiar white-haired man in the crowd. His strands of unkempt hair and rosy cheeks glowing under the fluorescent light were unmistakable. It was Fred from the park bench!

How sweet of him to come. Nora had told him about her book tour a few weeks past when she delivered her latest batch of pickles.

Nora gave him a little wave and proceeded to finish the passage. The crowd clapped as Nora sat down in her metal folding chair. The store manager stood up at the front of the room. This was the moment Nora expected to hear the news that Sonny Coultren couldn't make it. She cringed as he began to speak.

"May I present to you now, the man of mystery and San Francisco's favorite poet, Sonny Coultren." The crowd erupted in applause. Nora's eyes darted around the room. Was he *actually* here? To Nora's amazement, Fred stood up and hobbled toward the podium. What was he doing? *Oh no*, Nora thought, *is someone going to stop him from this embarrassing mix-up?* But then the store manager stepped to the side, smiling from ear to ear, as Fred sat down on the bar stool in front of the podium and grabbed his book.

The color drained from Nora's cheeks. Fred was *the* Sonny Coultren this whole time? Her mouth dropped open to the point her tongue dried out.

Fred opened his book, licking his finger before flipping to his page. The room became silent as he began to speak.

"Hello," Fred said, clearing his throat. "I'm Sonny Coultren, and today I'm going to read a few of my poems from my most recent book, *Doves of Grey*. I hope you enjoy it. This first poem is called 'Chance.'"

*Yes!* Nora's heart raced. It was one of her favorites. Her mind reeled as she watched her friend, *Sonny Coultren*, speak in front of the ecstatic crowd.

He spoke slowly; his gravelly voice was rough, but his words were sweet.

Fred flipped the page and looked up at the audience, a secret glint in his eye.

"This next poem is dedicated to someone very special in my life."

"To the ocean in your heart.
Phantom shadows of yesterday,
Misdirect the wings of tomorrow.
Let me in.
To sail your ocean blue..."

Fred continued with other poems. Some happy and some sad. His words were perfectly chosen and artistically executed. As Fred finished his last poem, everyone stood up and clapped, including Nora. A stream of tears stained her cheeks.

She allowed the rush of people that swarmed Fred after the reading to clear before she approached him. Nora gave Fred a big hug, wrapping her arms as best as she could around his checkered shirt. He smelled of beets and sourdough bread.

"I don't know if I'm more surprised that you are *the* Sonny Coultren, or that you actually showed up this time!"

Fred chuckled. "Well, I finally had a fellow author worth showing up for. It was about damn time."

Nora blushed.

"Nora, I'd like to introduce you to my wife, Jane." Fred turned toward the sea of folding chairs and beckoned for one of the women to come over.

"You have a *wife*?" Nora gasped.

A woman with a kind face walked up to Fred's side. She wore several strings of beaded necklaces over a frocked dress. Her salt and pepper hair hung loose and low down her back.

"I'm so glad to meet the woman behind the delicious pickles that Fred brings home," Jane said.

"If I had known Fred was sharing them with someone, I would have given him more." Nora shook her head in disbelief. The whole time she'd thought Fred was lonely—but he wasn't alone at all. He had a beautiful wife. A successful career. And a pathetic friend who thought he was homeless the entire time. Nora's ears burned from embarrassment.

"You know, Nora, I was so enchanted by your beautiful reading voice," Jane said.

"Really? Gosh, I always thought I sounded like a mouse."

"No, it is really soothing."

Nora giggled. "I can't say anyone has mentioned it before."

"You should do your own audiobook! Fred had a paid actor do his because of his old grouchy voice." Jane gave Fred a playful nudge.

"Well, thanks. I guess I hadn't thought of doing that before."

"Excuse me, Mr. Coultren? Ms. Ashbury? It's time to sign copies," a frail older man said.  His balding head was only partially covered by thin silky strands of ash-brown hair. He ushered them to their seats at a folding table at the back of the room, and the line of people formed in front of them.

"I still can't believe I'm signing books beside Sonny Coultren," Nora said.

"The honor is all mine," Fred said.

"No, really. I had no idea you were a writer. How did you keep it a secret for so long? Why didn't you tell me?"

"I'm not one to talk about my work with anyone but my wife. I prefer to listen and observe."

"It's just this whole time I thought you were just sitting there! Doing nothing. I feel so foolish."

"You were partially right." He winked.

Nora shook her head in disbelief.

# Chapter 18

The coffee machine gurgled as it made its last few drops of coffee. Nora wiped the sleep out of her eyes, anxiously waiting to fill her soup-bowl-size coffee cup with her wake-up juice. Taking a deep inhale, she let the coffee fumes warm her nose as she stepped onto her balcony. A twinkling jungle of San Francisco apartment buildings, kissed by the early rising sun, spilled into the glittering bay. Birds chirped in the palm trees, and a flock of small, wild parrots flew overhead.

The sun broke free from the horizon line, and soon the city started to wake up. A humming bus made its way across Corbett Avenue. Police sirens echoed up the hill, making their journey all the way from downtown. The clanking sound of bottles and aluminum cans led Nora's eyes to a man carrying a large clear plastic bag. He dug through a recycling bin, taking out valuables to add to his collection.

Nora's phone rang, letting her know someone was trying to video chat. She went inside to see who it was.

Mom. Nora pursed her lips, not sure if she had the energy for her mother so early in the morning. She hadn't even finished her cup of coffee yet. Their relationship had been strained ever since Nora stormed out of their house two years ago. Nora refused to talk to her father at all, so her mother tried to sneak in calls while he was at the community center, or asleep in his La-Z-Boy chair.

Nora accepted, and her mom's face appeared on the screen with blurry precision.

"Nora, I have some news."

"What is it? Is everything okay?"

"Everything is fine, I suppose. But we had to close down our community group."

"Really? Why?" Nora grabbed her coffee mug from outside and took a seat on her white fluffy couch.

"People in the community were starting to do some strange things," Nora's mom went on. "I think it's time you spoke to your father."

"Mom, I don't think that's a good idea—"

Just then Nora's father came into view. Well, his mustache came into view. He talked into the phone with his mouth only inches from the video camera.

"Nora. I need to talk to you. This is important," he said.

Nora held back an eye roll, bracing herself for another fight she didn't have the mental capacity for.

"I know things between us haven't been good."

"You think?" Nora snapped.

"Listen…pumpkin. I'm really sorry that I let our relationship fall apart. I was too hard on you."

Nora waited for the catch, but her father just moved the phone down so she could see his eyes. He was sad—remorseful, even. Why now? After all these years?

"What's this about the community center?" Nora asked.

He released a guttural sigh. "It started a few months ago when people showed up to our door with flowers and baskets.

It seemed nice at the time. I didn't think much of it really. They were thanking us for all that we were doing in the community, and that felt pretty good. But then one day I came into the community center, and there was this portrait of me, painted by some artist from Gaylord, I was told, and it was hanging in the lobby of the building. It was the first darn thing you saw when you walked in."

"Oh gosh," Nora said.

"It was a lovely painting, but it was a little much," Nora's mom chimed in.

"And then it wasn't too long after that I noticed these flyers with my face on them posted all over town. I knew we were going to advertise to get more people involved, but I wasn't expecting my face on there."

"People started coming from all over to see your father. They were bowing to him, kissing his knuckles like he was a saint or a king or something," Nora's mom said, her eyes wide with concern.

"Treating him like a cult leader, perhaps?" Nora asked, not able to keep herself from taking the jab her father deserved.

Nora's father huffed under his ruffled mustache. "People lost sight of what we were trying to do. And although it pains me to say this, they started worshipping *me* instead of God. I guess you were right all along. It was turning into a cult, and I should have prevented it. If only I had listened to you…" His voice trailed off for a moment.

Tears fought against her resolve to stay strong in front of her father. She almost couldn't believe his words—she was sitting in a parallel universe where her father actually acknowledged she was right.

"I had to put an end to it all. It had gotten too out of hand."

Her father frowned.

"I'm sorry, Dad. I know how much that community group meant to you."

"I'm sorry I didn't listen to you before, pumpkin."

The lump in Nora's throat was almost too much to overcome. "It's okay," she said weakly.

"In other news, we started a new book club," Nora's mom said.

"Well, that's great," Nora said. "I'm happy you have something to keep you busy now."

"We decided to let the group decide which books to read. You want to know which book was picked first?"

"Let me guess…a book about Lewis and Clark," Nora said. "No, George Washington, the biography." Her parents had always been interested in historical nonfiction. It took up most of their bookstore, back when they owned it. Nora wondered what the bookstore was like now that it was run by someone else.

"Actually, the group wanted to start with something lighter. Something fun. And I swear to heaven I didn't suggest it, but one of the gals in our group wanted to read *Coffee, My Love*, written by the very talented Molly Ashbury," her mom said.

"Your book club decided to read my book?" Nora asked, her face scrunched up in confusion. She couldn't believe what she'd just heard.

"It wasn't my first choice, but it got the popular vote," her father said. "And you know what? It was actually pretty good."

"You read my book?" Nora couldn't hold back her tears anymore. They streamed down her face, dripping from her chin until she could grab a tissue. Her heart was so full, it nearly burst.

"Your father liked the book so much, he couldn't wait to tell the book club it was written by our sweet little Nora," her mom said. "Of course, your father waited to hear what everyone thought first. Everyone loved it, and then your father couldn't hold in the secret anymore."

"The problem is nobody believed me," he said gruffly. "They all thought I was seeking out attention, that I was craving the spotlight ever since I stepped down as community group leader."

"They didn't believe you?" Nora asked.

"So, we were wondering if you might join our book club as a guest speaker one day," her mom said. She readjusted the phone so the video camera was properly framing her face. "Your father is now the laughingstock of the book club. We need to prove to these people that he's not a liar." She looked desperate.

"Are you kidding me?" Nora's voice reached an all-time high pitch. "I jumped through hoops to protect you both from the shame of my 'trashy' novel and now you want me to completely undo everything I've built to protect you?" Nora laughed at the absurdity.

"Well, no, but if coming home is too difficult, maybe you could mention it in your next newsletter?"

Nora smirked, shaking her head. They had subscribed to her newsletter too?

"I'll think about it," Nora said.

Her mother jumped up and down, dropping the phone. Nora watched through her phone screen as her mother's slippers shuffled over the fuzzy carpet until she scrambled to pick up the phone and point it back at her face.

"Thank you, thank you, thank you, Nora!" her mother cried.

"You have no idea how much this means to us."

Nora shook her head with an incredulous smile on her face.

"When's your next book coming? We're dying to read it," her mom said.

"Well, I just published my second one. Maybe start there. I'd like to write a third, but I'm in a slump. My muse is long gone."

"Your muse? What do you mean?" her mom asked.

"Nothing. It was nobody. Just a ghost from my past."

***

Nora rushed up the steps to Evelyn's home, anxious to see her. It had been too long since they'd gotten together for their monthly brunch. Evelyn had just gotten out of surgery but was insistent that Nora visit. She needed the distraction, as she said.

Evelyn's apartment was in the posh Pacific Heights neighborhood. Everything was white, except for the black and white photographs hung pristinely on the walls. Nora walked in to find Evelyn lying on a large white sofa, wrapped in a cashmere blanket, sipping a cup of tea. Evelyn's hair had grown back just long enough to be styled into a pixie cut. She looked frail. A vase with white hydrangeas was placed in the center of her square coffee table, next to a pot of tea on a hot pad and an extra empty cup.

"Please help yourself to some tea," Evelyn said. Nora poured herself a cup and sat in the matching white loveseat next to Evelyn. Evelyn's fragile arm reached for the remote control to turn off the television.

"How are you feeling? From your email, it sounded like the

bone marrow transplant was a success?" Nora asked.

"It went about as expected. It's been a tough recovery, but I am so happy to see you," she said. "How did the book tour go?"

"Oh my gosh, you're not going to believe this. My last signing was with Sonny Coultren, and he actually showed up!"

"No way! You got to meet him?" Evelyn's eyes sparkled.

"It turned out I knew Sonny Coultren this whole time. I thought he was Fred the Homeless Guy who sat at the park bench in front of my old apartment."

Evelyn's face contorted, tilting her head to the side as if she were computing what she'd just heard. "Wait a minute. Sonny's real name is Fred?"

"Yes."

"And you thought he was *homeless*?"

"Yeah, can you imagine how idiotic I felt when I learned he was *not* homeless? But how was I supposed to know? He'd been sitting on that park bench in front of my apartment all day, every day for years!"

Evelyn's shoulders shook with laughter. She had to put her tea down to keep from spilling. It was good to see Evelyn laugh again. It had been a long time. Over the past couple years, she'd been through hell trying to fight her leukemia. Chemotherapy had taken its toll, leaving her body sickly. It damaged her bone marrow so badly she had to undergo a transplant.

"You look good," Nora said. "Do you feel okay?"

"I'm doing fine. Just taking it day by day," Evelyn said with a forced smile. Just then Antonio came in from the back room.

"Bonjourno, Nora. It is good to see you." Antonio walked

over to Evelyn, giving her a kiss on the forehead. "Do you need anything, mi amore?"

"No, thank you," Evelyn said.

"I'm going back to the studio. Call me if you need me to pick up anything on the way home."

"I will, darling. Have a good day," Evelyn called.

"You two are cute together." Nora smiled.

"He's a good man," she said. "Now tell me. Did you ever make up with your friend? What's her name, Jolie?"

Nora shook her head. The anger she felt toward Jolie had drifted away with time, but she never mustered the courage to call her back. Too much time had passed, even though it still hurt to have lost her best friend.

"Maybe it's time to give her a call." Evelyn's words felt less like a suggestion from a friend, and more like direction from a mentor. "Do you forgive her?"

"I'm not sure I do."

"You need to find it in your heart to forgive her, or you'll never be free from it. Jolie is your best friend."

"Was. She was my best friend."

"Well, Nora. You know how much I love you. I adore you. But I can't fill that void for you. Lord knows I won't be around forever. He's making it hard enough for me as it is."

Nora frowned at the thought of losing Evelyn. She didn't want to hear it, even if there was some truth. Evelyn was her mentor. But not her best friend. She needed her best friend.

Nora nodded in silent agreement, taking a thoughtful sip of her tea. She would have to find the courage to text Jolie later.

"Good. I'm glad that's settled," Evelyn said. "You ready to pitch some book ideas?"

"Are you sure you're up for it? I'm fine if we just relax and hang out this time if you want."

"No, I want to. It helps my brain come out of the fog. I need some sort of creative interaction."

"Okay," Nora said, pulling out a list and a pen from her purse. "All right. A girl escapes her privileged life as an heir to a multibillion-dollar diamond business. She finds herself in Costa Rica to get away for a while. She walks by one of her family's jewelry shops, and she realizes it's being robbed. She's spotted, and the three robbers snatch her before she can make the call."

"I love a good damsel in distress," Evelyn said. "Go on."

"Well, then I got stuck after that. I was thinking the robbers were brothers. The youngest one was handsome and kind. He saves her somehow."

"Oh, that's good. You could create some serious conflict between the brothers."

"Right. And then maybe they go off on an adventure in Costa Rica, escaping the other brothers."

"Maybe your female character knows a secret about her father's business that could make them rich, and they go and search for it."

"Oh! And maybe that was her ploy to get him to save her the whole time. So, she never really knows if he saves her for the money, or for love."

"I love that," Evelyn said.

"Yeah, I guess it wasn't a bad idea after all."

"There are no bad ideas. Just seeds for a new one," Evelyn said.

Nora smiled, happy to hear Evelyn's go-to phrase.

After a few other book ideas, Evelyn's eyelids grew heavy, shading the sparkle behind her eyes. Nora took her cue and gathered the teacups, bringing them to the kitchen sink. The counter was littered with a dozen pill bottles, a plastic pill organizer and a heating pad. It looked like a miniature pharmacy.

"Can I get you anything before I head out?" Nora called.

"No thanks, Nora. I appreciate you coming to see me."

"Thank you for the brainstorming session. That was a lot of fun."

"It was." Evelyn yawned.

"Oh, before I forget. I just made a new batch of pickles. These might be my favorite so far. I brought you some." Nora pulled out a jar from her purse and set it on the kitchen counter. "They say pickles help the medicine go down."

Evelyn chuckled and then couldn't fight her eyelids any longer. She closed her eyes and gave Nora a friendly wave.

"Don't forget to call your friend," she mumbled.

"I won't. Thanks for everything. Have a good nap."

***

Nora pulled out her phone, thinking of what Evelyn had said. She pulled up Jolie's Instagram screen, and sure enough, life had moved on for her friend. She'd posted dozens of pictures of herself wearing hardly anything, in yoga poses all around the city.

She was wild, but Nora missed her. She pulled up her messages and sent her a text.

# Chapter 19

The doorbell chimed, and Nora finished washing her mason jar, setting it on the counter with the rest of them. The jittery feeling in her stomach grew with each step toward the door. She peered through the peephole. Jolie stood outside her door, distorted by the fisheye lens. When Nora opened the door, Jolie gave her a weak smile. Her hair was pulled up in a loose bun. Her flawless face was free of any makeup. She looked as pretty as ever, wearing a denim jacket over her tight-fitting yoga outfit.

"Hey," Nora said. "Come in."

Jolie tip-toed her way into the hallway, setting her purse down on the floor. She looked around the apartment, studying each picture frame on the wall and each potted plant in the living room.

"Your place is really nice," Jolie said. "I like what you've done with it."

"Thanks. Can I get you something to drink?" Nora asked, already reaching for the open bottle of wine on her kitchen counter. Her ability to make amends after so much time had passed would require alcohol.

"I'll have what you're having," Jolie said, taking a seat on the barstool along the kitchen island. Her fingernails clicked against the countertop tile.

Nora poured two heavy glasses of a pinot noir while Jolie studied her kitchen. Her brow furrowed after her first sip.

"Do you not like the wine?" Nora asked.

"Why did it take you so long to text me back?" Jolie asked. "It's been over two years, Nora."

Nora swallowed a big gulp of wine, the bitter tannins scraping her dry throat. "I wasn't ready to forgive you. What you did was pretty shitty, Jolie."

"You're right. I was a horrible friend, and I'm so sorry."

"Why do I feel like there is a 'but' at the end of that statement?" Nora asked, putting her hand on her hip.

"Because there is. I'm just not sure you're ready to hear it."

"Try me."

"What I did was terrible. I know. But it was so obvious that you were in love with Kellen. Not Jack. You were using Jack to make Kellen jealous."

"That's not the point. The point is that you betrayed me. I told you I was interested in Jack, and yet you still made out with him."

"I know. That was awful. I am so sorry."

"It obviously wasn't just Jack that I was upset about. You've stolen countless boyfriends from me before. You always have to be in the spotlight, and I just couldn't take it anymore."

Jolie looked down at her nails and fidgeted with her cuticles. "I deserve that," Jolie said. "I was too drunk to think straight, but you're right. I had just broken up with my ex and I was seeking attention. And I might have been a little jealous."

"Jealous of me?" Nora laughed. "That's a riot. How could you ever be jealous of me? You're beautiful, and smart, and can get any guy you want."

Jolie snorted. "Are you kidding? You have everything going for you. A successful career as an editor and a published writer. I have nothing. My blog is losing followers, and my Instagram count isn't going up. There are too many other girls on the internet just like me, but prettier, funnier, and better at writing. I'm not able to keep up with my bills on my own…." Jolie's words trailed off as she grabbed her wine glass and took a big gulp. And then another. And another.

"I had no idea." Nora walked around the island and put her arms around Jolie, giving her a tight squeeze. "You've been struggling all this time, and I wasn't there for you. I am so sorry."

"Can you ever forgive me for what I did?" Jolie sniffed, mascara collecting under her teary eyes.

"Can you forgive me too? I've been a terrible friend."

They squeezed each other for a long time. Nora felt at peace in Jolie's arms, like a heavy weight had been lifted from her chest. She finally had her best friend back, and she was ready to be a better friend too.

"No more kissing boys I like, okay? Even if they are assholes."

Jolie giggled. "I promise."

"And I promise I'll never shut you out again without a conversation."

"Are we sisters from other misters again?" Jolie jabbed her shoulder.

"You bet. Now come on, sister, and help me can these pickles. I have a special delivery to make to *Sonny Coultren* tomorrow."

***

Fred was sitting on the bench looking up at the sky as if he were reading the clouds. His hands rested in his lap. No notepad, paper, or pen. He just sat and watched.

"At what point do you write down your thoughts?" Nora asked.

"I usually don't. It's all in here." He smiled and pointed to his head.

"Wait a minute.… You don't have a notebook? A computer? Then how—"

"When I get home, I recite my poetry to my wife. If she likes it, then she'll type it up for me."

"What an interesting method."

"You should try it sometime. Giving your brain the freedom to think of whatever you want, with no commitment to writing the words down. It's freeing. It opens the mind to new places it wouldn't ordinarily go."

"I don't know. I feel like I'd forget everything, but maybe I'll try it sometime. In the meantime, I've brought you my latest batch of pickles." She sat on the park bench next to Fred and pulled out a jar from her oversized tote bag. His eyes lit up as he accepted them.

"Jane and I love your pickles. That reminds me." Fred reached into his pocket and pulled out his wallet. Within the old leather folds, he took out a business card and handed it to Nora. The thick white cardstock was embossed with solid black letters that read, "White Rabbit Studios." Nora traced the grooves of the indented letters with her finger.

"What's this?" Nora asked.

"Remember how Jane suggested you read for one of your own audiobooks? This is the studio we used. They're based in San Jose, but worth the drive."

"Thanks," Nora said, locking on the name at the bottom of

the card. Kellen Atwood.

*Kellen Atwood* at *White Rabbit Studios.* Nora's mouth went dry. The city seemed to swirl around like a tornado, whisking her away into a churning storm of fate.

"Is everything okay? You look like you might have seen a ghost," Fred interrupted her trance.

"Oh, sorry, I just recognize this name. Kellen Atwood."

"Kellen? Nice guy. Lots of tattoos, if I recall. His studio does all kinds of stuff."

Nora swallowed hard. It was *him.*

It felt like the universe was telling her she needed to go to him. Could this be fate?

She had to find out.

# Chapter 20

Nora parked her silver Audi convertible in front of a tall building with black windows. The address matched the business card she held tightly in her hand. She had to take a few shaky breaths before she could pull the keys out of the ignition.

Fingers trembling, she dropped her keys on the sidewalk in front of the building. She was a wreck, unsure if Kellen would be there—or what he would do if he saw her.

She should have called first.

Inside the building was a large directory with several names in gold letters. She scanned the directory for White Rabbit Studios. Floor sixteen.

She stepped into the elevator. The butterflies in her stomach were nearly coming out of her throat.

The elevator opened, and Nora stepped out into the hallway. She stood in front of the door to the studio for a breath before she gathered the courage to step inside.

A desk was placed in the middle of the small waiting room. The walls were painted black and displayed framed images of album covers and advertisements. She walked the walls, noting all of the accomplishments he'd made since he was let go from Quest Productions.

Nora heard footsteps coming from behind the back wall, and her heart started to pound. She pulled some of her hair behind her ear and sucked on her lip as a young man entered the room. He wore a brown plaid shirt, cowboy boots, and had a dusty brown mustache to match.

"Can I help you?" he asked in a heavy Texan drawl.

Nora's eyes darted around the room, hoping she hadn't come to the wrong studio.

"Hi, I'm Nora. Is Kellen here?"

"I'm Brian. Kellen's in the studio with a client right now. What brings you to White Rabbit?"

Probably better not to tell him that she followed her heart there, sitting in traffic for two hours, fantasizing about the very moment she'd leap into Kellen's arms.

"I'm interested in recording an audiobook. A friend of mine, Fred—I mean, Sonny Coultren—sent me here."

"Oh, yeah, I know Sonny. We can certainly help. Were you planning on doing the vocals yourself?"

"Yep, that was the plan."

"All right then, I'll just need to review some information with you, and then schedule you in for some recording time. Sound good?"

"Yes. I was actually hoping to speak with Kellen first, if that's okay. We… know each other, but it's been a while." She had to see him, or she would combust. Her nerves were like a ticking time bomb.

"No problem. He should be done in the next fifteen minutes or so. Do you mind waiting?"

Fifteen minutes? Her hands began to sweat.

"Not at all, thanks."

Nora took a brochure and sat in one of the black leather

chairs. She nervously applied a thin layer of lip balm and smoothed out her little black dress. Her jean jacket felt heavy, so she took it off and folded it on her lap. She fidgeted with her pearl drop necklace, letting the smooth round surface of the pearl run between her thumb and index finger.

What was Kellen's life like now? Did he spend all of his time in the studio, or was he hanging out with the musicians photographed and framed underneath their albums? Would he be too busy and important for her book? Oh God, she was in over her head.

The round white clock behind the desk taunted her as fifteen minutes crawled by. Then twenty. Then twenty-five. Thirty.

The door beyond the desk opened, and Nora started in her chair. Two men with long hair walked out, both carrying guitar cases. They politely nodded to Nora and walked out the door toward the elevators. Nora watched the door for Kellen. She held her breath as it creaked open again and Cowboy Brian walked through.

"Come on back. He's in Studio A."

Nora adjusted her purse over her shoulder and walked through a doorway that led to three different rooms. The door was open to Studio A, where Kellen sat facing the audio board. His headphones were on, and he bobbed to the beat of music only he could hear, pulling dials and pressing buttons while the large computer screen in front of him illuminated the dark room. Beyond the audio board was a large window pane looking onto an empty room with carpets and rugs pinned to the walls.

Kellen turned his head and noticed Nora standing in the doorway. He froze. His eyes fixated on her for a long moment while Nora struggled to remember how to breathe normally.

She gave him a soft smile, hoping for a smile in return. Instead, Kellen pulled off his headphones and stood up slowly. His jaw was clenched shut, shadowed against the blue glow of the flat screen.

"Nora?"

She barely heard him through the rush of blood pumping in her ears. She couldn't read his body language. Was he mad? Stunned? He gave nothing away, which made standing there in his doorway that much harder. Her dream of running into open arms—crushed.

"Hi." Nora gulped.

"What are you doing here?" He stood by his chair, motionless. Not approaching. The distance between them felt thick like putty.

Nora unfolded her jacket, wishing she hadn't come. She cursed her naive impulse. She looked down at her ballet flats and thought about making her exit.

"I, uh, got your business card through a friend. Sonny Coultren. He recommended your studio for… It doesn't matter. I can see you're busy. I should go," Nora babbled as she backed out of the studio. She strode toward the exit sign, passing Brian in his cowboy boots, too flustered to say anything before walking out of the lobby. Her cheeks felt hot, and she fought the urge to break down into tears before she had a clean getaway. She pressed the down button on the elevator once, twice. *Come on.* Three times. Finally, with a light ding, the doors glided open. As she stepped in, a large hand stopped the doors from closing. Kellen appeared, his tattooed arms crossed.

"What are you really doing here?" he asked.

Nora tried looking away, but a gravitational force sucked

her into his honeycomb irises.

"An audiobook," Nora said quietly. She swallowed hard. "I should have called first. I could see you're busy—"

"Is this for your first or second book?" His eyes softened.

Nora's mouth parted slightly. "You knew I wrote a second book?"

"Of course." The faintest hint of a smile tugged at the corner of his mouth.

Nora's chest warmed.

"I was thinking of starting with the first book, and then possibly doing my second book if the first goes well."

"I'm sure we can accommodate that. I'm sorry if I came off aloof a moment ago. I just wasn't expecting you."

Nora relaxed and inhaled deeply. "It's fine. As I said, I should have called first."

"You look really good."

And there it was. The side smile that curved in, and the dimple that made Nora's knees weak. She looked down, nervously smoothing out her dress again.

"We'll need to schedule some recording time, but perhaps we can talk through the details over a drink?"

"A drink? Now?" *Like a date?* She wanted to ask, but couldn't bring herself to.

"Yeah. What do you say? There's a bar just down the street. Come with me."

***

The dive had dimly lit red lamps that hung over a long wooden bar. College-aged students clustered around a few high-top tables, and a pool table was featured in the back.

Kellen signaled toward the bartender with two fingers in the air. The bartender seemed to understand, and Kellen guided Nora toward the pool table.

"What brought you to San Jose?" Nora asked.

"I have a couple buddies from high school that moved out here. They let me crash on their couch while I got my business up and running."

"Still sleeping your way to the top, I see," Nora quipped. Kellen laughed.

"I deserve that. I was a real jerk before."

"Yep," Nora said, crossing her arms. They shared a smile.

"Do you play pool?" Kellen asked.

"I don't." Nora rested her purse on the chair in the corner. She looked at the pool table as if it was going to swallow her up.

"I'll help you," Kellen said.

"Do you normally take your clients here? To talk about their projects?"

A mischievous grin swept across his face.

"No." He pulled two sticks from the rack, handing one to Nora.

What did that mean? The ball of nerves in her stomach ached for more information.

While he set the pool balls into the triangle, the bartender appeared with two bottled beers and set them down on the table next to Kellen.

"Thanks, Ralph. You can put these on my tab. Nora, would you like a beer, or something else?"

"Beer is fine, thank you," Nora said, reaching out for one of the cold brews.

"Can I get you two anything else?" Ralph asked.

"Just one round of pool. I'm going to teach this lady how to hit a cue ball."

"You got it," Ralph said, walking away back toward the bar.

"So, you want to make your own audiobook? Have you ever recorded your voice before?"

"I can't say I have."

"Well, you've got an amazing voice. I'm sure it'll turn out great."

"Thanks," Nora said.

Kellen slammed his stick, and the triangle of balls scattered for their lives. A solid red ball and a blue striped one made their way into opposite pockets. He walked around the pool table and coolly searched for his next move.

"Based on the studio name, I assume you finally caught your white rabbit and found what you've been chasing?"

The edge of Kellen's mouth curved in, and he looked into Nora's eyes, hitting the cue ball and knocking a solid orange one in the corner pocket.

"Not quite," he said. "Here, you take a turn."

His hands cupped her shoulders as he positioned her body in front of the pool table. Shivers ran down her spine. Nora placed her stick on the fuzzy green surface, accidentally bumping one of the balls. It rolled a few inches down the table.

"Oops," Nora chuckled nervously.

"Here, you hold the stick like this," Kellen demonstrated, letting Nora peer over his shoulder. "Now you do it."

Nora tried mimicking what she thought she saw, and Kellen came up behind her. She felt the warmth of his body against her hip, his arm lightly grazing against hers. He adjusted her hands and slid the pool stick back and forth so Nora could get a feel for the movement. He let go, and Nora attempted to make her first strike. The white ball jumped from the table and went the opposite direction she'd intended.

"Try again," Kellen said, smiling.

"I'm terrible at this," Nora said.

"It was only your first time. I'm letting you practice."

Nora made her second attempt, with only slightly better aim. "I never got a chance to thank you for punching out that guy."

"Which time?" Kellen teased.

"The last one." Nora smiled.

"You really ought to stay out of alleyways."

"I know."

"It was a good thing Jack was there for you," he deadpanned. "How's he doing, by the way?"

The crack of the cue ball rang in Nora's ears. A blue solid ball flung into the back corner pocket, and Kellen set up his next move.

"Jack? Why do you say that?"

"Since you two were back together and all that, it was a good thing he was there."

"Jack and I weren't getting back together. What are you talking about?"

"You were meeting him at the coffee shop, right? Crying in his arms when shit got bad. He told me you were working things out."

*Wait, what?*

"Jack told you we were working things out?"

He nodded.

"Oh my God, Jack is such an ass. I didn't intentionally meet him at the coffee shop. He cornered me to negotiate a deal."

Kellen looked up from his crouched position over the pool table.

"So…you weren't dating him?"

"God, no. After he showed up at the hospital, I couldn't get away from him fast enough."

Kellen put down the pool stick and placed both hands on his hips. "This whole time I thought…"

Nora shook her head, and then it dawned on her. The reason Kellen didn't show up at the hospital. The reason he left San Francisco without saying goodbye. He had thought she was with Jack the whole time.

They stared at each other across the pool table, the heavy glow casting shadows on his features. "Why were you in the alley, Nora?" His voice cracked. Eyes glossy. "You weren't coming to tell me about you and Jack, so why were you looking for me?"

"I wanted to finish the conversation we started in the coffee shop."

"What was it you wanted to tell me?"

Nora took a drink of her beer, the emotions from two years ago flooding back. She remembered how she'd felt running after Kellen. And the truth was, she'd never stopped chasing him. Now was her time. She needed to tell him how she really felt about him. But could she put herself out there only to be left in the dust again?

"What is it?" he asked softly.

The gentleness in his voice calmed her nerves. "I wanted you to understand how I felt about you."

"And how did you feel about me?"

The words caught in her throat. She wanted him. She'd wanted him then. And she wanted him now.

She took another swig of beer and lost the courage to tell him the truth. "It doesn't matter now, does it? It's been years. I'm sure you have a girlfriend now, and…" She was babbling again. "Can we just forget it? Give me that stick. It's my turn."

Nora grabbed the stick out of his hands, not really sure if it was her turn or not, but she needed to change the subject. She lined up her stick with the white ball and hit it with all her strength. It shot across the table, hitting the eight ball into the back rail. The eight ball rolled across the table and into the nearest corner pocket.

Nora beamed at her victory. Ignoring Kellen's protest, she did a little dance with her pool stick still in hand. Kellen crossed his arms and smiled at her, watching her shake her hips from side to side and shimmy her way back to Kellen.

"I got one!" Nora squealed in delight.

"You did. But you sunk the eight ball, which means you lost the game."

"Wait, what? I lost?" Nora's natural high came crashing down to reality.

"Well, no. We're just practicing. But generally, when you sink the eight ball before the end of the game, then you lose."

"That's a silly rule." Nora pouted.

"It is. I agree. See if you can knock the other balls in. I want to see you do another dance."

Nora cocked her eyebrow and gave him a playful jab. She lined up her next shot, pulling back her arm, ready to strike.

"I noticed your second book had an interesting scene," Kellen said, interrupting Nora's concentration. The pool stick rammed into the green felt, leaving a long blue streak.

Nora knew exactly what he was talking about: the scene when a girl was tracing scars on the male character's back. Like the time Nora traced her fingers along Kellen's tattoos—one of the most intimate, sensual experiences of her life. She had to capture the feeling in the book. Instead of going to sleep, the scene ended with a night of passionate lovemaking, fulfilling the fantasy Nora had created since that night with him.

Nora blushed and looked away from Kellen's knowing stare. "I don't know what you're talking about," Nora lied.

"Yes, you do." Kellen's sly grin spread from ear to ear. "It was a good scene. And everything about it would have come true in real life… if the timing was right."

Kellen walked up to Nora, closing the distance between them. The smell of cedarwood and ocean air made the cells in her body shimmer. She watched his lips as he played with them between his teeth.

"Nora?"

"Yes?" Nora's lips parted.

"I need you to move so I can get the yellow ball in the center pocket."

His eyes sparkled with mischief.

"You are bad." Nora stomped toward the table and grabbed her beer.

"That's what I've been trying to tell you."

She watched him maneuver around the table, calling his shots before sinking every last ball.

"What do you say? Shall we head back to the studio and give you a free practice round at recording your audiobook?" Kellen asked as he set down his empty beer.

"Do I really need to practice?"

"It doesn't hurt to get you set up and comfortable with the microphone. Plus, recording an audiobook is harder than it seems. There are professionals that do it exclusively. It's an art."

"I see. Then yes. I may need some practice."

"Let's head back, and I'll show you the ropes."

Kellen led Nora into the office building. His hand gently brushed against hers as he led her through the door, creating a frenzy of butterflies in her stomach. Only a few lights were left on, as most people had left for the day. He punched the up button for the elevator, and they silently waited for the doors to glide open.

"Are you still making music?" Nora asked.

"A little bit, yeah. I'll come back to the office after hours and mess around."

"Do you have anything I could listen to before we get started?"

"Sure." Kellen smiled.

The studio room was dark except for the lamps shining on the large board filled with knobs and dials. Kellen sat down in one of the leather chairs and ushered Nora to sit.

"I'll play you something I've been working on." Kellen turned on the computer and maneuvered the mouse through his folders of music. As he clicked his mouse, music filled the studio. The beat sounded like something out of a hip-hop video, not that Nora knew anything about that kind of music. She liked it, though. Her body caught the wave of the rhythm, and she bobbed to the beat.

"Now, check this out." Kellen tinkered with the dials, adjusting one lever and then the next. The muscles in his forearm flexed with each movement. He moved his head to the beat, the dim glow from the computer screen illuminating his concentrated brow.

"Okay, listen now compared to when it started. Can you tell

the difference?" he asked.

"I think so… it sounds more…"

"Full."

"Yeah."

Kellen finished typing something into the computer and swiveled in his chair to face Nora. They let the music come to an end, and Nora smiled.

"It's really good," Nora said. "What do you do with one of these when they're done?"

"I've been selling some of my beats online. I also keep a library of them in case I meet an artist who's interested in working with me."

"That's really cool."

"So, what do you say? Want to give your book a trial run?"

Nora wasn't sure she was ready, but she let him lead her into the soundproof room. She grabbed her book from her purse, then nervously sat on the stool in front of the microphone. Kellen adjusted the microphone so it hovered a few inches from her mouth.

"Are you comfortable?" he asked.

Nora nodded; she wanted to get this over with. What if she sounded silly? How would he ever find her attractive if she fumbled over the very words she had written herself?

Kellen carefully placed headphones on Nora's ears and walked to the darkened room. A single light shone down, highlighting his features. He smiled and reached over to press a button.

"You good? Want to take a practice run at it?"

Nora opened Chapter One and read a few sentences. The quiver in her voice came through her headphones. She looked up at Kellen, pleading with her eyes. This was too much.

"It always takes a few sentences to get rid of the jitters. It's perfectly normal.  Keep reading," Kellen said into his microphone.

Nora tried again, reading through the first couple pages—transporting herself out of a studio room and into her story.  As she finished the third page, she finally felt comfortable.

"Whoever suggested that you read your own story was brilliant. I can already tell it's going to be good. Try reading a part where there is dialogue between a man and woman."

*Oh, gosh.* Nora really didn't think through this situation. With a gulp, she flipped through several pages to find a certain point where she knew there was a lot of dialogue. She read several more lines, deepening her voice to mimic her hero, Luca, and then laughing at how ridiculous she sounded.

"Maybe don't go so deep?" Kellen said over the speaker.

Nora bit her lip before trying again—more subtle the second time.

"That's good. Now can you try reading the part when Luca and Emery get physical?"

"Do I have to?" Nora's hand on her hip.

"You'll want to get over the jitters now so you can ride the flow when you're recording later. Trust me."

Nora pursed her lips and flipped to the part she knew he was referring to. After scanning the chapter before reading it aloud, she cleared her throat and proceeded.

*"Luca pinned Emery's arms and pressed her against the window. The window was cold, and the sill dug into her hip, but she immersed herself in the heat of his chest and the softness of his lips.  Luca lifted her legs around his waist, and he leaned into her."*

Nora looked up at Kellen's intense gaze.  His lips parted

slightly; he nodded to her to go on.

*"Emery drew in a sharp breath as she felt his desire between her legs. The rain pounded on the window and echoed in the room. She heard her own breath getting stronger and louder as Luca pressed his body into hers. He grabbed her waist, lifting her up off the floor and carrying her to the bed."*

Nora looked up again, but Kellen wasn't standing behind the glass. Had he left?

"Was that okay? Kellen? Where did you go?"

Nora felt the headphones come off her ears, and they dropped to the floor. She turned around and found Kellen standing behind her.

"I don't have a girlfriend."

"What?" Nora asked.

"I've thought about you every day since I met you in the coffee shop and you spilled coffee all over yourself. You've had me under your spell for eight years." He cupped his hands around her face and whispered, "I should have done this a long time ago." Kellen's lips captured Nora's mouth. He was soft at first, but the desire between them grew stronger. His tongue penetrated her parted lips, caressing her tongue so gently it drove her wild. He was perfect. Everything she had imagined and more.

His hands caressed the sides of her rib cage before exploring her back and pulling her closer. Nora felt the strength of his embrace—holding her so tight, as if telling her with his hands he would never let go again.

She nibbled on his jawline and ran her hands up his shirt, feeling the flexing muscles of his stomach and chest. He picked her up, swinging her legs around his waist while he continued to explore her mouth, her neck, and the sensitive spot under her ear. He felt so good, she had forgotten where she was until he carried her into the computer room and set her down on the desk next to his keyboard. He pressed his hips between her legs, and Nora drew in a sharp breath as he pushed harder, deliciously caressing the ache in her core. His kisses trailed down her neck, and Nora arched her back, rubbing herself against the hardness underneath his jeans.

Kellen unbuttoned her blouse, slipping his hands around her shoulders, dragging her straps down with them. Kellen pulled his shirt over his head, exposing his tattooed chest and arms. Nora's fingers explored his soft skin and sucked gently on his bottom lip. She worked her way down his chest, leaving a trail of kisses. Circling his nipple with her tongue, she heard a soft whimper come from Kellen's lips. Nora craved every inch of him. She reached for his belt, but Kellen's hands softly clasped hers before she could pull.

"Wait," he said, panting. His eyes were closed and his lips were swollen.

"What is it?" Nora asked.

"I really like you."

"I like you too."

"No, I mean… I like, really like you," Kellen said. "I don't want to ruin this."

Nora cradled his face in her hands. "You're not ruining this. I want you. I've wanted you since the moment I met you."

He put his hand over his heart like she had touched him there with her words.

"If you want to go slow, we can go slow," Nora said, placing her hand over his. "Or you can take me back to your place and make up for lost time."

He bit his lip. A low moan came from deep in his throat.

"God, I really want that."

"Then take me now. We've waited long enough."

# Chapter 21

Kellen poured a beer into a glass. A cigarette hung from the end of his mouth. The head of the beer hissed and fizzed as he handed it to Nora across the white Formica countertop of his kitchenette. His studio apartment was the size of a shoebox. It was bare, undecorated, unlived in. The walls were beige, without a single picture frame. One black leather couch sat across from a small TV. A full-size bed was tucked in the back corner against the only window in the room.

"Nice place," Nora said, taking a sip of her frothy beer. Kellen chuckled as he poured his into a glass.

"It's a place to sleep. I'm never here."

"Where are you, then?"

"I spend almost all of my day at the studio. Or at the bar I took you to. That's about it. I'm trying to build up my library of music so I can start working with a big record label one day."

"Must be pretty lonely working all day and night all by yourself," Nora said, watching Kellen as he put out the cigarette butt in his ashtray.

"Yeah, well, it's paying off. I'm actually meeting with this guy from BEAR Records on Sunday. He's flying all the way from New York to meet with me and a few other guys, looking for someone to create beats for some of their artists."

"Are you serious? That is so exciting."

"Yep. I've been waiting for this opportunity my whole life. I could get a chance to work with the world's top musicians. And the royalties… I would be making so much more money."

"Wow. I'm so happy for you."

"I'm pretty excited." He sat on his couch and patted the seat next to him. Nora obliged, sinking into the cool leather cushions. She looked around the room, noticing he didn't have a kitchen table or chairs. She wasn't sure where they were going to eat their Chinese food when it arrived.

"Remember when you were working at the coffee shop in my building?" Nora asked.

"How could I forget?"

"You weren't much different than you are now. Maybe a little scrawnier. But I remember thinking you were just another hipster San Francisco barista, just like the rest of them."

"Gee…"

"I mean, what I'm saying is, I've learned that you are so much more than that. You've come a long way. I'm really proud of you, working so hard that you can't even find time to put a picture frame on your wall, your big dreams nearly in reach. You said something at the bar earlier, when I asked you about your white rabbit. Is this big record label thing what you've been chasing? Is this your white rabbit?"

Kellen wrinkled his nose. He took a big gulp of his beer and set it down on the side table next to the couch.

"I don't know. Maybe. Enough about me. How does it feel to be a big-time successful author, with *two* published books?

Are you working on another book now?"

"Sort of. I've got a book idea in the works, but not a lot of momentum yet."

"Are you needing a little bit of inspiration?" A sparkle appeared in his eyes.

"What do you mean?" Nora sank further into the couch, knowing exactly what he meant.

"Do you need me to save you in another alleyway to get your juices flowing again? Because if you do, there are tons of alleys in this city. I'm sure we can find you one with a sketchy character. I haven't broken my knuckles yet, so I'm sure I've got a few good punches left in me."

Nora laughed, playfully jabbing his chest. Kellen swiftly grabbed her wrist, bringing her into his arms. He stared deep into her eyes. The soft black halo of his eyelashes made her heart flutter. Kellen took the beer from her hands, set it on the counter, and then lunged at her mouth. His lips were soft, loving and caressing, nibbling on her bottom lip, which sent electric bolts through her body.

He wrapped his arms around her and weaved his hands into her hair. She breathed him in, relishing his scent, his touch, his closeness. Nora offered her tongue, caressing his with hers as she gave him everything in their kiss. Her hands explored under his shirt, stroking the rippling muscles of his abdomen, stretching around his ribcage and along his broad back. Their bodies rocked into each other, moving together, breathing together.

Just then the apartment intercom buzzed. The Chinese food delivery had arrived. It took every ounce of willpower to peel herself off of Kellen and sit back down innocently on the couch. Kellen stood up, giving Nora a kiss on the forehead before heading to the first floor to pick up their food.

Nora reached for her phone inside her tote bag and found three new text messages. They were from Antonio. *What could he possibly be texting about?*

*Nora, if you can, give me a call when you get this.*

*Nora, we need to talk.*

Nora's heart raced faster and faster as she scrolled down through the third and final message.

*Nora, I really wanted to tell you this in person or on the phone, but since you're not answering your text, I don't have another choice. I'm sorry to tell you that Evelyn passed away today. I believe she is at peace now and is no longer in discomfort.*

Discomfort? Evelyn had been fine just weeks ago. Wasn't she? Why would she have made it sound like everything was fine? Tears welled up in Nora's eyes. She couldn't help but feel angry at Evelyn for not being honest. Why couldn't she have just told the truth?

Just then, Nora realized where she was. Kellen walked in with a white plastic bag filled with stacked to-go containers. The smell of sesame orange chicken turned Nora's stomach. The smile on Kellen's face immediately vanished when he walked in.

"Nora, what's wrong?"

Nora was too shocked to know what to say. Her face reddened and the tears billowed down her cheeks. Kellen set down his bags and wrapped his arms around her, letting her sob into his chest, without an explanation. Nora soaked the front of his black band shirt.

"I just found out my mentor, I mean my *friend,* passed away," Nora said between sniffles.

Kellen squeezed her tighter. "God, I'm so sorry. Is there anything I can do?"

"I really should go," Nora said, gathering her bag. "I can't stay."

"Are you sure? Maybe you should eat something before you go—"

"I'm sorry," Nora said, wiping her eyes. "I'll call you later, okay?"

Kellen nodded in defeat and watched her walk out of his apartment.

# Chapter 22

Nora numbly walked into Evelyn's office. Manuscripts were piled on her desk. Books covered her walls from the floor to the ceiling. She had kept all her "precious gems," as she used to call them. She was so proud of her work, she'd collected each book like they were treasure.

Nora's eyes caught on *Coffee, My Love*, tucked between a row of other romance novels Evelyn had collected. Her heart warmed at the thought of how supportive Evelyn had been from Nora's very start. Without her, Nora's life as she knew it wouldn't have been possible.

Nora started gathering Evelyn's things. Separating items to send back to Antonio and manuscripts that she would help take on until Calico could hire a new young adult editor.

Shipping tape screeched across the cardboard box. It bulged at the top, overstuffed with stacks of books. Nora tried lifting the box, her lower back straining to pick it up only an inch off the ground. She gave up, shoved it toward the wall, and used her black Sharpie to write "Evelyn's books" on the top.

After she'd left Kellen's, Nora had visited Antonio and learned that Evelyn had been suffering from graft-versus-host disease, a condition after a transplant where the donor bone marrow attacks the body. Evelyn's lungs had filled with fluid, and her bones decayed. She was a strong woman, never letting others know how much she was suffering. But Antonio knew. He was devastated to have lost the love of his life but comforted to know she was free from her pain.

Nora caught the falling tear on her cheek before reaching for the small potted plant by Evelyn's old computer monitor. The leaves were brown and wilted. Nora carried the plant to her office down the hall and poured a drink of her Evian water bottle to see if she could revive it. If not, she would keep the pot on her desk to remind her of her great mentor. Surely Antonio wouldn't mind.

Footsteps from down the hall caught Nora's attention. She wasn't expecting anyone else to show up at the office today. It was Sunday, after all. She reached for her phone, not sure if she should be ready to call 911 or not. Her heart pumped in her chest as she waited. The footsteps grew louder as they grew nearer. Nora clutched her cell phone in her hand as she slowly peeked out the office door. Standing in front of Evelyn's office was Kellen, peering in the only room with the lights on.

"Kellen? What are you doing here? I thought you were supposed to meet with the big-shot record guy today."

Kellen walked in and gave her a hug. He smelled so good, Nora rested her head on his chest and breathed him in.

"I told them I needed to reschedule. I wanted to be here for you," he said into her hair. He ran his hands up and down her back, stroking her with such gentleness that Nora's heart almost burst. She looked up into his eyes, melting into their golden embrace.

"You didn't have to do that. We could have—"

"Shh. It's fine. They're going to call me later." Kellen held Nora tighter.

"How did you know where to find me?" Nora asked.

"When you texted me that you were going to pack Evelyn's things, I remembered you saying something about the eighth floor. Do you need a hand with any of her stuff?"

Nora remembered the heavy boxes in Evelyn's office.

"Actually, yes. I packed the boxes so full that I literally can't pick them up."

"Of course, let me help you."

Kellen lifted one of the boxes of books. His biceps rippled as he steadied the weight between both arms. "You weren't kidding. This box is very full. Where should I take it?"

"Let's start with taking these two boxes down to the lobby, and then I'll bring my car to the front."

Kellen staggered down the hall, panting by the time they reached the elevators. Nora pushed the down button, and Kellen's face and neck started to turn pink.

"How were you planning on getting these boxes down by yourself?" Kellen puffed as he got into the open elevator.

"I hadn't thought that far ahead, I guess." Nora shrugged. "It's a good thing you came."

"Are you taking these back to your place?" Kellen asked.

"I am. Antonio said I can have the books. But first I have to drop off some paperwork at his house."

The veins in Kellen's neck looked like they were about to pop. Once they reached the bottom floor, Kellen had to rest the box onto the tile floor of the lobby.

"Good God that was heavy. I'll run up and grab the other one if you want to stay here."

"Sounds like a plan." Nora reached over and gave Kellen a

soft kiss on the tip of his nose.

***

Kellen stepped back on the elevator, happy with his choice to help Nora with Evelyn's things. After Nora had rushed out of his apartment the other night, Kellen couldn't wait another minute to see her again. The moment she walked back into his life, everything became so clear. He knew what he had been chasing after. *Her.* And he needed to prove to her he wasn't the fuckup he had been. He could finally make it on his own.

Kellen couldn't lose her again. Not this time. Getting a record deal could wait. He had to make sure she was okay. Safe. Close.

As he stepped off the elevator, he looked both ways to find the office with the light on. As he approached Evelyn's office, he noticed a woman sitting in the desk chair. Kellen startled at first, recognizing the woman, but he couldn't remember from where. Was this Evelyn's ghost? A spike of adrenaline rushed through his veins, and he stood still, waiting for the ghost to say something.

"Hey, I know you," the woman said. "You're Kellen, right? Hot Coffee Shop Guy."

"I'm sorry, do I know you?" Kellen asked.

"I'm Jolie, Nora's friend. I came here to help her pack, but I see most of it is already done."

Kellen let out a sigh of relief. "Oh, right, I remember you now. I'm sorry I didn't recognize you. Last time I saw you, you had Jack's paws all over you." His words came out more bitter than he intended, but whatever. She deserved it as far as he was concerned.

"Yeah, Nora and I worked that out. Anyway, where is she?"

"She's waiting downstairs with one of the boxes. I was going to bring the last one down before we took off."

"I see. Hey, before we head down, I wanted to ask you something."

"What's up?"

"What is a tall, dark, and handsome man like you doing with a bookworm like Nora?" Jolie asked coyly.

Kellen narrowed his eyes, noticing that Jolie had unzipped her leather jacket, exposing her floral chest tattoo atop her drool-worthy cleavage.

"What do you mean a 'bookworm like Nora'? You mean a successful published author? I like that about her. I'm really into her."

"Yeah, but how do you know she's going to be able to hold your attention? You're the type of guy who looks like he needs excitement. A little danger. Someone a little naughty perhaps?" Jolie stood up and sauntered towards him.

"I don't need any of that shit. I just want Nora." Kellen clenched his jaw as she came closer.

"Oh, come on. Haven't you ever wondered what it would be like to be with me? Most guys do. I've made a whole living off of it, men pining for me across the internet."

"You've got the wrong idea then. I'm not interested in you. I'm in love with Nora. End of discussion."

Jolie pouted her lip and crossed her arms as Kellen bent down to pick up the last box of books. It was every bit as heavy as the first box. He struggled to walk out of the office, and when he did, he saw Nora standing in the hallway. A potted plant tucked in her left arm. Her mouth was shaped in an O.

*How much did she hear?*

"You love me?" Nora asked softly.

*Shit.*

Kellen set the box down and put his hands in his front pockets. He hadn't put much thought into it before, but saying the words to Jolie had come so easily. He'd always known on some level he loved Nora, but the word had never traveled out of his mouth. He looked into her eyes and nodded. He searched her expression, looking for a hint that maybe she felt the same way. Nora set the potted plant down on the floor before leaping into Kellen's arms.

"I love you too," Nora whispered, wrapping her arms around his neck, giving him a delicious kiss. She sucked on his lower lip as he softly set her back on the ground.

"You do?" He kissed her again, cupping her face, cherishing the moment while trying to ignore the white elephant in the office.

"Do you think you can bring this last box downstairs on your own? There are some quick things I need to do. I'll be right down," Nora said.

"Sure," Kellen said, looking towards the office door. "Um, in case you didn't know, your friend is in there."

"I know," Nora said. Her expression grew dark.

# Chapter 23

"How could you?" Nora demanded, closing the office door behind her. Jolie sat casually in Evelyn's office chair, her legs crossed and resting on top of the white desktop, her hands loosely behind her head. "And how can you be so casual about this? You just hit on the guy I've been chasing for years!" Nora could feel her temperature rising. Her pulse quickened. She was ready to pull the hair out of her best friend's head. *Ex-best friend.*

"Nora, calm down. I was just messing with him," Jolie said nonchalantly.

"*Messing* with him? What the heck does that mean?"

"I wasn't hitting on him *for real*. I'm not interested in stealing your man. I promised you I wouldn't do that again. I was just making sure he legitimately liked you. I can't have him bailing on you again, can I?"

"How can I believe you after what you did in Colombia? How can I ever trust you again?"

"Here's how. Open up your phone and check your voice-mail."

"What?" Nora asked. "Are you crazy?"

"Do it."

Nora pulled the cell phone from her back pocket and saw

she had two missed calls from Jolie. The first timestamp was from two hours ago. The second timestamp was from less than thirty minutes ago. Nora pressed the speaker button.

*"Hey Nora, it's Jolie. I just got your text message. I'm so sorry to hear about your mentor. I know how much she meant to you. I'd like to come and help you at the office. I won't take no for an answer. I'll head over in a little while. See ya."*

Nora pressed the second message and hit the speaker button again.

*"Hey Nora, I just got to your office building, and you're not going to believe who I just saw walk in. It's the Hot Coffee Shop Guy you've been crushing on! What the heck is he doing here? Oh my God, he just got in the elevator.... Is he here to see you?"*

There was a long pause before Jolie continued.

*"Okay, I'm giving you my fair warning.... As your best friend, I feel obligated to make sure he won't disappear on you again. I may have to corner him. Don't be mad."*

Nora looked up at Jolie's smug face. "See? It was premeditated. I did it for you, and guess what? He fucking *loves* you, Nora! He said 'I love you!'" Jolie shot out of the chair and wrapped her arms around Nora, jumping for joy. Nora stood in shocked silence as her friend bounced up and down.

"Okay, next time, maybe let's not test the man I'm dating by trying to seduce him. Okay? I don't love that technique. Although grudgingly, I find it reassuring that your seduction didn't work on him."

"See?! I knew you would see it my way eventually." Jolie gave her a shove. "Now, let's head back downstairs to meet up with your *looooove*."

***

Nora walked up the hill, a coffee in each hand. It was a dark foggy morning. The street lamps offered a hazy glow, illuminating the damp sidewalk. She approached the park bench to find Fred sitting in his usual spot, his feet crossed at the ankles. His long scraggly beard reached the first button on his collared shirt. Nora handed him a coffee and sat down next to him.

"How did it go?" Fred asked.

"The funeral was beautiful. There were bouquets of every color filling the auditorium with so much life. I couldn't believe how many people were there. Antonio, her husband, gave a beautiful speech that made everyone burst into tears. A few authors got up and spoke too. It is amazing how much of an impact she had on people's lives outside of my own. When I would meet with her, she made me feel so special. Like I was the only person who mattered to her in that moment. And it turns out she made others feel the same way too. In some ways that was comforting to know, and in other ways I felt a little jealous. But overall, the celebration of life ceremony was about as perfect as her. Beautiful, comforting, and sophisticated."

Fred nodded, indicating he was listening, but encouraging her to go on.

"I miss her a lot more than I would have thought. She had a greater impact on my life than I realized. Just the other day, I thought of a new book idea. I wrote it down, and I thought, 'I can't wait to share this with Evelyn. She's going to love this one.' And then I remembered she was gone. I won't get to share my book ideas with her anymore. Gosh, we had so much fun doing that, going back and forth with ideas. One-upping each other with plot twists and dramatic turns. It's going to be hard not having that be a part of my life anymore."

Fred took a sip of his coffee, nodding some more, then curling the end of his beard around his finger, deep in thought.

"I'm sorry, I hope I'm not disturbing your work by sitting here and chatting with you. I was going to try your method today. Sit and do nothing but free my mind and open myself to new ideas. Is that all right with you? Do you mind if I sit next to you while I try it out?"

"I would love the company," Fred said. "And you're not disturbing me at all. You can talk as much as you'd like."

Nora smiled, putting a hand on his shoulder to thank him for his kindness.

The next hour was spent in complete silence. Nora observed the way the fog dissipated into the sky. As the sun came over the horizon, the colors of the apartment buildings turned from dingy pastels to brightly colored hues. Dog walkers and tourists occasionally came into view. Nora noticed the way they walked, dressed, or talked with or without their hands.

The smell of baked bread brought Nora's attention down the street, where a local bakery opened its doors, setting out tables and chairs on the sidewalk. Nora's stomach growled at the thought of a freshly made croissant. She wondered if Fred would take breaks for food. She decided to wait and see for herself.

By noon, Nora's mind wandered from rooftop to rooftop, but without anything concrete enough for a book idea. Her phone buzzed, announcing a text message from Kellen.

*Dinner tonight? There's a burger place in Burlingame that's pretty good.*

*Yes. See you there at eight,* Nora replied. She smiled to herself as she put her phone back in her purse.

"I see someone has captured your heart," Fred said sweetly. "The look on your face says it all."

"You must know me pretty well then. Tonight is going to be our first official date. I've known him for a long time, but he kept disappearing on me. He's kind of been my muse, for lack of a better word. When I'm with him or thinking about him, I'm inspired to write."

"This guy is your muse?" Fred asked.

"Well, yeah. I mean, the only times I've ever decided on book ideas worth pursuing, it was because of him. Either something he did or said. The way he made me feel. All of that spilled into my writing."

"Well, what are you doing here, then? You have your muse. You should go to him!" Fred boomed.

"I wanted to give your method a try. See if I could have any success by freeing my mind."

"Forget about all that crap I said. Have you thought of any ideas from sitting here this morning?"

"No, not really," Nora said.

"I've written two poems in my head," Fred said. "San Francisco is my muse. You apparently have a date with your muse tonight. No sense in sitting around here doing nothing, now, is there?"

"I guess not." Nora chuckled.

"Go get yourself some lunch from that bakery over there. I know you were thinking about it," Fred teased.

"Hey! How did you know that?" Nora scoffed.

"When their doors opened, you were breathing in so hard through your nose, I thought you were going to catch a fly."

# Chapter 24

"Do you have a reservation?" the hostess asked. Her hair was pulled back so tightly in a ponytail, her eyebrows made her look permanently surprised.

"Yes, I think so. It should be under the name Kellen," Nora said. She checked herself in the mirror behind the hostess, pressing her lips together to blot the red lipstick she'd applied just moments earlier. Nora wore a sleeveless blouse tucked into high-waisted chino shorts and strappy sandals. She styled her hair down, with loose waves of brown hair kissing the tops of her shoulders. Her bangs lay neatly above her eyebrows and thick lashes.

"Come right this way." The hostess smiled, leading Nora through the dimly lit restaurant. The nervous ache in Nora's stomach compounded with each step forward. She followed the hostess past the kitchen window, where cooks with white chef hats feverishly attended to their grills. The smell of barbequed burgers reminded Nora of her summers at home, when her dad grilled burgers in the background. The memory helped calm her nerves. Then Nora saw Kellen sitting at a booth in the far corner. His face lit up when their eyes met. His hair was styled back, his strong jawline perfectly shaven, the dimple in his cheek on full display.

Kellen was wearing a black buttoned-up collared shirt with rolled sleeves, showing off the tattoos on both of his strong arms. He stood up, towering over Nora before leaning down for a light kiss on her cheek. Shivers ran down her spine at the contact. By the time she pulled her wits together and sat down, she noticed the hostess awkwardly gawking at Kellen. Nora waited for her to tell them the specials or something, but the hostess stared in awe.

Nora cleared her throat, releasing the girl from her trance. She muttered something about a pulled pork special and then scurried off.

"You look absolutely gorgeous," Kellen said.

"As do you, and I can see from the look on our hostess' face that I'm not the only one who thinks so," Nora teased.

"I have a surprise for you," Kellen said.

"A surprise? What is it?"

"You'll see in about two seconds," he said, proudly crossing his arms.

Just then a large tray came into Nora's periphery. A platter full of twelve different kinds of pickles was placed on the table between them, each pickle in their individual tiny grooved section. Nora's eyes grew large.

"Is this…?"

"A flight of pickles? It certainly is," Kellen exclaimed. "And they're all yours. I can't touch the stuff."

Nora took a bite from one of the small pickles. It was so tart it made her mouth water. The second pickle was dill. The third was a spicy Thai flavored pickle. She urged Kellen to try it, but he stood his ground and refused.

"I am so happy," Nora said, munching on the fourth pickle.

"I never thought I'd say this, but I'm also very happy,

watching you eat pickles. You're like a kid in a candy store. Also, I should tell you there is one more surprise tonight."

"What's that?" Nora asked.

A server arrived with a pint of beer and a martini glass. The martini glass had a pickle garnish. It was placed delicately in front of Nora.

"Now this might be too much, but I also ordered you their pickle martini."

"Are you kidding? This is a thing? I think I might have died and gone to pickle heaven."

Kellen took a sip of his beer and read Nora the burger menu while Nora focused on her pickles. They both agreed the Burlingame Burger with bacon and avocado sounded the best.

"How was your day sitting on the park bench?" Kellen asked.

"It was… well, it was boring. It's so much harder to sit still and do nothing than it sounds. I tried freeing my mind as Fred suggested, but I could never get to a place in my head where I was thinking of book ideas. I gave up right around lunch time."

Kellen chuckled into his beer. As he swallowed, Nora watched his Adam's apple go down and back up again. She resisted the urge to reach across the table and lick his neck.

"Any word from that record label?" Nora asked.

"Nah, not yet. They were supposed to call me by today, but it's looking like that didn't quite work out. It's all right. I'll find my big break some other time."

Nora felt a pang of guilt. He'd walked away from his chance to meet with a big-time record label for her. She wondered how often those types of chances would happen again. She played with the napkin in her lap, not knowing what to say.

"Hey, don't worry." Kellen lifted her chin with his fingers

and locked onto her gaze. "It's going to be fine." She stared at his features, the angles of his nose, the way his bottom lip pouted farther than his top lip. His perfectly angled jawline.

*You really are so beautiful*, Nora thought.

Their food arrived at the same time Kellen's cell phone buzzed. He stared at the screen, his eyebrows furled together.

"Do you mind if I answer it? I think it's BEAR Records."

"Of course! Answer it!" Nora urged. Kellen answered the call, confirming it was the record representative with a nod.

"Yeah. Okay. What time? Right now? Um… hold on one second, okay?"

Kellen muted his phone and looked up at Nora.

"This is Rick. He got bumped off his flight back to New York. He said all the other audio engineers he met with here were crap. He wants to meet with me now. Downtown San Francisco in thirty minutes kind of now."

"Obviously you have to go, then," Nora said. "Or you're going to be late."

"I can't just—"

"Go," Nora said.

"You sure?"

"Go!"

Kellen got back on the phone. "Rick? Yeah, I'll head over right now. I'll see you around nine." Kellen hung up and gave Nora a kiss on the forehead. "I'm so sorry to leave you here on our first date."

"Just go. It's fine! I'll take care of the food."

Kellen took off, rushing down the aisle. If he hurried and found parking immediately, he would probably be able to make it. Nora looked at the table. Two gigantic burgers with piles of french fries sprawled before her, but Nora had lost her appetite. Of course he needed to take that meeting. He'd missed his first chance because of her. She couldn't let him miss a second chance just because they were on their first date.

Nora bit the head off of a french fry, then flagged the waiter to bring her boxes and the check.

***

Ready for bed, Nora had tucked herself under her cool down comforter when her cell phone vibrated on the nightstand.

"Hey," Kellen's voice came over the speaker.

"Hey. How did it go?"

"They loved me. They loved my work. They think I could be a real asset to their company," he said cautiously over the phone. He didn't sound as excited as she would have expected given the news.

"Congratulations. I'm proud of you."

"Thanks," he said quietly.

"What's wrong? This is good news. Aren't you happy?"

"They want me in New York full-time. I was hoping I would be able to keep my studio and work from San Jose, but they said a lot of their musicians live and work out of New York. It would be an unnecessary expense to have them fly out to California to work with me."

"Oh," Nora said, letting the weight of the information sink in.

"They're offering me a ton of money to sign a contract, and a full-expense-paid trip to New York to check out the studios in Manhattan and meet some of the musicians I would be working with."

"Wow," Nora said. "That's amazing."

"They want me on a plane tomorrow, and a signed contract by the end of the week."

"I see," Nora said. "Well… um. This is your dream, right? This is what you've been working for?"

"Yeah," Kellen said.

"So, you leave for New York tomorrow, then?"

"Yes." The finality of his response grew heavy on Nora's heart. It was all coming to an end before it could even begin. Again. Nora swallowed the lump in her throat, begging herself to stay poised. She couldn't let him know that she was devastated.

"I am so happy for you, Kellen. Congratulations again."

There was silence on the other line.

"What time is your flight?" Nora asked.

"It's at six a.m."

"You'll need your rest then. Have a good night, and safe trip to New York."

"Nora… I…" Kellen's words drifted away like bubbles flying into the sky.

"I'm going to miss you," Nora said. "Good night."

***

Mary put on her glasses, sliding them down the end of her nose while she tried to figure out where to look through the video camera lens. Her face became pixelated, frozen in space, and then she zoomed back to normal, nodding, listening to Nora pitch her idea over their video chat.

"So, what do you think?" Nora asked nervously.

*Smack!* Nora heard Mary's hand slam against the table so

hard her glasses fell off and into her lap. Her eyes glittered with excitement and a slow, steady smile spread across her face. "Do I like it? Are you kidding? I love it! Nora, this is your best idea yet. How far along are you?"

"I'm a few chapters in. I'll send them to you today."

"Excellent. Oh, Nora. I'm so glad to see your sweet face, but I'm even happier to hear you're writing again! This is wonderful news."

Nora gave her a polite smile. She wished she was as excited as Mary, but the truth was, Nora's heart hurt. It had been five days since Kellen flew to New York, and she hadn't heard a single thing from him. Her despair was too much to bear, and she found herself each day lying in bed or stalking her apartment in her pajamas and pouring her emotions into a new book idea. She should have been thankful for getting out of her slump, but she was too miserable to feel anything else.

"Oh, by the way, I've decided to have your first two books translated into German. We're breaking into the European market with some other authors, and I was thinking you could do a publicity tour in Europe in about six months or so. Do you think you could have our third book rounded out by then? It would be great to offer up a trio set."

Nora nodded. "Yeah, I think I might be able to be done by then."

"Fabulous, honey. All right, it's time for my smoke break. Send me those chapters. I can't wait to read them."

"Will do. Bye, Mary." Nora closed her laptop. Someone knocked softly on her front door. Nora couldn't remember if she was expecting a package or not, but they usually left them down in the lobby area. Looking down at her sweatpants and baggy T-shirt, she shrugged before trudging toward the door.

She looked through the peephole and gasped.

It was Kellen. He was back. Her heart skipped a beat as she pulled the door open.

He was wearing a white T-shirt and jeans. A suitcase rested by his feet. Was he coming or going? She wasn't sure she could handle the answer.

"Hey," Nora said uneasily.

"Can I come in?"

Nora looked down at her clothes and wished she were wearing something other than frumpy sweatpants.

"Sure," she said. "I was just about to get dressed."

"Don't change. You look cute."

There was that word again. Cute. The same thing other boys told her before they dumped her for Jolie. She pushed her insecurity down and raised her chin high.

"Want some coffee?"

"Please." He followed Nora into the kitchen, rolling his suitcase behind him. Nora pulled her coffee beans down from the cabinet.

"How was New York? Did you just get back, or are you heading out there for good now?"

"I just got back. Came straight here from the airport. New York is a really cool city. BEAR Records is badass. I would have been really happy there, I think."

Nora froze. She pressed the brew button and turned toward Kellen.

"Would have been?" Nora repeated.

"Would have." Kellen smiled. "I told them I couldn't leave the Bay Area."

"But… it was your dream job."

"Yeah. It was a risk. But they decided to let me stay in

California and work for them out of my studio after all."

"No way."

"Yes way. When I told them that moving was a deal breaker, they totally changed their story. It turns out there's a ton of ways to work remotely. They just ask that I travel to New York from time to time."

Nora jumped up and down, dancing her little jig—the same one she danced every time she got excited. "So, does this mean…"

"Yep."

"You're staying."

"Yep."

"You're not leaving."

"Yep."

"Oh, Kellen. How can you be so laconic in a time like this? You've finally caught your white rabbit."

Kellen closed the distance between them. He cupped her face in his hands and looked deep into her eyes, catching the single tear that fell from her cheek.

"I'm done chasing white rabbits. I've already caught myself one right here." He pressed his lips against hers. Nora reached for him on her tiptoes, wrapping her arms around his neck. She pulled him closer and parted her lips—caressing his tongue with hers.

"You're mine now," Nora said into his mouth.

"I'm yours," Kellen said. "And you're mine."

# Acknowledgement

I'd like to thank my incredible editing team; Bethany Robison, Alexandra Ott and Anne Victory. Thank you for everything you have done to whip this book into shape.

Special thanks to my beta readers, Maria and Annie, for taking the time to read my work before my editors fixed it up. Your support means the world to me.

Thank you to the talented book cover photographer and designer, Erik Ebeling. You continue to amaze me. I am so happy with the cover and all the marketing assets you've provided.

Thank you to my supportive family and friends. I love you all so very much. This book wouldn't be possible without you.

Last but not least, a special thank you to all my subscribers, followers and readers. You all have made this journey an incredible experience. Thank you for your support, your encouraging words and your honest reviews! I am so blessed.

# About the Author

Alicia Crofton is a romance novelist and a sucker for a good love story. She lives with her husband and two children, nestled in Portland, Oregon's jungle of roses.

Join her mailing list for updates on upcoming books.

**You can connect with me on:**
- http://www.aliciacrofton.com
- http://www.facebook.com/aliciacroftonauthor
- https://www.instagram.com/aliciacroftonauthor

**Subscribe to my newsletter:**
- https://mailchi.mp/31aee60d4ff1/aliciacroftonsignup

# Also by Alicia Crofton

**Coffee, My Love**
Emery Smith, a Chicago-born workaholic, wants to prove herself as a strong female leader in a male-dominated company. Assigned a task that would impact the lives of coffee farmers, she puts on her big-girl-VP pants and travels to Colombia to set up negotiations.

Luca Mendoza's coffee plantation is on the brink of bankruptcy. His plans to confront the bigwigs are set aside when he rescues an enchanting American from an uprising led by his unhinged brother.

Deep in the exotic coffee fields of South America, Emery finds love, passion, and inspiration that could help the Colombian farmers ... but to save them, she must risk the precious career she has worked so hard to build.